MW00781698

Fracture of the Soul

By

Geoff Loftus

Saugatuck
Books

Books by Geoff Loftus

Double Blind (2012)

Engaged to Kill (2012)

The Dark Saint (2013)

and the Jack Tyrrell novels:

Murderous Spirit (2016)

Dark Mirage (2016)

The Last Thing (2017)

Dangerous Purpose (2018)

No Traveler Returns (2020)

Fracture of the Soul (2020)

Published by Saugatuck Books

Fracture of the Soul

© 2020 by Geoff Loftus

ISBN: 978-1-7346558-2-7

Fracture of the Soul is a work of fiction. Any resemblance to actual people is unintentional and coincidental. A serious attempt has been made to portray the details and geography of the New York metropolitan area accurately, but the needs of the story may have driven me to exercise poetic license, even with some actual places, buildings and even organizations. I want to emphasize this with regard to the NYPD's 24th Precinct. I hope the reader will excuse this.

Cover design by Tom Galligan, Green Thumb Graphics.

Published by Saugatuck Books.

For my siblings,
Jill, Mark, Kit, Andrea, and Patrick

The journey wasn't always smooth or safe,
but I'm glad we made it together

Mary Debenham: To a man with a hammer, every problem is a nail. You live crime. You see evil every day.

Hercule Poirot: Not so. I see enough crime to know that the criminal act is the anomaly. I believe it takes a fracture of the soul to murder another human being.

Murder on the Orient Express (2017)
Screenplay by Michael Green
Based on the novel by Agatha Christie

1

You can be excused for wondering just how I ended up standing in the rain on a mid-November evening in New York City, preparing to charge into an Upper West Side townhouse. My mission: To beat the hell out of a gang of neo-Nazis and rescue a number of young, Jewish women who were being held against their wills and abused as sex slaves.

So . . . how did I end up standing in the rain about to launch an attack on some very unsavory types? What's my story?

Once upon a time, I came home from serving my country in Afghanistan as a member of the U.S. Army's Special Forces, popularly known as the Green Berets. Like many combat veterans, I suffered from PTSD but managed to hold it together enough to become a deputy in the U.S. Marshals Service. I was lucky enough to meet and marry a wonderful woman named Maggie. All was well. Except . . .

I was still struggling with PTSD and self-medicating with alcohol. I got angrier and angrier with almost everything. I loved my Maggie, but instead of trusting her with my feelings, I suppressed the ever-loving hell out of them.

Much as I'd like to tell you that I emerged from this

dark night of the soul with my spirit and dignity intact, I can't. The anger and depression raged inside me, and eventually, I convinced myself that it was all right if I took a bribe from some members of the Mafia who wanted information on some mope in witness protection. It was a terrible idea, but one of the many reasons I was able to convince myself that it was okay was that there was no way I could actually deliver the information the Mafia was asking for. I didn't work in the Marshals Service Witness Security Program, and there was no way for me to get the info I had been bribed to get.

You might not be aware of this, but it was a very bad idea to take a bribe from the Mafia and not deliver. Really bad. Horribly bad.

My mob acquaintances shot me. They also shot Maggie. I survived. Maggie didn't. My wife, my love, was dead. And it was my fault.

Did the shock of these events and my culpability snap me out of my alcohol-fueled PTSD funk? Of course not. I dove deeper into depression and booze. I resigned from the Marshals Service and became a low-level "enforcer" for some very ugly people. Mostly I drank.

And then . . .

On the fifth anniversary of her death, Maggie appeared to me. Yes, Maggie. My late wife. Now a ghost. Exactly the way Marley's spirit appeared to Ebenezer Scrooge in *A Christmas Carol*.

She visited me in our old apartment. She told me

she still loved me and wanted me to become the man she had married. And she had interceded with the Highest Authority to get me a second chance.

That chance would come to me in the form of a guy named Harry.

As you might imagine, I thought I was going crazy. Suffering from alcoholic hallucinations. Overwhelmed by PTSD, depression and paranoia. Absolutely and completely out of my mind.

There was no possible way that my dead wife had come to me and told me I was going to get a second chance and that a guy named Harry was going to guide me.

But Harry appeared to me and explained that Maggie had interceded with the Chairman, who was granting me a second chance to live a better life.

"The Chairman?" I asked. I was informed that the Chairman was exactly who I thought He was. The Higher Power. God. The Big Guy in the Sky.

What was I going to have to do to live a better life? Harry was going to help me right wrongs for people. *Other* people. I couldn't work to benefit myself. In other words, I had to be selfless. The Chairman wouldn't guarantee that I would survive my attempts to right wrongs, however, the Chairman did guarantee that He would give me whatever I *needed* for my missions. Harry and I had many conversations on the subject of *need* but had never found a precise definition of it.

Helping others was how I came to be outside a

neo-Nazi house of prostitution on a rainy Wednesday night at the corner of Riverside Drive and West 91st Street in Manhattan, just eight days before Thanksgiving,

Okay, Tyrrell, time to ride to the rescue. Or to be more precise, time to bust up the neo-Nazis goons who ran the place and rescue the Jewish women who were being raped and abused.

I cannot tell you how much I hate neo-Nazis. And men who victimize women. There just aren't enough words to cover my loathing for these animals who think they are the Übermenschen. Please excuse me, I shouldn't have said "animals." That was an insult to animals everywhere.

Harry and I were standing with our backs to Riverside Park, scouting out the front of 341 West 91st Street, a four-story building about a hundred feet east of Riverside on the uptown side of the block.

Its facade had none of the brownstone charm that its immediate neighbors did. It was a simple, weathered red brick structure, built much later than the other buildings on the street. But given its location, whatever it lacked in elegance was made up for in purchase price.

"How the hell does a neo-Nazi thug have the scratch to own that building?" I asked.

"His family's real-estate business has owned it for decades," Harry replied.

"Oh, I see, he got it the old-fashioned way. He inherited it. Just like the new President-elect."

"Exactly."

4

"I'm guessing Adolf's family is loaded."

"Yes, they are. And you know that his name is not Adolf."

"Franz? Fritz? Heinrich?"

Harry gave me his icy, "you are not amusing" look.

"Sorry. But if I don't amuse myself somehow, I'm going to puke in disgust."

"Don't you think you should pay attention to the job at hand?"

"I guess so." I yanked the hood of my navy-blue rain jacket farther forward, trying to keep the water off my face. It was an improvement, but not much. Now only my chin was getting wet. Underneath the rain jacket I was wearing a gray, long-sleeved T-shirt, a charcoal-gray wool sweater, and black cargo pants. I was damp, but I was ready for special ops. "How much security?"

"Cameras over the front and back entrances. Cameras inside in the first floor living room and the upstairs hallways. The back yard is surrounded by a high metal fence that I would recommend you not attempt to climb in these wet conditions. That's assuming you could get to the fence from one of the next-door buildings."

"Okay, I get it. A frontal assault. Once I'm through the front door, then what?"

"The door opens onto a hallway. The foot of the stairway is about 10 feet straight ahead. To your left is a large living room, opening off the hallway. The hall runs to a small bedroom, a bathroom, and the kitchen."

"The johns wait their turns in the living room?"

"Yes."

"How many neo-Nazi goons are guarding the front door?"

"One at a small desk that sits in the living room arch, facing the front door. Another in the living room."

"Out of sight when someone, like me, enters?"

"Yes."

"Hmm. They're not complete idiots. Too bad. Are they armed?"

"Both carry 9mm pistols."

"What's the layout upstairs?"

"All the apartments on the top three floors were gutted and converted into small bedrooms. Fifteen young women in all. None of them is eighteen-years old. The women live in a barracks-style set-up in the basement. The basement is accessed by a door under the stairs in the front hall. The young women eat all their meals in the kitchen."

"They're really just girls. Are there more of them than bedrooms?"

"Not at the moment."

"All Jewish? All kidnapped by the neo-Nazis?"

"Yes."

"All shot full of drugs so they can't resist?"

"Yes."

"How old are they?"

"Seventeen or younger."

I felt a hot coil of anger in my gut. Stay focused on

the job, Tyrrell, or you won't be able to help these girls who so desperately need help. "Aren't there missing persons reports out on all these girls?"

"You probably have a better idea than I do of how many young women go missing in the New York metro area each year."

"The metro area?"

"Yes, they were kidnapped from different parts of New York City, Westchester, New Jersey, and Connecticut. Even from Massachusetts and the Philadelphia area. Different law-enforcement jurisdictions."

"Which means that no one has noticed a pattern."

"No."

"How did these Nazi jerks find all these girls? It's not like Jewish teenagers wander the streets with religious labels on their clothing."

Harry said nothing, waiting for what I had said to sink in. "Religious labels . . ." I muttered. "These bastards staked out synagogues, yeshivas, and Jewish community centers to find their prey."

"Yes."

Calm down, Tyrrell. You're about to wreak havoc on Nazi scum. But first, focus on the task at hand. "What about other security? More guards all with guns?"

Harry glanced skyward, as he often did, then back at me. "Yes. There are two relaxing in the first-floor bedroom. Another one on each on the three floors above to make sure there's no trouble."

"A total of seven guys. And one of them is Mrs. Schörner's nephew, little Willi Axmann."

"Not so little."

"I remember the description: 6 feet, light brown hair, hazel eyes, slender. As long as he's not big and tough, I don't care."

"Do you mean as big and tough as you are?"

"Well, now that you mention it . . ."

"Remember, Mrs. Schörner is our client. You agreed to help her nephew."

"I agreed to do what I *could* for him. That may or may not include help."

"Mrs. Schörner is of the belief that you will help her nephew," Harry pointed out.

"Yeah, well, since he's a part of this neo-Nazi gang, he's involved with kidnapping, illegal drugs, and prostitution—not to mention what probably constitutes a hate crime—the only thing I can do for little Willi is turn him over to the law."

"If that is the result, I don't think Mrs. Schörner will feel that you helped him."

"He'll be alive. Best I can do."

I watched a man carrying an umbrella walk down the 91st Street block in our direction. He stopped in front of No. 341, pressed a buzzer, leaned over, and spoke into an intercom. I asked Harry, "Is this place by appointment only?"

"Yes."

"And the house has a policy that all of its customers have to walk so there's no procession of taxis to the front of this building?"

"Exactly."

"I'm guessing that just to be ultra-secure, our ugly little pimps probably have arranged protection at the local precinct. Right?"

"Yes."

"They don't miss a trick. No pun intended."

"No, they don't."

I pulled off my backpack, selected a pair of smoke grenades from inside, tucked them into the jacket's pockets, and smiled at Harry. "I'm going to come down on these animals like something biblical. Pillar of fire. Plagues. Wrath of God."

"The term 'wrath of God' strongly suggests that acting that way does not fall to you but to the Chairman."

"Okay, I'll be His avenging angel."

"As you may recall," Harry said, "I *am* the angel in this scenario."

I took a very deep breath. "Fine. Nothing biblical. No avenging. But I'm going to enjoy every moment of mayhem."

"Stay focused on the mission."

"I will. Someone's gotta rescue those women." I pulled a dozen plasticuffs out of the backpack, tucked them into a pants pocket, and handed the pack to Harry.

As I stepped off the curb into Riverside Drive, I asked, "Care to join me? *You* could be the avenging angel."

He shook his head with a tiny, Mona Lisa smile that came and went faster than a thought through Einstein's brain.

When I reached the opposite sidewalk, I unzipped my jacket so I had easy access to a pair of shoulder-holstered 9mm Ruger SR9 pistols with 17-shot magazines. I strolled to the door of No. 341 and pushed the buzzer.

"Hello. Who is it?" the man's voice sounded fuzzy, thanks to the intercom system.

"Jones," I mumbled into the speaker plate.

"What?"

"Jones," I mumbled again. Maybe I should have said "Adolf."

With exaggerated slowness, the man said, "What—is—your—name?"

"Jones." A slightly less garbled mumble on my part.

There was a pause of a few seconds. I dug my right hand into my rain jacket pocket, grasped the smoke grenade, and prayed that the guard inside would open the door.

The door buzzed, and I pushed through with my shoulder. I had the grenade out of the pocket and stepped inside.

A short, stocky guy with a dark crew cut, bright blue eyes, and a bristly dark mustache was coming toward me as I entered. "Who are you?" he asked. "What's your name?"

"Jones," I replied, yanking the pin and tossing the smoke-hissing grenade at him.

He dodged to the side into the hall. The grenade sailed past him and hit the living room floor as smoke continued to billow. His head jerked around to look at it, then twisted back to me just in time to catch my foot in his chest. He slammed back into the little desk at the archway and toppled straight over it.

Another man, aiming a pistol at me, rushed through the smoke-filled room and hallway toward me. He was 6-feet tall, light brown hair, slender. Willi the nephew.

I stepped toward him, blocking his gun hand outward with my left hand while smashing my open right hand into his Adam's apple. He gasped in pain and staggered backward, his gun was idly waving at the end of his arm. Clearly, he was hurting too badly to even aim. I hammered him with a right cross to the jaw, and he hit the floor like an anvil dropping on a cartoon character.

His gun bounced across the floor of the living room. I stepped over the gasping Willi and spotted the gun at the feet of a man sitting on a couch. Given the guy's startled, wide eyes and gaping mouth, I assumed he was a paying customer and not a threat to me. I leaned over Willi, gave him a love tap on his forehead with the butt of my Ruger—just wanted to make sure he slept tight. I grabbed Willi's pistol, a Glock, and slid it into the jacket pocket I had yanked the grenade from.

The room was full of smoke. But I could see that there was a total of three men sitting on some well-worn, upholstered furniture, coughing and rubbing their eyes.

"You," I growled, pointing at one of the men, who looked like Benjamin Franklin, "come here!" He got up and took two steps over to me, closer but not too close. He probably thought I was going to smack him around, and I have to admit it was a tempting idea. Instead, I handed him two pairs of plasticuffs and told him to cuff the other men.

"But—" one of them started to protest.

"—What? You already paid?" I interrupted him. "You let this guy cuff you or I'll beat you senseless and leave you for the police. Your choice."

Mr. Protest looked at the other two men, who were shrinking from me in fear.

"Cuff 'em," I growled.

Ben Franklin did as he was told, securing the other two, then meekly submitting to being cuffed. They stood nervously in a row, like schoolboys waiting to be dressed down by the principal.

"I'm sorry about what comes next," I said but wondered whether I was really and truly sorry. "Actually, let me correct myself. You deserve this." I hit the foreheads of the two guys nearest me with the butt of my Ruger, smashing each to the floor. Ben Franklin was the last. He jumped away, but I have long arms. I grabbed him, spun him around, applied the butt of my Ruger to his forehead, and dropped him unconscious next to his fellow johns. I turned and headed for the stairs.

"Hold it," a very tall, string bean of a man grunted from midway up the stairs. There was a pistol in his hand, aimed in my direction. "Show me your hands."

I raised my right hand with the Ruger, hoping his eyes would lock on my gun. Like a magician working a magic trick, my left went into the jacket pocket for the second smoke grenade. "Both hands up!" he said angrily, his attention focused on my pistol.

I pulled the pin on the grenade and flung it at him. He started to back up the stairs, then stopped, and began firing. As soon as I released the grenade, I dropped to the floor, rolling over and over into the living room, stopping once I was out of his line of sight behind the arch. I came out of the roll onto my feet, my Ruger still in hand. I reached around the arch, aimed in String Bean's vicinity, and fired four times. Then I crouched low, poked my head around, and fired twice more, catching him in the chest with both shots.

He crumpled downward, toppling face first on the stairs, bumping all the way to the first floor, and stopping in a lump at the bottom of the stairway. Three guards down, four to go: two in the back bedroom on the first floor; two somewhere upstairs. What with all the commotion and shooting, I was expecting they would arrive with pistols ablaze.

There was a barrage of gunfire from down the hall

from the rear of the building. Bullets chewed up the walls, the stairway railing, and the molding that framed the living room arch. This was no time to be fastidious about personal hygiene: I hit the floor next to the body of the stocky guard, pulled out my second Ruger, and put both guns on the floor. Then I tugged his unconscious bulk on top of me and grasped both pistols, holding them close to my thighs.

The gunfire stopped. Through screams and shouts from upstairs, I heard footsteps approaching fast. I peered past Stocky Guard's right ear. Two men in black T-shirts and swastika tattoos on their forearms stood back to back in the foyer, scanning their surroundings for me. There was still enough smoke left from the grenades that it was hard for them to spot me immediately.

Then one of them glanced directly at Stocky Guard on top of me, did a double take, and grunted at his partner as he brought his gun to bear on me. The second man had just begun to twist around when I fired the Rugers, shooting both of the men. They were flung backward, landing in a heap on top of String Bean at the bottom of the stairs.

I shoved Stocky Guard's body off of me—geez, the guy needed a better deodorant—and stood up. I put a fresh magazine in one Ruger and holstered it. I moved quietly to the men in a heap at the bottom the stairs and checked their pulses. All were alive. Great! I thought. You are all winners of a set of free plasticuffs. I walked over to Crew Cut and Willi the Nephew, checked them and also awarded them free plasticuffs. Due to all the bullets flying around, I thought I should check the three johns on the living room floor. Turned out they were all breathing. None had been shot. The astounding amount of violence I encountered on my missions from the Chairman always made me grateful when people survived.

I stepped to the living room arch and listened. I heard deep, muffled voices, maybe the johns, maybe the remaining guards. I also recognized the soft sound of female whimpering. It sounded like more than one woman, but I couldn't be sure.

Well, what now, Tyrrell? If you go up the stairs, you'll be an easy target. If the remaining guards were to come down the stairs, then *they* would be the targets. So, it was unlikely anyone was going to be eager to use the stairs. How the hell are you going to save these women now?

Almost on cue, the remaining upstairs guards appeared, moving very slowly down the stairs from the second floor and crouching behind two women in the scantiest of lingerie. Both women's hair fell past their shoulders, providing more cover for their cowardly, neo-Nazi captors. The only thing I saw of the two men was their swastika-tattooed forearms, which were wrapped around each woman's neck. They held guns to each woman's waist with their free hands.

"Put your gun down," one of the guards said.

"Or else?" I asked.

"Or else what?"

"You're supposed to say, 'or else,' and then threaten the woman." I was stalling. Two men moving slowly, hiding behind innocent women, and aiming guns at those women, presented minuscule targets. The first hostage-and-guard pair was about halfway down the stairs, the second pair was a few feet behind. And did I mention they were moving? If I shot and missed, the odds were very good that I would blow one or both of the women away. But if I didn't shoot, one of the two guards would shoot me, leaving nobody to save the kidnapped women. This seemed an impossible situation.

"Put your gun down, asshole," one of the guards shouted.

I whispered, "Please, God, help me with this."

Without the tiniest hesitation, I swung my arm up and fired once at the guard closest to me. A micro-second later, I swung my arm over and shot the second man a micro-second later. I held my shooter's stance, gun at the ready, as the two guards went limp, releasing the women, and collapsed straight down onto the stairs.

The women were horrified, gasping for breath, looking down at the bodies, then at me, then back down at the bodies. Their fear kept them frozen in place on the stairs.

"Come down," I said, firmly but gently.

They stepped over the bodies on the stairs and made their way down to the living room arch where I was.

They glanced this way and that, trying to absorb the carnage.

"Are there any more guards in the house?" I asked.

One of the women, a sandy blonde with large blue eyes, was too stunned to answer. The other, a brunette with dark brown eyes, shook her head.

"Are there still john—" I stumbled over the word; it seemed inappropriate with these two young women. "Are there any more men upstairs?"

"Yes," the one who had shaken her head replied.

"Do you know how many?"

She shook her head.

"Is it a full house?"

"No, not tonight."

"You sleep downstairs, don't you? Do you have clothes there?"

"Yes."

"Why don't you go down there, get dressed, and wait for me? Okay?"

They both hesitated.

"You're all right now. Really. It's safe now. Go get dressed and wait for me. I'll come get you."

They lingered, still unsure what to do.

"Please, I'm going to be sending the other women down—I need you to help them."

The brunette nodded, grabbed the blonde by the hand, and gently pulled her toward the basement door.

I slapped fresh magazines into both Rugers and slid

them into their holsters, hoping I wouldn't need to use them anymore. I ran up the stairs quietly, landing on the edge of each step with my toes, pushing off almost as soon as I touched the step, and hoping to avoid creaking noises. When I reached the second floor, I looked down the hallway and listened. I could hear young women crying softly. There were no male sounds except one: to my right, I could hear the huffing and grunting of a man trying to achieve orgasm.

Really? I wondered. There's been all kinds of noise, shouting, and shooting, and you're still in there humping away on some poor, drugged-out young woman. You're either a drunken moron not to have stopped and hidden, or you're so desperate to get your rocks off that you didn't stop to find out what was going on. Or, most likely, you're both: a desperate, drunken moron.

I walked down the hall toward the grunting and stopped outside the door where the sounds were coming from. I brought my knee up to my chest then extended my leg in a hard, swift kick. The door rocked on its hinges and separated from its frame by an inch. Without delay, I brought my knee up again and extended forward in another ferocious kick. The door exploded inward.

The balding, pot-bellied john was scrambling off the bed like a crab scuttling backward. The young woman grabbed for the dingy sheet and pulled it over her nakedness. Tears ran down her face.

"What the fuck?" the john shouted in a raspy voice.

"Who the hell are you?"

"Your worst nightmare," I said calmly.

He was trying to yank up his pants when I hit him with a right cross. I think maybe the Chairman allowed me to utilize the wrath of God, because the john rocketed backward through the air, crashed into a wall, and slid to the floor. He was unconscious, and I was pretty damn sure his jaw was broken.

What the hell? I thought. Let the punishment fit the crime: I stomped on his gonads. I'm a big boy. Six feet two, two hundred twenty pounds of muscle. When I stomp, it's significant. The john moaned in pain even though he was unconscious. I left his pants still down around his ankles and plasticuffed his wrists. Not a pretty picture.

I turned to the girl. The corner of her mouth was curling up the tiniest bit in an uncertain smile.

"Thank you," she whispered huskily.

"You're welcome. Go all the way to the basement and get dressed. Wait with the others, okay?"

She nodded.

"Go now."

She nodded again and was gone.

Two of the other bedrooms on the second floor produced two sleeping girls—probably from the drugs they'd been given. In the last two rooms, two johns cowered behind little wooden chairs while the girls remained in the beds, covering themselves with sheets. The johns both had their pants pulled up and shirts on, but the shirts were unbuttoned. The girls turned from me to the johns and back to me.

I asked the two girls to come into the hall, asked them to wake up the two sleeping girls and help them get to the basement and get dressed. While they did as I had asked, I collected the two johns into a single room.

"Drop your pants," I said.

Their bodies were rigid with fear; their hands held stiffly over their heads.

"Don't make me tell you again."

They reluctantly began to do as instructed.

"And your underwear."

"Hey, come on," one of them wailed.

"I've taken out eight men so far. You want to be nine and ten?"

They dropped their underwear to the floor.

"Stand back to back and raise your arms out from your sides."

They followed instructions, and I plasticuffed the men together at their wrists.

"Sit on the floor."

They complied. I plasticuffed the ankle of one of them to a cast-iron radiator leg.

"Comfy?" I asked, not waiting for an answer. "Good. Sit tight and the police will be by to arrest you."

"Oh, come on!" the one who liked to wail wailed again. "It's a victimless crime."

"Oh, really?" I knelt on one knee, but I still

towered over the man. "These girls have all been kidnapped, drugged, prostituted against their wills, and they're all underage. Have you any idea how long you're going to prison for?"

"No, no, wait a minute—" this from the other man. "Can't we come to an understanding? I can make it worth your while—"

"Shut up," I said, cutting him off. "There is good news in this scenario: once you go to prison, the sex is unlimited and free."

They both looked as if they had swallowed scorpions. After a moment of panicked silence, they began jabbering. I stuffed their underwear in their mouths.

Two more floors to go. Two more floors of frightened young women and despicable low-lifes. The thought exhausted me. I was disheartened but walked slowly to the top of the next flight of steps to the third floor. I barked in an imitation of my boot-camp drill instructor.

"Hey, assholes! Yes, I mean you, you gutless pieces of animal feces. Stop whatever the hell you're doing, step away from the women, and go to the corners of your rooms. Do it *NOW*, or I am going to feed you your own testicles. And I'm going to make sure you chew thoroughly and swallow. *NOW*—go!"

I could hear footsteps on the third and fourth floors. After about 10 seconds, everything was quiet.

In a gentler, but still penetrating, tone, I called out,

"Girls, please wrap yourself in a sheet or blanket and come out into the hall. Please. You're safe now. Come on out."

There was a soft shuffling of feet, and the doors on the third floor opened and five young women, wrapped in bedding of some kind, appeared.

Speaking much more quietly, I said, "You're safe now. Please go to the basement and get dressed and wait there. The police will be here soon. "

They paraded downstairs, slowly but steadily. I ran upstairs to the fourth floor and found three more girls and three more johns. I left the johns standing in the corners of the bedrooms and gathered the girls, draped in sheets, in the hallway.

"Is this everyone on this floor?"

One of them, a slender girl with reddish brown hair, shook her head and whispered, "There's one more man in the last room." She was pointing down the hall to a door on my right. "He's really bad. Scary."

"Okay, I'll take care of him. You're safe now. Please go to the basement and get dressed."

"Will . . . will we be going home?" asked another girl who appeared to be barely thirteen-years old.

"Yes. Soon."

After the girls went downstairs, I collected the johns in the hallway. It was amazing: now that they were dealing with a large, obviously angry, obviously dangerous man, they behaved like sheep instead of men dominating girls. None of them said anything, obediently doing what I told them to do. A far cry from bullying and raping teenage women. I had the men form a small circle. They were facing outward and their wrists were plasticuffed together. Their male apparatuses were exposed to the world. I plasticuffed two men's ankles to stairway railing posts.

"You all just wait here. The police will probably come by in the next 10 minutes or so."

I glanced down the hall to the room where the really bad man was. The door was shut. My attention hadn't been solely focused on it, but I was pretty sure that the man inside had not opened the door, not even wide enough to take a peek at the goings on in the hall.

The man nearest that door, a scrawny, brown-haired man with a bad complexion, begged, "Please, mister, can't we—"

"Shut up," I hissed, inches from his face. "Be quiet, or I'll kill you right here, right now."

He pulled his head back away from me and nodded.

Time for a final charge, Tyrrell. One more "really bad" man and then you're finished. I rushed along the hallway on tip toe, stopped to listen at the door, and heard nothing. Then I made my final appearance on the Capture the Bad Guys Tour.

2

I pushed open the bedroom door and stepped over the threshold. The john, hiding behind the door, slammed it shut against me, crushing me against the frame and stunning me.

The man slammed me with the door again and shouted, "I'm a cop, asshole!"

He didn't even attempt to give me my Miranda rights. He aimed a small 9mm pistol at me.

"Don't move!" He was a balding, burly guy with hairy forearms and chest. His only apparel was a pair of boxers. He stepped close and jabbed his gun into my chest. "Freeze you mother—"

I was a bad boy: I didn't freeze. I spun, my left hand blocking his gun hand away from me, my right fist connecting with his jaw, rocking him back against the wall. When he hit the wall, he fired, and the bullet whined past me into the hallway. A thumping sound came from the hall, the sound a body makes when it hits the floor.

Burly Cop turned toward the sound then twisted back to me. Too late. I smashed into him with a full body block, my right shoulder catching him under the chin and snapping his head back off the wall. His gun fell to the floor. I kicked it away. Burly Cop was disoriented, but he had plenty of fight left. He came at me with his fists flying. He knew how to punch and hit me with a very solid left that made me see stars.

"I'm a cop," he repeated in a grunt. "I'm going to beat the ever-loving shit outta you, then arrest you for assaulting a police officer." He stepped in close, pummeling me in the belly and lower ribs.

He was too close for me to punch back. Headbutting him was out; he was about 3 inches shorter than I was and I couldn't get the appropriate angle. At the rate he was hitting my ribs, I wasn't going to be able to breathe in a few seconds. If I didn't take this guy down, who knew what would happen to the girls I was trying to help. I kneed him in the groin. He doubled over with a low, gurgling moan that would have done credit to someone dying in a horror movie.

I brought my knee up again, this time catching him in the face and standing him straight up. I finished him off with a left-right combo that would have given a rhinoceros pause. His eyes rolled up in his head as his body sagged to the floor.

"Are you really a cop?" I gasped between breaths. He didn't answer. I rolled him onto his stomach, plasticuffed his wrists behind his back, then cuffed his ankles. I found his T-shirt on the back of a chair, balled it up, and shoved it into his mouth.

I went through the rest of his clothing and found cash, keys, a phone, a leather cover for the man's gold detective's shield, and a wallet with business cards identifying Detective Patrick Costello of the NYPD.

"You are a disgrace to the Hibernian race and the NYPD," I muttered.

I grabbed the small pistol with an 8-bullet magazine, probably his off-duty weapon. I yanked the magazine, ejected the shell from the chamber, and tucked both the mag and bullet into my pockets.

Out in the hallway, I found Scrawny Guy dead from a bloody wound in his gut. The one shot Costello had fired had done a lot of damage.

Back in the bedroom, I checked through Costello's one more time. Like many police detectives, Costello had a small black notebook and a pen in his jacket pocket. I wrote a note on a blank page in the notebook:

To whom it may concern at the NYPD,

This man is a detective in your department. He shot and killed the man in the hallway. He is probably on the take, accepting cash and free services from this establishment.

He is also guilty of statutory rape of a drugged girl.

I recommend that you use the murder and rape charges to get him to cooperate and give up the information regarding the owner of this establishment.

Sincerely,

Your Friendly Neighborhood Spider-Man

I left the note and Costello's personal belongings, including his now-empty gun, on the bed. I pocketed one of Costello's business cards. You never knew when you were going to need the services of a corrupt cop.

My business with the guards and johns was complete. Time to get the girls out of this hell hole. I went downstairs to the basement. The barracks-style room made prison seem appealing. Cinderblock walls with a pair of naked lightbulbs hanging from the ceiling. Tiny beds with metal frames, thin mattresses, and tattered blankets. The women were dressed in a ragged assortment of clothing: sweats or leggings with T-shirts and ratty sweaters. They were looking at me as if I was about to lead them to the land of milk and honey.

"You're safe. All the men are cuffed and can't hurt you anymore. I'm going to contact the police now, and they'll take care of you."

"Will we be able to go home?" one asked.

"Soon," I nodded. "Very soon."

"The men . . . upstairs. What will happen to them?"

"They're going to be locked up for a long time."

"Are you sure?"

"Yes. They'll never hurt you again." I paused before going back upstairs. "Please wait here. I'll tell the police where they can find you here."

"Are you leaving?"

"Not until the police are close by."

"Will . . . will we ever see you again?"

"Maybe. I don't know," I smiled. "You're safe now, that's the important thing."

As I climbed the stairs, I was certain of one thing: none of them would ever remember me.

*   *   *

Harry was waiting for me in the living room on the first floor. "What are you planning on doing now?"

"I'm going to call the police, and once we hear the sirens approaching, I'm hoping you will whoosh me and little Willi here to a secure location."

"I'm glad you remembered that helping Willi was tonight's mission."

"Finding Willi was just a job. Saving the women in this house was the mission I was called to." I dug my phone out of my pants pocket and dialed Charlie Winfield, Detective First Grade at the 6th Precinct.

"Winfield," he answered. His tone was neutral.

"Charlie, it's your favorite confidential informer."

"Hello, Jack. Am I happy to hear from you?"

"You're going to be. I just, er, discovered a house of prostitution at 341 West 91st Street. All the bad guys are wrapped up and ready for arrest. One of them is a Detective Patrick Costello. He shot and killed a man while attempting to escape. The women are in the basement, waiting to be rescued."

"Ohhhhh, God," he groaned. "Oh, so many questions. Okay, first, are you playing vigilante or informer?"

"Can't I be both? But if I have to choose, I'd say informer. *Confidential* informer."

"Got it. Now, West 91st is way the hell out of my precinct. Why are you calling me?"

"I have it on the very best authority that some of the cops in the local precinct may be on the take from the people running the prostitution house."

"Shit. Is Costello one of the cops on the take?"

"That would be my guess."

"Why didn't you call Vice?"

"I don't know anyone who works over there. Besides, I wanted you to get the credit."

"Give me the rest of the details, and I'll reach out to Vice."

I gave him the address, and explained that there were two dead bad guys, and a bunch of men cuffed and helpless, including the johns. And the aforementioned Detective Costello. "Please have the responders go in softly. Those young women have been through hell."

"How many women?"

"Fifteen. All Jewish, under-age, and drugged to some extent. This is really ugly."

"Got it. Did you say some of the bad guys had been shot?"

29

"Yes, two dead. Others are wounded. You're going to need ambulances."

"Did you shoot them?"

"I will neither affirm nor deny that. But circumstances arose that made shooting some of the men a necessity."

There was a heavy silence on Charlie's end of the call. Finally, he said, "Okay, I'd better make this happen fast."

"Yes, please."

"Thanks, Jack."

"For you, Charlie, anytime."

We disconnected. Harry and I looked down at Willi. I shook my head and muttered, "Hard to believe that this young jerk is the reason this entire operation came crashing down."

"The Chairman works in mysterious ways," Harry said.

"Yeah, so I heard."

Police sirens wailed in the distance, growing louder very quickly.

I said to Harry. "Let's whoosh. And please bring Willi."

Harry's eyebrows arched up, then—

He and I were standing on a sidewalk in Riverside Park. It was still raining. Willi was on the ground, still unconscious.

I asked Harry, "You couldn't whoosh us someplace

dry?"

"There was no need."

"No *need*? On a rainy night?"

"The more time you waste expressing your dissatisfaction with the situation, the more time you spend getting soaked."

I didn't have a suitably sarcastic riposte, so I turned my attention to Willi. I put the toe of my right shoe into the small of his back and pushed. He groaned but remained unconscious.

"Vake up, *Villi*," I said in a faux-Prussian accent. "Come on, *aufwachen*." I continued nudging him in the back with my shoe.

Willi groaned and rolled onto his chest, with his face resting in a tiny puddle. He spluttered in surprise, woke up, pulled at his cuffs to no avail, and realized he had better roll out of the puddle to save himself from drowning in an inch of water.

"What the hell?" He was groggy but managed to sound angry, too. "What's going on?"

I grabbed him by his left arm and dragged him away from the puddle. "Your aunt sent me," I said.

"What?" His surprise seemed genuine.

"She's worried about you. She thinks you hang out with a bad crowd. She asked me to find you."

"Are you fu—"

I gave him a relatively gentle kick in the gut. Although I doubt he would have agreed with the kick being classified as relatively gentle. "Don't talk like that about your aunt. The only reason you're not dead or under arrest is because of her."

"Oh."

"But I need to clarify something for you."

"Yeah?"

"You could still end up dead. Or arrested. Got it?"

"You won't kill me."

"Really?"

"You would have done it already."

I had to admit he was thinking pretty well for a guy in his predicament. "You might be right. But I won't hesitate to throw you to the police."

"Didn't my aunt send you to help me?"

"I told her I'd *find* you."

"Could we get the hell outta the rain?"

"Not until I get some answers."

"Like what?"

"Who runs the prostitution house? Who owns the building on 91st Street?"

"I don't know."

"Really?"

"I swear, I don't know," his words came fast, sounding like desperate truth.

"Okay, how did you end up working there?"

"I can't tell you."

"Of course not."

I grabbed him by the arm again, dragged him to the

puddle and pushed his face into the shallow water.

"No, no wait!" he spluttered out of the side of his mouth.

"How did you end up working there? Was your aunt right to worry about you hanging with a bad crowd?"

"No, no, she worries about nothing."

"Let's get something straight: You were working security at a house of prostitution where the women were taken against their will and are younger than seventeen. That's kidnapping and statutory rape. They were also drugged, which probably means you can be charged with some drug distribution charges."

"But I didn't arrange any of that. And I never touched any of the girls. They're Jewish skanks."

"What?" I pounded my fist down on the back of his head and smashed his face through the inch of water into the sidewalk. Then I curled my fingers in his hair and jerked him out of the puddle.

He was gasping for air, "I never touched them, I never touched them."

"The fact that they're Jewish makes this a hate crime on top of everything else. If you say anything that disrespecting any of them, I will drown you right here in this puddle. Got it?"

"Got it," his gasping was slowing down. His nose was bleeding, and the rain spread the blood over his upper lip, around the edges of his mouth, and down his chin.

"Are you a neo-Nazi?"

His eyes went wide with fear.

"I'm sure the idea of ratting out your Aryan brothers is abhorrent to you," I growled, "but if you don't, it's back to the puddle. Are you part of a neo-Nazi group?"

"I . . . I belong to the . . . they'll kill me."

"It seems to me that you have bigger problems than a bunch of guys who might, I emphasize *might*, kill you in the future. I'm about 30 seconds away from killing you right now. Or, if I'm struck by a sudden, generous impulse, I'll turn you over to the police. And you will go to prison, where you'll be raped more often than the girls in the house."

His eyes were as wide as they could possibly go. He was breathing fast, his mouth gaping open. "I can't. Please. . . ?"

"Tell me."

He panted a few more seconds then began sobbing. "I belong . . . I belong to the Supreme Order. *Oberste Ordnung*."

"Who's the leader of this club?"

"I don't know. He hides his identity."

"You better get off the hidden identity crap, or it's off to prison and all the intimate relationships you could ever want."

"I swear, I don't know."

"Where does this club of yours meet?"

"We meet at *Gesellschaft der Deutschen*. It's a little club on East 85th Street, about halfway between Third and

Second Avenues."

"Smack in the middle of what used to be German Yorkville."

"Yes, yes, it's one of the last German places left in the neighborhood."

I released my grip on his hair, took hold of his arm, and helped him stand up.

"There, that wasn't so bad, was it?"

"What are you going to do to me now?"

"Oh, I'm turning you over to the police."

"But you promised—"

"Nothing. I didn't promise a thing."

Harry spoke for the first time, "What about his aunt?"

"I'm sorry for her, I really am. But this clown aided and abetted kidnapping, prostitution, and illegal drugs. He belongs in jail."

Willi began sobbing again, "But they . . . they're going to . . ."

"Look at it this way, kid," I said. "Maybe you'll get lucky. Maybe you'll be in a cell with someone who appreciates a nice little white supremacist like you." I turned to Harry. "What's going on back at 341 West 91st Street?"

"The police are loading up the bad guys?"

"Could you whoosh him inside the prisoner transport van?"

"Yes."

And Willi was gone.

"I thought you were going to argue more about helping Willi out," I said.

"Because of Mrs. Schörner?"

"She does happen to be our client."

"Yes. But as you so eloquently put it, her nephew belongs in prison."

"He certainly does."

"Would you like me to transport you home?"

"Could I ask a question first?"

"You just did."

I shook my head in faux disgust. "I liked you better when I made all of the jokes."

"When was that?"

"Ouch. Will any of the girls remember me?"

"What do you think?"

I exhaled slowly. "No. That's not the deal I have with the Chairman. I make things right for people, but they don't remember me. That way it's selfless."

"Given your understanding of your 'deal,' why did you need to ask?"

"I wondered what the girls are going to think happened?"

"They'll remember a tall man saved them. But they won't be able to describe you. They won't remember the color of your eyes or the sound of your voice."

"They're safe. That's all that matters."

"Yes." Harry smiled. A real smile. "May I

transport you home?"

"What's the ringleader's name?"

"Excuse me?" Harry seemed genuinely surprised.

"Who's the leader of the Supreme Order? And please don't waste my time telling me that if I need the name, I'll be given it—if the Chairman didn't want me to go after these clowns, why did he send me here? And how the hell can I go after them if I don't know the name of the evil leader?"

Harry turned his face up, seeking guidance from above, then said to me, "Gerhard Fuchs."

"Thank you."

"Now," Harry said with a microscopic hint of impatience, "may I transport you home?"

"Kim's place, please, and could you dry me off—?"

I found myself standing just inside Kim's front door, completely dry. "Thanks, Harry," I whispered, then I spoke loudly like the Dad in a 1950s sitcom, "Honey! I'm home!"

Kim Gannon, with sparkling blue eyes and long, glorious red hair, was sitting on the couch. She closed her laptop and put it on the couch, stood up, and came to meet me. She kissed me very tenderly on the lips.

"Tough day at work, honey?" she purred.

"Oh, yeah."

"Is that a bruise I see on your right cheek?"

"Probably."

"Were you mixing it up with bad guys?"

I nodded and collapsed into her spot on the couch.

"Hey, I was sitting there," she said.

"Sit next to me. Please?"

She picked up her laptop and put it on the coffee table. Then she sat next to me, clasping my right hand in both of hers. "Was it bad?"

"Yeah. Very bad. Fifteen teenage girls had been kidnapped, drugged, and forced into prostitution."

"Oh my God. That's horrible. Did the Chairman send you to rescue them? You did rescue them, right?"

"Of course."

"Was that your mission?"

"Not exactly. This particular house of prostitution was run by a gang of neo-Nazis. The old-lady aunt of one of the Hitler Youths wanted me to track down her nephew."

"And you found him at the house?"

"Harry led me there."

"Neo-Nazis running teenage prostitutes . . ." she realized there was something else. "Were the girls Jewish?"

"Yup."

"That . . . that's so ugly. It's disgusting. It's . . . there isn't a word that really captures how horrible it is. I can't believe people behave that way."

"Believe it."

"Did you get all the bad guys?"

"Every last one of them. The johns, too."

"And the girls are safe now?"

"They are."

She stared at me for a long moment. "You didn't get the ringleader, did you?"

"He wasn't there."

"Do you know who he is?"

"I've got a name. Gerhard Fuchs."

*   *   *

NIGHT – GERHARD FUCHS'S HOME
PALISADE AVENUE, RIVERDALE, THE BRONX

GERHARD FUCHS stared at the computer monitor as the security video from his West 91st Street property played on the screen. He was blond with blue eyes, a straight nose, and a well-defined chin. A lean physique, not quite six-feet tall. He wore a dark-blue suit over a white shirt but no tie. He sat at a large wooden desk in his den. The room had thick, cream-colored, wall-to-wall carpeting and wood paneling that climbed the walls top within a foot of the ceiling. All of the wooden furniture was large and dark.

A tiny woman with cold, gray eyes and a hard face stood next to Fuchs's chair. Her posture was straight and rigid as if she were standing at attention, like an army officer reporting to a superior.

Both Fuchs and the woman watched the computer's screen: A large man moved quickly and quietly about the 91st Street building, incapacitating the guards then

39

capturing the johns. He rounded up the prostitutes and sent them to the basement, where they dressed and waited for the police to arrive.

"One man was able to subdue every one of my guards?" Fuchs asked. "And the johns? Including the cop?"

"Yes, sir."

"Are there any clear pictures of his face? Something we could give to our friends in NYPD to discover this intruder's identity?"

"No, sir."

"Ms. Aschgrau, how many cameras are there at 341 West 91st?"

"A dozen."

"And not one single camera produced a clear enough image to identify this man."

"I'm sorry, sir, but that's correct," she replied.

"How was it possible for this intruder to do that?"

"I'm sorry, sir, but I have no idea."

Fuchs stared at the monitor without really seeing it, softly drumming his fingers on top of his desk while he pondered the video. "Maybe he's a magician."

Aschgrau shrugged, uncomfortable because she had no solid information for her employer.

"Maybe I should recruit him. Convert an enemy into an ally." Fuchs smiled bitterly as he continued to scan the images on the monitor. "Someone that . . . proficient would be quite an asset. What do you think?"

"Yes, he would, but I haven't a clue how we would

go about finding him, never mind recruiting him."

"You're right." Fuchs stood up and walked around to the front of the desk. "I wonder if this man, whoever he is, was solely interested in the house on 91st Street or is he coming after us. Coming after *Oberste Ordnung*."

Aschgrau had nothing to offer.

Fuchs held his hands out from his sides, palms up and empty. "I realize you don't have an answer." He paused, thinking. "Are all the guards and johns under arrest? Did anyone escape?"

"They're all under arrest."

"That's unfortunate. And there are no clues to the intruder's identity?"

"I'm sorry, sir, but we don't have access to the building. The NYPD was on scene before we had time to do any analysis of our own. And we had to cut the video feed so the NYPD couldn't trace it back to us."

"Good work." Fuchs was thinking out loud, "So. We don't know if the house on 91st Street was the target or just the beginning of. . . ." He paused, staring at his desk without focusing. "Did the intruder take any of our money?"

"No."

"So this was about stopping the business and might be the beginning of operations against the *Oberste Ordnung*." He paced back and forth. "I wonder if he's an agent for the Jews in New York. If they somehow got wind of us, they might pay a man of this . . . *type*, to protect them. Of course they'd never dirty their own hands."

He stopped pacing and turned to speak directly to the woman, issuing an order, "Double up security at the *gesellschaft*, the König facility, and Colgate in the Bronx."

"I'll see to it immediately."

"Thank you, Ms. Aschgrau."

Fuchs walked to a window and stared through the glass into the night.

After waiting for a moment, the woman said, "Was there something else, sir?"

"Were all of the . . . young women taken away by the police?"

"Yes."

"Including Diane?"

"Yes."

"That's a particular problem for me. Contact Rolf Jäger. Make sure he eliminates the problem."

"Yes, sir."

*　　*　　*

"Before I'm done," I said to Kim, "I'm going to know this fucking neo-Nazi inside and out. Pardon my French."

"Your French seems very appropriate in this situation. Does 'done' mean you're going to wreck this gang of neo-Nazis?"

"It does."

"That wasn't part of your original mission, was it?"

"Do you think the Chairman would have had Harry lead me to that place if He didn't want me to take care of these bastards?"

"I guess not."

I sagged down on the couch, resting my head on the back, and closing my eyes. "I'm exhausted."

"Fighting with neo-Nazi slime balls will do that to you."

"You are so right about that."

"Do you need a cappuccino?"

I opened my eyes and smiled, "Always."

She went into the kitchen and I followed her like a puppy who can't be away from its master. If I had a tail to wag, I would have been wagging it.

"Wow," she said, grinning, "the mere mention of cappuccino seems to have revived you."

"It's the magic elixir of my existence."

Kim had the espresso dripping and the milk steaming within seconds, moving smoothly and efficiently around her kitchen. She made a second cup for herself, and we returned to the couch. After a few sips, I felt completely rejuvenated.

We drank in silence, staring out the windows of her tenth-floor apartment, taking in her scenic view of some of the Upper West Side. Well, I was gazing out the window. As I was finishing my cappuccino, I realized that Kim was watching me.

"What?" I asked.

"What, what?" she replied.

"You're doing a visual analysis of my emotional state. Why?"

"I have this feeling that something else is going on with you. Am I right?"

"What do you mean?"

"Ever since we got back together, you've been," she smiled weakly, "and I mean this in the gentlest most loving way, you've been depressed and angry. Are you still upset about our being on a break?"

"No. Absolutely not."

"What is it then? Have you decided that you need to talk about my brief flirtation? The bearded guy you saw me with at Café Sabatini?"

"No," I shook my head and grinned. "He wasn't your type."

"Oh? What's my type?"

"Tall, rugged, government-trained guys with blue eyes and a devastating smile."

"I can't imagine whom you're referring to. And your smile isn't that great."

"But I am tall and blue-eyed."

"Yes, you are," she admitted. "Do you need to talk about Lauric?"

Why would I need to talk about Laurie Mandelbaum, I asked myself. Well, Tyrrell, you randomly ran into the first woman you ever loved and the two of you had proceeded to have the romantic encore to end all romantic encores. But, realizing that Kim was your true love now, you had ended the relationship with Laurie.

"Jack?" Kim whispered. "Do you need to talk about Laurie? If not to me, maybe to Dr. Hoffman?"

"I find it a little unsettling that you can see right through me."

"It's a gift," she replied. "You loved Laurie, she was Jewish, and she was only a few years older than these young women when you first dated her. Sorry to tell you this, but you're not all that hard to figure out.

"Shucks, I always wanted to be a man of mystery."

"No chance." She waited on me to say something. But when I said nothing, Kim added, "You're still beating yourself up over her death."

"She was my client. I was supposed to stop her murderer."

"This is the point where you would tell me that it must have been the Chairman's will that she die."

I shook my head, "My job was to help her."

"Help her, not save her. Maybe the help she needed didn't include her being saved."

"You spend too much time with Harry; you sound like him."

"I'll take that as a compliment." She gave me a quick kiss on the cheek and stood up. "Do you want another cappuccino?"

"I do, but first—I think I would like to take a hot

bath, if you don't mind."

"I don't mind. And you're a shower guy. What's with the bath?"

"I need to soak my aching body. A soon-to-be ex-cop gave me quite the working over."

"Does that mean no sex tonight?" she grinned.

"Well, let's not get hasty."

3

"So," Kim said smiling widely, "sex with a punch-tender tummy is possible."

"Only thanks to your gentle yet erotic ministrations." I took a first sip of my morning coffee.

"I may just have to patent 'gentle yet erotic ministrations.'"

"I hope you'll share the credit."

"You came up with the terminology. I'm the one who invented the ministrations."

"Yes, you did."

"How 'bout waffles and bacon for breakfast?"

"What's the occasion?"

Kim pushed her laptop across her dining room table to me. On the bottom of *The New York Times* home page was the headline: *Prostitution Ring Broken Up By Spider-Man*.

"Gee, the *Times* headline writers have a sense of humor."

"That's what you were talking about last night, isn't it?" she asked.

"Yup."

"I read the story. Did you really leave a note signed by Spider-Man?"

"No. I left a note signed by 'Your Friendly Neighborhood Spider-Man.'"

"Pardon me for being imprecise. Why Spider-Man?"

"He's my favorite comic book hero. Always has been."

"Did you leave the bad guys trussed up in webbing?"

"No, I had to resort to plasticuffs."

"Well, Spider-Man, in order to celebrate your triumph of last night, do you want waffles?"

"Yes, please."

I drank more coffee as I watched Kim make and pour the batter onto the heated waffle iron. She put a double layer of paper towels on a plate, stretched uncooked bacon strips on the paper towels, covered the bacon with another layer, and popped the plate into the microwave.

The well-done bacon and hot waffles arrived in front of me within minutes. Kim joined me with a single waffle and a single bacon strip adorning her plate.

She delicately bit off the tip of her bacon. "What are you going to do about the neo-Nazis?"

"I'm not sure."

"Why don't you ask Harry?"

"Maybe I'll ask Harry," I said.

"Gee, why didn't I think of that?"

"Cause you're not a government-trained private detective cum troubleshooter?"

"Just remember that whole government-trained verbiage was mine."

"I promise I won't forget. As if you'd let me."

"These waffles are good," she said. "If I say so myself."

"And you do."

"And I do. Anyway, why not get in touch with NYPD's counter-terrorism unit? See what they've got on this neo-Nazi group?"

"Why not?" I muttered and shrugged my shoulders. "Maybe I should just ask Harry to whoosh me straight into one of the neo-Nazi meetings."

"Would he do that?"

"He would if he thinks I *need* to be whooshed. If I don't *need* it, he won't do it for me."

She chewed on the meaning of the word "need" while she chewed on her waffle. "Harry only helps you out when you *need* his help—who decides whether or not you *need* help?"

"The Chairman."

"Your tone suggests that you're not always in agreement about your *needing* help."

"I'd say the Chairman and I are rarely in agreement."

"Did you feel you needed His help when your last—" she hesitated, "when Laurie was killed?"

"Absolutely."

"Were you angry with Him?"

"Absolutely. Still am."

"Don't you think you should be careful about getting angry with the Chairman?"

"I wouldn't recommend it as a way of proceeding. On the other hand, I figure if anyone can handle my being angry at Him, it's the Chairman."

Kim nodded as she mulled that over. I thought she was about to ask something else, but she plopped more waffle in her mouth instead.

"Man, this is a good waffle," she said.

"The genuine maple syrup doesn't hurt."

"No, it does not."

*　　*　　*

After breakfast, Kim went to work. It was a short commute since her second bedroom was her office. Once she went into her office, she was all business. She emerged occasionally for a cup of coffee or ice tea or to use the bathroom. If I happened to be at her place during a work day, it wasn't unusual for us to exchange a grand total of ten words.

One of the joys of having moved into a new apartment a month earlier was that I now had a second bedroom in my home. Tiny though this bedroom was—it served as my office. But when I spent the night at Kim's, I either had to commute to my place in Greenwich Village or improvise at Kim's. Sometimes the dining room table, sometimes the coffee table. Today however, I had no clients to keep happy. I could devote my full attention to Gerhard Fuchs, modern-day Nazi.

I dressed from the limited collection of clothing I kept at Kim's: today's choice was blue jeans and my dark-gray wool sweater. I poured myself a very large coffee in a thermos-style mug, threw on my Barbour jacket, and went to the roof of Kim's building. I ignored the patio area with its tables and chairs and walked to the railing on the west side of the building. I could see all the way across West End Avenue and the Hudson River to the Palisades in New Jersey. About five miles to the north, the George Washington Bridge spanned the river, joining Manhattan with the Garden State.

I soaked in the view and drank coffee for a few minutes.

"What's wrong, Jack?" Harry asked.

"Hello. I was just about to call out to you."

"I spared you the effort. What's wrong?"

"I want to get this guy Fuchs. Is his being a neo-Nazi after all enough to justify my going after him? I mean, do you think it's enough?"

"He espouses hate, and he supports his efforts with a criminal enterprise that exploits young women. Shouldn't that be enough?"

"Yes, of course. I just . . . I . . ."

"But your desire to go after him isn't motivated by the noblest of feelings?"

"Uh, no. Not noble at all."

"You hate him personally."

"I do," I admitted reluctantly, "and I hate his swastika-tattooed, asshole followers, too."

"That's a lot of hatred."

"Yeah, probably not good for my work. Hard to keep focused when you're driven by hate."

"Sounds like a topic of conversation for you and Dr. Hoffman."

"Okay, I'll take my emotional turmoil to my shrink, but—" I extended my hand to stop him, "before you leave, I need some help."

"What, pray tell, do you need?"

"Pray tell?" I shook my head, "Never mind, I don't know what to do next. I don't know a damn thing about Fuchs."

"Why don't you ask for help from your friends in the law-enforcement community?"

"My plans—vague as they are at the moment—go beyond the scope of law-enforcement work."

"Does that mean you will be pursuing vigilante justice?"

"It means the police and FBI have to work with evidence. Something that will stand up in court. I don't have to follow those kinds of evidentiary standards. Come on, help me out here."

Harry was staring in silence across the river without any sign that he was going to respond any time soon.

"Harry, that prostitution operation that I broke up last night is probably not the only criminal activity that Fuchs has going. Depending on his plans, he needs capital to fund his activities. Someone has to pay for all the black clothing, swastika paraphernalia, and weapons. Bad intentions are not enough for neo-Nazis. My guess, and it's just a guess at this stage, is that Fuchs has more than a couple of ongoing criminal enterprises. And I'd like to know what they are, stop them, and then confront Fuchs."

"He has a drug lab where heroin is laced with fentanyl and then distributed through his network. Not to mention a separate team, whose sole task is robbing banks."

"Oh boy. Do you know where or when any of this stuff is happening?"

Harry glanced skyward then gazed at me. "No. Sorry."

"That's not helpful."

He shrugged.

If Harry was finished briefing me on Fuchs, I needed a different way to gather information. I asked, "Is Costello being interrogated today?"

"Detectives will be talking to him later today."

"Would you whoosh me into that interrogation? Whoosh me invisibly?"

"Yes."

"How 'bout whooshing me straight into Gerhard

Fuchs's lair?"

"So you can put an end to his criminal activities by putting an end to him?"

"I just thought maybe you could provide me with a short-cut into Fuchs's heart of darkness."

"No. You need to work this one step at a time."

"Okay. How 'bout whooshing me to Costello's interrogation?"

"I can do that."

"Thank you."

"You still have plenty of time to see Dr. Hoffman beforehand."

"What about any of the other bad guys who got caught with Costello? And Willi the nephew? Have any of them been interrogated?"

"Some. Most of them know nothing."

"Yeah, Fuchs would never let the underlings know enough to screw him."

"You could use this time to visit Dr. Hoffman," he reminded me.

"You are such a noodge."

He disappeared. I could swear his tiny little Mona Lisa smile was on his face as he vanished.

"Damn," I muttered.

As if by miracle, when I called Dr. Hoffman, he said he was available for a session. I knocked softly on Kim's office door, poked my head inside, and blew her a kiss. She blew me a kiss in reply. Having a woman I loved in my life was a truly joyous thing. That must have been why I had proposed to her. And spent all that time and money selecting a piece of purple yarn to act as an engagement ring. We kept telling each other that we were going to pick something a little more traditional, but that never seemed to happen. I suspected that Kim actually liked the yarn ring.

I caught a No. 1 train at West 79th Street and Broadway and rode it all the way to Christopher Street in Greenwich Village. From there it was a brief walk to my shrink. Dr. Hoffman's office was on the fourth floor of a pre-war building at the southwest corner of Washington Square Park. Two rooms with a bath. Probably subdivided from a larger apartment.

Dr. Hoffman held the door to his inner sanctum open for me. "Why don't you come in?" His Bavarian-flavored German accent was softly inviting.

The good doctor had recently had the place redecorated, but it was hard to spot the difference from the old decor.

"Who did your decorating? Or was it some kind of package?"

"Why do you ask?"

"Your walls used to be painted the faintest mint-tinged off white. Now they're cream-colored. And your artwork used to feature paintings of beaches and shoreline—now you have paintings of beaches and shoreline, but they're slightly different. New but hardly noticeable. Even your couch and armchair have fresh upholstery but in almost the exact same shades of blue and maroon as before. Is that so patients don't freak out at the change?"

"What do you think?"

"I'm guessing you wanted to freshen the place up but not disturb anyone. A lot of your patients won't even notice."

"That's a reasonable guess. I hope you won't mind if I point out that *you* noticed."

"Was that a question?"

"No. Did you take it as such?"

"I probably did. No, scratch that, I did."

"Why do you think you noticed?"

"Because I'm a government-trained troubleshooter cum private detective."

"Any other reasons?"

"Because I'm openminded and receptive to new things?"

Dr. Hoffman managed to squelch the smile pulling at the corners of his mouth. "Do you really think you're openminded?"

"Actually, yes. I embraced the idea that I could work directly for the Chairman, for God. That I could be partners with an angel. That I could right wrongs for others."

He nodded, "Yes, that is definitely openminded."

"Thank you."

"Are you still attending AA meetings?"

"Speaking of being open?"

"Yes. Are you going? Do you find them helpful?"

"They're fantastic. I love them."

"Good. Now that you've reassured yourself about your own openness, why did you want to see me today?"

"I'm . . . I'm working on a case with neo-Nazis, and it's disgusting and unpleasant. I just broke up the operations of a prostitution house that kidnapped, drugged, and enslaved Jewish girls."

"That is horrible."

"Yeah . . . I gotta admit, I didn't think of this before I got here, but it's kind of awkward to be talking about Nazis with you."

"Because I'm from Germany?"

"Yes."

"But we're talking about you, not me."

"Yeah, but . . . and hey, I don't mean to suggest you have Nazi leanings or anything. I'm sorry if I made you feel that."

"You didn't. But thank you for your concern."

I was uncomfortable and didn't speak for a long moment.

Hoffman asked, "What is it that concerns you about neo-Nazis? Specifically, what are your feelings about them, and why do those feelings worry you?"

"My feelings . . . I, uh, I . . . freakin' loathe and detest those guys."

"I think many people share your feelings. I do myself."

"I get that, I really do. But I'm trying to . . . take a bunch of them out. And hating them makes me angry and hurts my focus. Which might end up getting me hurt. Or dead."

"What exactly are you hoping to accomplish in this session?"

"Can you help me work through my anger toward them? I don't mind being motivated by it, but I can't be blinded by it."

"Or the result could be your death."

"Yes. So how do I handle my hatred?"

"That's extremely difficult."

"That's extremely unhelpful."

"I'm sorry," he smiled. "You've admitted to yourself the true nature of your feelings and identified the problem with those feelings. That's an excellent first step."

"What's my second step?"

"Well, what is the second step in AA?"

"Came to believe that a Power greater than ourselves could restore us to sanity."

"And the third step?"

"Made a decision to turn our will and our lives over to the care of God as we understood Him."

"Do you think those steps are helpful?"

"Absolutely."

"Then I suggest you take them."

I blinked in surprise. "Okay, let me be sure I understand you. You're saying I should work AA's first three steps on neo-Nazis?"

"Yes. Work the steps to understand and cope with *your feelings* about neo-Nazis."

"If I work the steps and come to a better understanding of my feelings, can I still go ahead and kill these disgusting excuses for human beings?"

Hoffman stared at me for a long moment. "I believe that is for you and the Chairman to decide."

We sat quietly for a couple of minutes. I was about to stand up, thank Hoffman for his time, and leave, but found myself posing a question that had been bothering me ever since I had confronted Mrs. Schörner's nephew Willi.

"These neo-Nazis, these people who are trying to emulate Hitler, are they crazy? Or are they evil?"

"What do you think?"

"I'm not sure. I think . . . I think maybe they're both."

"Why do you say that?"

"Well, this might be an overly simplistic compared to what you'd say, but I think the hatred is driven by fear. Fear so huge and corrosive that they become deranged and believe that it's all right for them to do evil."

"Are you sure they know their behavior is evil?"

"They must know their actions are wrong. There are laws against kidnapping and rape. The neo-Nazis are aware of the laws, or they wouldn't carry on illegal activities in secret."

"By your definition these neo-Nazis are legally sane: They *know* they are breaking the law."

"I agree, but . . ."

"But you are having trouble accepting their abominable behavior. You want it to be evil and not the actions of the mentally ill."

"Yes, I do."

"Because if they are evil, you would be justified in doing whatever you do to stop the neo-Nazis."

"Yes."

Hoffman glanced out his window, something he almost never did, and pursed his lips as if considering what he was about to say. "This is my non-professional opinion: Neo-Nazis are evil. If they are mentally ill, their illness is caused by the evil within them. It appears that your current mission is to confront this evil. But, since this is only my opinion, you might want to talk with Harry about the Chairman's will for you."

I let his words sink in. After a moment, I replied, "Yeah. I should talk with Harry."

"I hope you'll allow me to shift this conversation in a new direction. Do you feel that you failed Laurie Mandelbaum?"

"Yes. I'd say that when your client gets killed by the bad guy you're supposed to stop, then yes, you obviously failed her."

"Do you say that solely because she was your

client? Or because you loved her once?"

Despite having discussed this very issue with Kim earlier, it was hard for me to answer Hoffman. "Both. She was my client. And my first love."

"Do those two facts have equal weight for you?"

"No," I hesitated. "She was my first love."

"You were unable to save your first love, who was Jewish. Then you become involved in a case where the villains are neo-Nazis. By definition they are anti-Semitic. Is it possible that some of your current feelings are due to your feelings about Laurie?"

"Yes."

"That's going to make it harder for you to let go of the hatred and maintain focus on finishing this job."

"You are such a comfort."

"Ah, you are getting better already. Your poor attempts at humor are resurfacing."

"I don't come here for criticism of my wit."

"No, but it's yours as a free bonus."

"Is our time up?" I asked with faux desperation.

"Yes, actually, it is."

4

"Take the damn handcuffs off," Costello growled. He was sitting at a steel-topped table on a stainless-steel slat-backed chair in a dank little room with cinderblock walls. Across the table from him were two more, slat-backed chairs, but these chairs had padded seat cushions. Occupying those cushions were a pair of detectives. The man was tall and skinny and had mousy brown hair that flew in all directions and a thin, bristly mustache. The African-American woman dressed a lot better and had close-cut dark hair. On the wall behind them was a mirror. Given this was a standard interrogation room, I figured the mirror was transparent from the opposite side.

"I hope this goes quickly," I whispered to Harry.

"You act as if we have never attended an event with the participants not being able to see or hear us," he responded in a normal tone of voice. Nobody in the room was checking to see where our voices were coming from.

"Sorry, but I still haven't gotten used to it. Names?" I asked, pointing at the two detectives.

"The man is Mazzeo. The woman is Cunningham."

While we were talking, Mazzeo unlocked the cuffs and pulled them from Costello's wrists. "You've been Mirandized, right?" Mazzeo asked, sliding the cuffs into his jacket pocket.

"Yeah, sure. I don't need you to read me my rights."

"Do you want an attorney?" Cunningham asked.

"Not for right now."

"Are you sure?"

"You don't think I can handle you two?" Costello grinned.

She smiled in response. An icy expression that would have frozen my toes if directed at me.

"Who's paying you off?"

"Nobody."

"Really?" Cunningham was still smiling. "We have it on very good authority that you're on the take. Again, who's paying you off?"

"I'll speak slowly for those of you who don't have good English," Costello said. "N – O – B – O – D – Y. Got it? Understand?"

Mazzeo interjected, "Cut the crap. We've got you cold for patronizing a prostitute and statutory rape. And since the young woman was Jewish, we've got you for a hate crime. Your fingerprints are all over the room, your DNA is in the victim's rape kit. We've also got you on felony murder since you stupidly shot one of your fellow johns. We have your fingerprints on your off-duty piece and gunshot residue on your hand. So, do you want to cooperate or tell me a fairy tale about mistaken identity? Either way, I can guarantee you'll be going to prison for a long time. Gee, a convicted cop in prison, I wonder what a great experience that must be."

Costello looked back and forth at the two detectives, then down at the table. "I've been in rooms like this one a lot of times."

"So you know how this works."

"Yeah."

"Just tell us what we want to know."

"What kind of deal can I get?"

"The DA told us he'll knock the felony murder to manslaughter. And drop the patronizing charge."

"Shit, patronizing is a misdemeanor. You're not giving me anything."

"Manslaughter instead of murder is quite a break."

"What about the rape charge?"

Mazzeo shook his head.

Cunningham said, "The DA has no interest in dealing on that charge. It's a hate crime. What you get is your felony murder becoming manslaughter."

"With a recommendation to serve the sentences concurrently?"

"No promises," Cunningham replied, "but we'll ask the DA."

Costello continued to look down at the table.

"You're going to prison," Mazzeo said after a minute. "The only question is for how long."

"Okay, okay. I get it."

"In that case, start with who's paying you off.

Which other cops are on the payroll? Who owns the brothel? What else has he got going on?"

"I should have killed that freaking guy," Costello muttered, staring up at the ceiling.

"What guy?"

"The one who broke up the party. The guy who cuffed everyone and left us for you to collect."

I pointed to myself and grinned at Harry.

"Your humility overwhelms me," Harry said.

Before I uttered a rejoinder, Cunningham snapped, "Stop stalling. You know what we want to hear. Get going."

"Okay . . . I don't know the owner, the guy in charge. He belongs to some neo-Nazi group called the Supreme Order. I don't know anything else about him. Really."

"You're a neo-Nazi?" Cunningham asked.

"No, I'm not. But their money is as green as anyone else's."

"The property isn't owned by a Supreme Order," Mazzeo cut in.

"What do you want from me?" Costello whined. He wasn't as tough now as he had been last night with a gun in his hand, trying to blow me to kingdom come. "The Supreme Order probably has two or three dozen shell companies. One company inside the other inside the other inside—"

"We get it," Cunningham cut him off. "Any ideas

what else these neo-Nazis are up to? Are they running more prostitutes? Other criminal activities?"

"I heard some of the security at the 91st Street house talking about running drugs."

"That's it? You heard something? What kind of drugs? Running them where?"

"They were a little drunk. One of them made a crack about 'retailing some interesting inventory' and another guy said, 'I never heard drugs called inventory before.' They laughed and then realized I was sitting there listening to them. They shut up. They were drunk but they weren't complete morons."

"Only partial morons."

Mazzeo pushed a notepad and pen across the table. "Write down the names of all of the neo-Nazis that you remember. Include addresses and phone numbers."

"I don't have any addre—"

"Shut up. Write what you have. Including the names of cops you know are on the take."

"I'm not doing that."

"Fine," Cunningham shrugged. "The deal with the DA is off."

Costello shook his head. "You people are screwing me over big time."

"You did that to yourself a long time ago," Mazzeo said and pointed at the pad.

Costello glared balefully at each of the detectives, and when neither of them flinched, he reached for the pad and shoved it till it fell off the table onto the floor.

"This little conversation has not been very helpful," I said.

"You don't know anything now that you didn't before."

"Not a thing." I paused, waiting for inspiration to strike. A thought popped into my head. Not sure it qualified as inspiration, but it was a good idea. I said, "Let's get some cappuccino."

"Yes, let's."

"Please whoosh us to Buona Tazza on Minetta."

My words still seemed to hang in the air as I found myself standing in front of Buona Tazza on Minetta Street at the corner of Sixth Avenue and Bleecker Street in the Village. The front of the café was all windows with a view of the tiny park at the corner where the trees were all bare this late in November. Inside, the café had a warm feel with its exposed-brick walls and blond-finished oak tables and chairs.

"Shall we go in?" Harry asked.

"I don't suppose you could whoosh my laptop to me?"

"You want to search the internet for the Supreme Order?"

"Since I know absolutely nothing about them, yeah, I thought I'd start online."

"You'll be wasting your time," Harry said, leading the way inside Buona Tazza.

We both ordered cappuccino then settled a table with our beverages.

"Why would it be a waste of time?"

"What are you expecting to find?"

"The Supreme Order probably has a website. With swastikas, maybe a picture or two of Hitler, and statements from well-known American Nazis explaining how the Jews are taking over everything, how they already control the media and the financial industries, and how they're polluting Aryan purity with inter-marriage, blah, blah, blah. Is that about the size of it?"

"Yes."

"But no clues to help that would help me unravel their criminal activities, right?"

"Right."

"Is Herr Fuchs planning something really ugly?"

"Yes."

"Really soon?"

"Yes. Within days."

My stomach dropped at that news. "How am I going to find out what this guy is up to?"

"Follow the money," Harry replied.

"What?"

"Follow the money. It's from the movie *All the President's Men*."

"I know: Deep Throat tells Bob Woodward to follow the money."

"Exactly."

"Great. Just how do I manage to follow the money?"

Harry said nothing.

"Oh, wait," I said, a light bulb going on and illuminating the vast, dim recesses of my mind. "I ask Naomi and Stewart to dig into this guy."

Harry nodded.

"Can we go see them now?"

"I'd like to finish my cappuccino first," he said.

"Good thinking," I replied and drained the last of my cup in a single gulp. Harry was daintier, taking three, slow sips to finish.

A second later, he had whooshed us inside a railroad flat, a long, narrow apartment full of worn, battered furniture that even the Salvation Army wouldn't have wanted. A half-dozen tables were scattered about, each with a computer, keyboard, and monitor. I wondered if the prevalence of monitors was because there was no view to the outside world: all of the windows had pale-blue paint on the insides of the glass frames. Even though I'd been here before, I remained clueless as to the location of this place.

A petite, very pretty Asian woman glanced up from her screen. "Hey, Harry, Jack."

Harry bowed slightly, with complete sincerity. If I had tried to bow, it would have come across as heavy-handed sarcasm.

"Hey, Naomi," I said. She had jet-black hair with

bright, neon-blue streaks in it. Not a look that I normally liked, but on her, it was fantastic.

A short, hairy man dressed in sweats walked in from the kitchen end of the flat. He reminded me of one of J.R.R. Tolkien's hobbits. He certainly appeared to consume a hobbit's normal menu of six meals a day. "What do you have for us?"

"Hello, Stewart," Harry said.

"Yeah, hey."

"I've got neo-Nazis," I said. "Right here in New York City. Led by a guy named Gerhard Fuchs."

Stewart responded by mumbling a string of epithets about Gerhard Fuchs. For a gentle-looking hobbit, Stewart had quite the mouth on him.

"Aside from being a neo-Nazi," Naomi said, grinning at Stewart, "do you know anything else about him?"

"His group is called the Supreme Order. In German: *Oberste Ordnung*. And I think he owns a house of prostitution at 341 West 91st Street. But the ownership is probably obscured behind multiple corporate fronts."

"Supreme Order, huh?" Her grin had a nasty twist to it. "Those Nazi pricks. Believe me, it'll be a pleasure digging into Gerhard Fuchs. But you have to promise me one thing, Jack."

"Yes?"

"You're going to mess him up."

"That's my plan."

"Do you have a personal address? Or know the names of any of his corporate entities?"

"Sorry, no personal address. Yet. But one of the Supreme Order members told me they meet at a place called *Gesellschaft der Deutschen*. It's some kind of social club on East 85th Street near Second Avenue."

Stewart spoke to Harry, "Will you be assisting us in these endeavors?"

"Of course."

Stewart sat at a computer and began clicking and typing away. Not a continuous stream of action, mind you. Stewart paused after some of the clicks, and a couple of times Harry gave Stewart guidance about where to click next.

Naomi watched them for a moment then turned to me. "With Harry's help, there's no one we can't hack, no code we can't crack, no accounting system we can't figure out."

"Thank you," he nodded graciously.

Naomi asked me, "We'll probably have a pretty full picture for you by tomorrow. Okay?"

"Tomorrow's great. Thanks."

"Jack?" Stewart asked, still focused on his monitor.

"Yes."

"Fuchs's home address is on Palisade Avenue in Riverdale. Some big fancy homes there, with views of the Hudson." Stewart spun around to face us. "Ironically, Riverdale's always had a substantial Jewish population.

71

Fuchs's house is just a few blocks away from three synagogues, and an assisted-living community for Jews."

"Our neo-Nazi villain is living in a heavily Jewish neighborhood."

"That's about the size of it."

He texted me the exact addresses of the *Gesellschaft der Deutschen* and Fuchs's home.

"Thanks," I said. "Call me when you have more."

"Will do," Naomi said. "Hope you'll come by to collect the information in person." She winked at me.

Stewart swiveled back to his computer. I could have sworn he was in a little bit of a huff.

Harry and I said goodbye and headed out the front door. We stopped in the hallway once the door was closed behind us.

"Your place or Kim's?" Harry asked.

"First a question: Care to go to Riverdale with me tonight?"

"Are you planning to scout out Fuchs's home?"

"*Ja, das Haus von Herrn Fuchs.*"

"Internal reconnaissance as well as external?"

"That would be my preference," I admitted.

"You expect me to transport you past his security so that you can gain access to his home, possibly even Fuchs himself?"

"Well, I'd rather leave his neo-Nazi personage out of it, but if we happened to run into him, I might be able to pose some questions to him."

Harry glanced up at the ceiling—a gesture he made on my behalf so that I would know when he was seeking divine guidance—and asked, "What time did you have in mind for this excursion?"

"I hadn't really thought about it—11:00 P.M.?"

"I will transport you at 11:00. Now, do you want to go to your apartment or to Kim's?"

"Kim's—"

I'm not sure I had fully enunciated the "s" sound in "Kim's" before I found myself standing on the sidewalk in front of her building. All by myself. No Harry. Gerry, one of the doormen, was holding the front door open for me. I knew Gerry didn't really care about me, but, like most people, he adored Kim, and since I was her boyfriend, he graced me with a big smile. I stifled the thought that he needed the attentions of a good orthodontist.

"Chinese okay for dinner?" Kim asked after greeting me with a long, clinging kiss.

I would have agreed to eat a can of Alpo dog food after that kiss. "Yes, that's very nice."

She studied my face for a moment; her right eyebrow arched quizzically. "Are you going out later?"

"Yes."

"Is this about the neo-Nazis?"

"Yes."

"Uh, oh. You're giving me one-word answers."

"That's all some of your questions require."

We walked to the dining room, where the table was

set with chopsticks and empty plates. The food containers were on placemats in the middle of the table. Kim sat at the head of the table; I was on her right like the guest of honor at a banquet.

"Given what you do, I know I'm about to ask a ridiculous question," she said as she served up the food. "But, should I be worried about tonight?"

"No."

She stared at me with the intensity of a mad scientist's laser weapon.

"This is just a scouting mission. In-out. Quick."

"No violence? No shooting or stabbing?"

"That would be my preference."

"You can be so frustrating. Is Harry going with you?"

"Yes."

"That makes me feel a little better."

Given that Harry had allowed me to be stabbed and shot several times on his watch, it didn't make me feel any better. But his whooshing me in and out of places almost compensated for his lackadaisical approach to my personal safety.

"What will you be looking for on this expedition of yours?"

"Harry told me that these neo-Nazis have got some criminal operations going in addition to prostitution. Drug running for one. Harry also told me that Fuchs is planning something big and I don't have much time to find out what

74

these goose-stepping jerks are doing."

"How do prostitution and drugs help with their Nazi agenda?"

"I'm not sure," I replied, after chewing and swallowing a delicious dumpling. "Maybe they need the funds. Or they're funding criminal ops that also push their hate agenda."

"Do you mean Fuchs is generating cash and humiliating those Jewish girls at the same time?"

"That's probably part of it."

"But . . .?"

"Harry told me that Fuchs is warming up for . . . more."

She thought about that for a moment as she deftly used her chopsticks to pluck a shrimp off her plate. "You think he's working up to an act of anti-Semitic terrorism?"

"Yes, and it terrifies me. New York City is full of targets for him."

"Can't you warn NYPD?"

"I can, but my warning would be a hell of a lot more effective if I had some solid evidence. Something better than 'I gotta bad feeling about this guy.'"

"But your bad feelings are based on years and years of experience."

"If Fuchs is as smart as his namesake—"

"His namesake?"

"Fuchs is German for 'fox.' You know: Clever like a fox?"

"Oh."

"Anyway, if I give the NYPD some evidence that will get them much closer to stopping this guy."

"They're not exactly without resources, Jack. They can find their own evidence."

"That's true, but—" I pointed up, as if to heaven, "nobody has the resources I do. I think I should do what I can to give them evidence of Fuchs's criminal activities."

"So off to his place to find something incriminating?"

"Exactly."

"I know I tell you this all the time, but please be careful."

"I will use every last bit of my government-training as a Green Beret and Marshal to exercise extreme caution."

"Why do I find that less than reassuring?"

"Because you know me?"

"Yup, that's it" she said, grabbing the last dumpling. "That's definitely it."

After we finished eating, and I did the tiny amount of cleaning up necessary (ah, the joys of takeout!), Kim resumed her work on a marketing presentation for one of her largest clients. I attempted to finish *Napoleon: A Life* by Andrew Roberts. Napoleon lived one hell of a life, and Roberts was one hell of a storyteller, but at about eight hundred dense pages, it was quite the challenge. Also a good workout for my arms since I had bought the trade paperback edition not a digital version. (Last time I do that,

I thought.)

A few minutes before 11:00, Harry showed up, holding one of my backpacks. "I prepared a go bag."

"Thank you."

"What's in the go bag?" Kim asked.

"Oh . . . just some of the tools of my trade," I replied. "All quite necessary, I assure you."

"Harry, will you please remember you are his guardian angel?"

"I will do whatever I can."

She shook her head in frustration and walked toward the bedroom, muttering, "One's as bad as the other."

Harry turned to me, "Was she hoping for a guarantee of your safety?"

"Really? You have to ask?"

5

As Harry so often did, he responded to my rhetorical question by whooshing me to a large, flat expanse of lawn in front of a Tudor Revival house. We stood under a leafless oak tree at the edge of the lawn. Even with the dim light from the nearest streetlight, I saw that the lawn was the brown color of autumn. The house with steeply pitched roofs, decorative half-timbering, and a grand, stone-embellished front doorway, stretched a long way from left to right. Azalea bushes were spaced out under the front windows, and tall holly bushes stood at each corner.

"Wow, Herr Fuchs lives well. Nice place for the Home of the Supreme Order," I whispered.

"No one can hear you," Harry replied.

"Will I remain undetectable for the duration of this little mission?"

"Not if you go inside the house."

"Why won't you keep me invisible even inside?"

"Maybe I enjoy watching you work."

"Maybe you enjoy watching me get beat up and shot at."

"Is violence on your agenda tonight?"

"I hope not." I looked behind us, across Palisade

Avenue. There wasn't a house across from Fuchs's home, which meant that only a few, devoid-of-leaves trees impeded his ability to enjoy a spectacular view of the Hudson River. I turned back and scanned the front of the house. There were lights visible through a few windows on the ground floor, but the second floor was dark.

"How many people are at home?" I asked.

"Three. Gerhard and two of his security men."

"Not a very big security team."

Harry said nothing.

"I'm guessing," I said, "that there are some canine guards on the premises. Right?"

"Yes. Two Rottweilers, both inside at the moment."

No wonder Herr Fuchs only had two human guards.

"What about alarms?"

"Only contact sensors at the doors and windows. No motion or sound detectors. Nothing a government-trained specialist can't handle."

"The substance of your answer should reassure me, but your tone is not instilling a sense of confidence."

"That is not my problem."

I shook my head in feigned disgust and quietly ran toward the edge of the yard where a line of small evergreens separated Fuchs's house from his neighbor's. I'm sure the distance to the evergreens was only a hundred feet or so, but I was in plain sight, which made it feel like a mile. Once I reached the evergreens, I stayed in their shadows and quickly headed to the backyard. You could have comfortably set a rugby pitch in the back. If you felt like filling the space with something more serene, you could have fit at least two par-3 golf holes.

Dashing across the space from the evergreen border to the house, I reached a rear corner and froze when I heard a door open.

A gruff voice spoke, "Get on. Do your stuff."

I crouched behind a rhododendron bush the size of a VW Beetle. From where I was hiding, I could barely see them through the rhododendron's leaves, but the Rottweilers' thudding paws and heavy panting made it easier to locate them. They were about 30 feet away from me when they both stood completely still and sniffed the air. I wondered if I could slip my gun out of my backpack without the dogs hearing but realized there was no way I could shoot a dog. Even a dog capable of ripping my throat out. Besides, if I managed to shoot one dog, there was almost no chance that I could shoot the second dog before it, well . . . before it ripped my throat out.

The Rottweilers moved slowly toward my hiding spot, heads down, sniffing more eagerly with every step.

The gruff voice came again, "What's up, boys? You find something?" A shadowy figure holding a pistol in his right hand moved slowly after the dogs, peering into the dark.

From my days in the Marshal Service, I

remembered a favorite phrase of my boss's: Somedays, you eat the bear. Somedays, the bear eats you. Tyrrell, today is the day you are on the menu.

The Rottweilers were on the far side of my rhododendron hiding place. The man came up behind them and pointed his weapon at the middle of the bush. Directly at me.

"Go, " he commanded softly.

The dogs circled the bush, one going one direction, the other the opposite direction. No escape for you, Tyrrell. When the dogs saw me, they stopped about 6 feet away, on my left and my right.

"Hands up," the gruff guy said. "Stand up slowly and walk out to my right."

"I'm coming," I said. "Assuming your dog doesn't turn me into a chew toy first."

"He'll let you pass. Walk slowly."

I did as I was instructed. The dog backed away to give me room to pass him. I glanced over my shoulder. The second dog was following right behind me.

As I stepped onto the lawn, the gruff man asked, "What's in the pack?"

"The usual. Guns. Plasticuffs. Twinkies."

He grunted. "Slide the pack off real slow then put it on the ground in front of you and step back."

I complied with his wishes.

He scooped up my pack with his left hand and gestured with the pistol in his right. "Keep your hands up, and we'll go inside."

The Rottweilers followed us. Another man, gun in hand, met us at the back door. Neither man was close enough to me that if I spun around, I would knock their guns away. And they were careful to avoid stepping into each other's line of fire. They might not have been as well-trained as I was, but they were pretty damn good. They were also ugly. One was a skinny, rat-faced man with dark hair. The other was stout with greasy, sandy blond hair and a blank expression.

"Walk straight ahead," the gruff-voiced man, Mr. Greasy Hair, said.

We walked down a narrow hallway with the kitchen opening on one side. The hallway ended in a large dining room with dark wood wall paneling and a huge wooden dining table with carved wood chairs that would have been perfect for the stage set of a Wagnerian opera. The dogs' nails clicked on the wood floor as they walked immediately behind the two gunmen.

Greasy Hair pointed me to the front foyer on our right. I could see the living room on the far side of the foyer. It wasn't quite as big as a basketball court, but it was close. There was thick, cream-colored, wall-to-wall carpeting, which meant the dogs moved silently across it. More wood paneling, more large, dark-wood furniture. I had a feeling the decorator had been living out some Ruritanian fantasy.

We walked through the living room to the rear of

the house, going through a pair of thick wooden doors into a room with the same dark-wood décor theme but smaller. Standing behind a desk at the far end of the room was a man with clear blue eyes, a straight nose, a chiseled chin and a blond buzz cut. He was about 6-feet tall and of trim build and was wearing a charcoal-gray suit over a white dress shirt, no tie. The Aryan ideal. A tiny woman stood at his right side.

"Gerhard Fuchs, I presume," I said.

"You have the advantage of me, Mr. . . . ?"

"Wouk. Herman Wouk."

"Ah, Mr. Wouk. Best-selling Jewish writer."

"Don't forget winner of the Pulitzer Prize."

"An honor given to a Jew by the Jewish-controlled Columbia University."

"Well, that's one peculiarly distorted way to look at it."

"I see you are one of those who's been brainwashed by the Jew establishment."

"If there's been any brainwashing, it was done by Hitler and Goebbels."

He waved his hand through the air as if brushing away flies or a foul odor. "Let's not continue this circular argument. I am certain that you are not really a 101-year old Jewish author."

"I can dream, can't I?"

He shook his head then opened his arms wide in a gesture of greeting. "Welcome to my home." He had the clear diction and smooth polish of a prep school alum. I wondered if that was an affect, or if he had actually gone to Groton or Choate. Not that I cared. I was disappointed that he didn't sound like the proverbial Nazi in a World War II movie. "Please have a seat," he pointed at a wooden armchair on the other side of the desk from where he stood.

Fuchs gestured at the woman to his right, "This is my second in command, Mina Aschgrau."

"*Guten abend*," I said and made an ironic bow of respect. At least I hoped they understood I was being ironic.

Greasy Hair grabbed my shoulder and pushed down hard to make sure I took a seat. I could have shrugged him off but chose not to. Save the violence for a time when you need it, Tyrrell.

As soon as my fanny touched down, Rat Face was secured my wrists with plasticuffs to each of the armrests. Greasy Hair handed my backpack to Fuchs, who began pulling out the contents one by one and laying them on top of his desk.

"Your pack is filled with interesting items," he said. "Ruger SR9, excellent choice; four extra magazines; four grenades; hmm, two smoke grenades and two flashbangs. And about a dozen plasticuffs. Were you anticipating trouble?"

"I just like to carry a basic tool set with me. You didn't mention Twinkies—aren't there any Twinkies in there?" I twisted around to glare at Rat Face and Greasy

Hair. "Did you guys eat my Twinkies?" Turning back to Fuchs, I said, "I can't stand it when the bad guys eat my Twinkies."

"You assume we are the bad guys."

"No, I *know* you are the bad guys."

"How do you know?"

"Because you're neo-Nazis. You people are *always* the bad guys."

"Really? We're bad guys because we want to save our country from being overrun by Jews? Because we want to stop the liberal pansies from giving America away to the so-called 'people of color?'" He spoke matter-of-factly, absolutely sure of *his* truth. "Why don't they all go back to whatever holes they came from?"

"There's so much wrong with all of those questions that I don't know where to begin."

"Wrong? Wrong with my belief that America is under threat from the Jews? Don't you know *they* control the media? Don't you know *they* control the financial services industry?"

"Wow. Grow a pathetic little mustache and shout in a harsh German accent and you could be mistaken for *der Fuhrer* himself."

"Your insults aren't at the level I'd hoped for. They reveal a small, angry mind."

"I guess as a neo-Nazi you know all about small, angry minds. By the by, all your crap about the Jews is just an excuse for *your* crimes. And when you follow Aryan ideals, you're not some kind of high-minded do-gooder. You're just a racist and an anti-Semite following the failed philosophies of a raving lunatic. A coward who hid in his bunker and killed himself."

Fuchs grinned and shook his head, clearly amused by the situation. "You're remarkably assertive for a man surrounded by guns and dogs."

"I guess I'm not the coward that you are."

My words bounced around in my head. Careful there, Tyrrell, don't let your anger and hatred for what this guy stands for drive you to underestimating him. Right now, you're acting like an overgrown adolescent trying to piss someone off. Royally piss them off. Which, as Fuchs had correctly pointed out, was probably not the best choice for a man cuffed to a chair and held hostage at gunpoint. Not to mention the Rottweilers eyeballing me as if I was their next meal.

Fuchs stiffened for a second at my comment then forced an insincere smile. "Why are you here, Tyrrell?"

"Oh, I don't know, I was kinda hoping I might find some evidence of criminal activities lying around. You know, kidnapping, prostitution, drug-running, and robbing banks. Did I leave anything out?"

Fuchs quickly glanced at the bookcase on one wall of his den then returned to me. His smile widened. "Since you're here, I thought we could engage in a gentlemanly conversation. But you're not interested in such a conversation."

"With you? No thanks."

"Why are you here?"

"I told you."

"My security cameras recorded your breaking up my business on West 91st Street. I assume you were the large, violent man on the video. Why did you do that?"

"You kidnapped and prostituted Jewish girls." I turned to Mina Aschgrau. "Did you know that's how your boss treats women?"

"Jewish women," she corrected.

"You're making a rather serious criminal charge," Fuchs said.

"It's a statement of fact."

"And you felt you had to intervene?"

"That's what I do. I make things right. I put people like you out of business."

"Well, the loss of 341 West 91st, while painful, is nowhere near enough to put me out of business."

"Maybe the NYPD will follow the clues they found at 341 and come here to your doorstep. After a big trial, you'll go to jail for a very long time. Your only hope is that whatever prison where you end up in has an active Aryan Brotherhood who will want to acknowledge you as *der Fuhrer*." To Aschgrau I said, "And maybe an Aryan Sisterhood for you, *fraulein*."

She ignored me.

Fuchs said, "I really am wasting my time with you. All you're interested in is forcing my hand."

"To do what, exactly?"

He picked up my Ruger, snapped the safety off, and pointed it at me. "I'm afraid I'm going to have to eliminate you. I caught you trespassing after all."

"You did. But it will be easier to sell the trespassing story if your fingerprints aren't all over my, uh, stuff. And if you don't kill me with my own gun. It could be difficult to explain how a guy your size managed to take my gun away from me and still felt so threatened that you needed to kill me."

"Good point." He withdrew a handkerchief from his pocket, wiped down my pistol, and slid it back into my pack. He did the same thing with each of the items. Then he tossed the pack to a corner.

"What about your dogs? And your guards? How did I get past them and threaten you to the point where you had to kill me to defend yourself?"

"Nice try. But I think we'll stage the rest of the scene after I kill you."

"Gerhard, do you mind if I ask you a question?"

"I suppose not."

"Have you ever killed anyone?"

"No, you'll be my first."

"Hmm. Good luck with that."

He opened one of his desk drawers and pulled out a Glock 17 pistol. "Don't worry," he said. "I have a permit for this gun. Kept specifically for home defense."

"You should really keep that in a locked drawer or

container somewhere. And store it unloaded. With the ammunition in another drawer. Keeps your little ones safe."

"I don't have children."

"Lucky them."

He aimed the Glock at me and smiled. Another icy, insincere smile from the neo-Nazi. "I think I'm going to enjoy this."

"Have at it," I said and lunged hard to my right.

Fuchs fired at the space I had just vacated, the bullet digging a hole in the cream-colored carpet. I crashed into Rat Face, my shoulder hitting his gun hand, his pistol firing into the floor.

I stood up—as straight up as I could cuffed to a chair, but straight enough—the top of my head caught Rat Face's chin and slammed him backward. His body arched and crashed into one of the dogs, sending it scurrying backward.

Greasy Hair aimed his gun at me. Still in my awkward chair-crouch, I spun around, forcing Greasy Hair to step back out of the way, stumbling backward as he did. I jumped forward, the legs of the chair smashing him down onto the floor. The impact of the chair hitting the floor shattered the chair legs and tore the seat and armrests from the back.

I was still cuffed to the armrests. I clubbed down on Greasy Hair's head, knocking him unconscious.

One of the Rottweiler's lunged at me, its jaws

closing on my right thigh. I'm not fond of being bitten by a dog. I really didn't want to hurt the animal, but I had to get him off me. I hit it on the head with an armrest, and it dropped to the floor.

Aschgrau had snatched up Greasy Hair's gun and was aiming it at me, her finger tightening on the trigger. I clubbed her arm with the same armrest I had used on the dog, sending the pistol flying. She jumped back, out of range of my armrest club.

At almost the same moment I had dealt with the woman, Fuchs had commanded the other dog, "Hold!" It did what it was told to do. As Fuchs controlled the dog, I dove over Greasy Hair's body, grabbed the gun that Aschgrau had dropped, and rolled up into a shooter's crouch, the gun pointed at Fuchs. We stared at each other across the expanse of his desk, aiming pistols at each other.

"Good for you," I said, "You managed to hang onto your gun all through that fight. But I'm sorry to say I told you so—well, actually, I'm not sorry—but it isn't easy killing a man."

"Yes, I see that now." Spoken with that damn smile.

Rat Face moaned from his spot on the floor. Without taking my eyes off of Fuchs, I dropped my left hand and shook it until the armrest slid loose from my cuff. Switching the gun to my left hand, I repeated the shaking process with my right. When the second armrest chunked to the floor, I switched the gun back to my right hand. I walked across the den, scooped up Rat Face's gun, and slid it into my pocket. The one conscious Rottweiler issued a low growl but held his position a foot away from me.

"Aren't you going to try to intimidate me by pointing two guns at me?" Fuchs asked with an arched eyebrow.

"I only need one gun. The two-gun intimidation thing is the kind of show you Nazis like to put on."

"Still insulting me, I see."

"If I was willing to insult you when you had all the guns and the dogs, why should I stop now?"

"You're a bit cleverer than you seem. That was a sly way of informing me that the odds have shifted."

"Ya think?"

"Have you ever killed a man?" he asked.

"Yes."

"Is it hard to do?"

"It depends."

"On what?"

"You figure it out."

"What about killing a woman?" he motioned toward Aschgrau. "Have you ever done that?"

"Yes."

"Was it more difficult than killing a man?"

"Killing someone is never a great option. I do what's necessary. But sometimes, like right now, killing actually seems appealing."

Fuchs nodded, relaxing a bit and letting his gun

stray a bit from pointing directly at my chest.

"Much as I'd like to stay and chat, it's past my bedtime," I said. "You need to put down your weapon."

"What if I don't?"

"You'll end up joining the sleeping beauties on the floor."

"Ah, yes." He pointed the gun straight up, ejected the shell in the chamber, released the magazine, and laid the pistol and mag on the desk.

"Nicely done," I said. I gestured at the bookcase, "Now, go over there and open your safe."

"No, I don't think I will," delivered with his ever-present smile.

"Okay. But don't blame me if I knock you and Ms. Aschgrau senseless, tear apart your bookcase, crack your safe, and take whatever it is you don't want me to take."

"My dog won't like it if you knock me senseless."

"I won't like killing your dog, but I'll do it."

He glanced at his dog, "I can't let you hurt my dog."

"Amazing how much you care about your pet but can't manage the teensiest bit of concern for your fellow man."

"When you say my *fellow* men, do you mean the Jews? They are not my fellow men."

"Okay," I sighed impatiently, "enough Hitler horseshit. If you don't open that safe right now, I'm going to show you what it's like to be on the receiving end of someone's sadistic cruelty."

"You'd kill my dog because I don't have any warm feelings toward Jews?"

"I'll kill your dog because I told you I would if you don't open the safe. But I'll torture and kill you because I am even less concerned about you than you are the Jews."

"Will you let us both live if I open the safe?"

"I'm not negotiating with you. Open the safe."

"It would seem you leave me no options." He turned toward the bookcase, "May I?"

"Please."

"Stay where you are, Ms. Aschgrau," I said and followed Fuchs to the bookcase.

He pulled a few books off a shelf and stacked them neatly on the edge of his desk. He pressed a button I couldn't see. There was a click, and the middle shelf and the back of the bookcase swung open. He quickly entered a sequence of numbers into a keypad nest to the safe then pressed his thumb on a small black screen. There was a metallic thunk as the tumblers fell into place, and the safe's door popped open.

"Step back and sit down behind your desk," I ordered him.

He did as he was told. I dug around in my backpack, found some plasticuffs, and cuffed him to his own chair. I had Aschgrau sit on the floor behind him, loop her arms around his right arm, and cuffed her wrists. I also cuffed Greasy Hair and Rat Face to each other. The conscious Rottweiler growled through this entire phase of operations but didn't move, so I was fine with the growling.

Finally ready to turn my attention to the safe, I found one thing, and one thing only. A Dell XPS 15 laptop.

"I'm guessing you went for the extra RAM and a huge hard drive. Am I right, Gerhard?"

He ignored my question. "You need a password to log in, and then all of the files are encrypted. It will take you hours to unlock all the data on that machine. And you said it was past your bedtime."

"Yeah, I need to get going." I slipped the laptop into my backpack.

"You need the expertise of the NSA to hack the files on that computer." His smile was firmly in place.

"I've got someone even better," I said evenly. I grabbed a pair of scissors from the desk and put them in the safe, shutting its door. No point in making it too easy for these folks from the head office of the Supreme Order to get free. I dumped the guns I had taken from Greasy Hair, Rat Face, and Gerhard into my pack, then swung it onto my back.

"*Auf wiedersehen,*" I said and headed for the back door. The dog turned its head to watch me go, clearly wanting to bite me but not making a move.

I walked through the house and out the back door and said, "Harry?"

In the tiniest bit of time imaginable, I was in my apartment.

"I thought you would appreciate a chance to fix your leg before Kim sees it," Harry said.

"Very thoughtful of you. Do I need shots?"

"Probably. But not because of the dogs."

"Ha, ha." I put my pack on the coffee table. My dog-bitten leg was throbbing painfully. Just as you might expect when a powerful Rottweiler had tried to tear it off. Actually, if that had been the pooch's intent, I think I would have been in much worse shape.

I hobbled off to the bathroom, where I slowly pulled off my bloody pants dumped them on the floor of my shower. The liberal use of hydrogen peroxide and some gauze pads cleaned up the blood on my leg and allowed me to assess the damage. Not too bad considering how big the Rottweiler's jaws were and how firmly they had been crushing down on my leg.

"Hey, Harry?" I called. "Could I get your medical opinion?"

He appeared next to me.

"Did you just whoosh into the bathroom?"

"Yes."

"Really? You wasted a whoosh on a trip from my living room to my bathroom?"

"Did you need a medical opinion?"

"Yes," I pointed at my right thigh. It was bruised and there were about nine cuts, four of which were quite deep. "Do you think I need stitches?"

He shook his head, "Liberal use of antiseptic cream

followed by butterfly closures will do the job."

"Thanks."

"Would you like me to handle this?"

"Well, if you wouldn't mind . . ."

He closed his eyes in an expression of impatience then went to work. He was swift and adept; in no time at all my wounds had been salved and closed with the butterflies.

"You do nice work."

"Thank you. Do you want me to take you to Kim's?"

"Could I change into an intact pair of pants first? And put away the weapons I seized?"

"Those are unusually good ideas coming from you."

I went to the closet, grabbed a fresh pair of blue jeans, and tugged them on. Then I stepped back to the closet, which at first glance seemed to be like any other closet. But appearances can be deceiving. In the month since I had moved into my new place, I'd installed a very special feature: A false, hinged panel that swung open just below the height of the closet's hanging bar. I pulled out my phone, sent a text message to a special number, and there was a click. The panel popped open about an inch.

"Pretty nice, huh?" I asked rhetorically.

"You should be very proud," Harry replied.

"I brought it from the old apartment and with a little bit of extra fitting to make the dimensions work, installed it here. Nobody but you and I know it exists."

"I am very impressed," Harry said, sounding anything but impressed. "You may remember that I watched you install it."

"You were here for all of a minute that day."

"Some of us only need a minute to comprehend what is happening."

"Oh, excuse me," I said without a trace of contrition. I opened my backpack and put the guns I'd taken from the bad guys on a shelf. Then I tugged out Gerhard's laptop.

"I don't suppose Naomi and Stewart happen to be awake, are they?"

"Yes, they are."

I placed my now-skinny pack on the floor of the hidden compartment and closed the panel. It clicked into the locked position with a nice solid sound. More of a tumbler thunk than a simple little click.

Now that the weapons were secure, I prepped for an overnight at Kim's. All this entailed was picking up what I considered my "normal" backpack, which contained any books I happened to be reading and my laptop.

"Before we go to Naomi and Stewart's," I said, now completely ready to depart, "should we bring them some refreshment?"

Harry treated me to his Mona Lisa expression and whooshed me into Buona Tazza.

"We're closing," said the barista behind the counter, a super tall, super skinny, badly groomed white kid.

"I'll take your order," said the other barista, a bright-eyed, brightly smiling Latina.

I spoke to Harry, "I don't suppose you know what Naomi and Stewart want."

He slowly closed his eyelids in his disgust at my remark, then turned to the young woman, and ordered, "A double espresso and a dirty chai tea, please."

"Let me guess," I said. "The double espresso is for Naomi. The dirty chai is for Stewart."

"Yes."

I waited for Harry to ask me how I knew, but he obviously had no intention of engaging me on the subject of other people's caffeine consumption.

The barista placed the drinks on the service bar as Harry handed her a twenty-dollar bill. "Keep the change. Thank you for staying open for us."

"You're very welcome."

We walked outside Buona Tazza. A second later, we were inside Naomi and Stewart's railroad flat, and Harry was giving out the drinks.

"What have you got for us?" Naomi asked with enough energy that I wondered if she needed a caffeine boost.

"The laptop of one Gerhard Fuchs," I said, handing over the laptop.

"Ah, the bad guy we've been analyzing."

Stewart stepped to her side, checked the laptop,

and said, "Hmm. Dell. Encrypted like crazy, I suppose."

"Probably," I admitted.

"Okay," he said.

"Give us till tomorrow," Naomi said. "And we'll have all the other information on Fuchs by then, too.

"That's fast," I said.

"Hey, with Harry's help, all things are possible."

6

The next morning, I lingered over my second cup of cappuccino at Kim's dining room table. I had popped a lot of ibuprofen because the bite I got from Rover the Rottweiler hurt like crazy. Hurt as in *OUCH*! But being a manfully manly man meant that I couldn't show pain to my fiancée, so I acted as if nothing was wrong. Kim had one cup of coffee and a bowl of some kind of healthy, whole-grain cereal, kissed me on the cheek, and made the long commute down the hallway to her office.

I took out my laptop, logged into e-mail, and started my workday at Tyrrell Security Consultants. When I wasn't busy righting wrongs for the pro bono clients Harry brought to me, I ran a small but very successful security consulting business. I didn't know if my success was due to my credentials as a combat veteran of Special Forces or my time in the U.S, Marshals Service or Harry and the Chairman funneling a number of clients to me. When you receive excellent word of mouth from on high, it tends to bode very well for your business.

This morning's agenda included reviewing a security proposal created for a prospective client—after three on-site visits—and putting out small fires for two existing clients. I made a few tweaks to the proposal and sent it off to the client. As for the fires, e-mails and a promise to stop by for an on-site soothed the fears of the existing clients.

Having dealt with the morning load in my inbox, I took a shower and redressed the dog-bite wound. I'm not a medical expert, but it appeared to me that the wound was closing pretty darn rapidly.

I looked to the ceiling and whispered, "Thanks for the shallow bite. But . . . it still hurts like hell."

There was no answer. Oh well, you can't have it all.

I got dressed in gray cargo slacks and a navy blue, long-sleeve T-shirt. I pulled on my Barbour jacket and wrapped my neck with a heavy woolen scarf to ward off the November chill. At Kim's office door, I knocked softly and pushed in. She was on the phone, speaking calmly and carefully to one of her clients. She gave me a wave. I kissed the top of her head and pointed toward her front door, mouthing the word, "Goodbye."

She nodded and blew me a kiss.

Outside her building, I walked uptown to West 96th Street where AA had a 10:15 A.M. meeting called First Things First. AA met in a basement room of Holy Name Church on the uptown side of the street. A couple of people were smoking out on the sidewalk, and we said hello to each other as I went inside. In the meeting room, after greeting a few more people, I chose a chair just as the meeting chairwoman called out, "Hello, I'm Soledad, and I'm an alcoholic."

People settled down quickly and listened to the meeting's speaker, Jennifer, talk about her story. One of the things she was struggling with at that particular moment was her anger.

"I'm angry with my ex, with my boss, sometimes with my kids, who I love dearly. But things don't always go my way, and I find myself so . . . damn angry. Then the little devil who sits on my shoulder starts talking to me. He says things like I'm completely justified to feel the way I feel. I should be angry with my ex, who doesn't fulfill—" Jennifer stopped, shook her head, and grinned. "There I go. I was about to rant about my ex. I'm justifying my anger to you right now, so that I can go on feeling angry. It's like a drug. I get a rush from it. It makes me feel powerful over the person I'm angry with.

"But I don't have any power over them at all. If anything, my ex would be glad that he makes me angry. And if anger is like a drug, if it's a mood-altering . . . thing, then I am powerless over it and need to turn it over. Let go and let God."

As Jennifer spoke, I shifted uncomfortably in my seat. I had been reveling in my anger at Fuchs and his band of neo-Nazis. But if I was honest with myself—and I didn't want to be honest with myself if it meant giving up my justifiable anger with the neo-Nazis—wasn't I just binging on rage? Wasn't I getting a rush from my hate-fueled anger?

But . . . but . . . Fuchs and his bunch were neo-

Nazis for crying out loud! They were evil. Talk about hate-fueled, these guys practically wrote the book on hate. Well, their patron saint, Adolf, did actually write the book. So, maybe anger was justifiable when it was directed at neo-Nazis? Maybe . . .?

Jennifer continued, "My problem is that I just can't handle the anger. The whole thing about it being justified is pointless. I can't handle anger. Justified or not. It's like booze. I can't handle it. If I want to live a sober life in recovery, I need to stay away from booze *and* anger."

I had to admit she had a very good point there. But was I ready to stay away from my anger in this case? I felt as if I needed it to motivate my crusade against Fuchs. Shit. Why was this stuff so hard?

When it was my turn to share, I said, "I identified with a lot of what you said, Jennifer. I spent the five years after my wife died drinking myself stupid and wallowing in my justifiable anger and resentments. Hey, my wife is dead! I'm entitled to be angry as hell, right? Only it never did a bit of good. Like you said, I couldn't handle the anger." I paused and mentally reviewed the last few months. "I'm getting a little better, but I have a feeling I may have a lot of work to do on my anger."

A number of people nodded and smiled as I spoke.

When the meeting concluded, I made it a point to shake Jennifer's hand and thank her for what she had said. I didn't have a clue as to how I could incorporate her words into my life, but I knew that it was something I needed to hear and think about.

Harry was waiting for me outside the church, holding my backpack—my go-bag backpack. The one that was usually full of the assorted tools of my troubleshooting trade.

"Good morning," he said. "Would you like some cappuccino?"

"Always. Are you going to tell me why you brought my backpack?"

"Over cappuccinos." He whooshed us to Café Sabatini. Because it was the place where I had met Kim, it occupied a special place in my heart.

"Did you drink as much cappuccino before your association with me?"

"No, you are solely responsible for my consumption of espresso-based beverages," he dead-panned as he ordered two cappuccinos from the barista.

"Very funny," I replied.

He flashed me the briefest of grins then spoke over the noise of the machine, "To be completely honest, yes, you *are* responsible. And I thank you."

"You're welcome. Glad I could have a positive influence on you."

"That might be overstating things." The machine stopped growling, and the barista handed our drinks over the counter to us. Harry paid and led the way to a café table.

"How does your leg feel?" he asked.

"It's been better. Do I have you to thank for the dog's not tearing my leg off?"

He pointed skyward.

I tilted my head up and whispered, "Thank you."

We drank in silence for a moment. When I'd finished, I considered ordering my fourth cup for the morning, but instead asked Harry, "Are you here for a reason besides cappuccino?"

"Unfortunately, yes."

"Unfortunately?"

"Yes."

"Oh, don't be coy, Harry. Blurt it out."

"I am not coy, and I do not blurt."

"Of course, you don't. But just tell me what it is you came to tell me."

"One of the girls you saved is in the hospital."

"Is she going to be all right?"

"Medically speaking, yes."

I mulled that bit of information over for a minute. "But she's not going to be all right in some non-medical way?"

"No."

"Is she in danger from Fuchs?"

"Yes."

"Is he sending someone to the hospital to kill her? And do I need to get there now?"

Harry glanced up as if consulting with the Deity (or Café Sabatini's ceiling) then at me. "We have a few minutes."

"Only one guy?"

"Yes."

"I wish I found that reassuring, but I don't."

"Given the gentleman in question, that is very wise of you."

"Please fill me in on his background."

"His name is Rolf Jäger. He is an extraordinarily dangerous individual."

"That's not very helpful."

"It's all you need to know."

"Does the guy have a kryptonite?"

"Kryptonite?"

"You know, Superman's weakness. Kryptonite."

"I see. No, sorry, as far as I know, he has none."

"This is getting better and better." I stared at the dregs in the bottom of my cup. "Why is Fuchs taking the risk of going after one of the girls? Why not the others?"

Harry waited; his eyes locked on mine.

"She's seen him. She can link him to the prostitution house."

Harry remained silent, waiting for me to realize the full picture.

"Oh my God," I said. "It's much worse than that. Fuchs raped her. Her testimony, along with all the other evidence, could convict him of rape."

"Yes," Harry affirmed.

"Was she the only one?"

"She was the only one in the group you rescued."

"So if Jäger dispenses with her, Fuchs stands a much better chance of getting away with his crimes."

"Yes."

"Okay. Can you whoosh me to the hospital?"

"What do you think?"

Before I could answer, I was in a hospital hallway. The walls were painted in a pale green shade, spearmint, I guessed. People in hospital scrubs moved here and there, talking quietly. Others, clearly visitors, had strained faces and body language that screamed stress.

Harry pointed down the hall past me. "Her name is Diane Eisenberg. She's in a single-patient room, No. 714."

"Can people see and hear us?"

"Yes. You can't interact without being seen and heard."

"Interact? Like smash Jäger 's face in?"

"Not the expression I would have chosen, but yes." He looked over his shoulder than back at me. "Jäger will be here in about 60 seconds."

"Gotta go." I shifted my pack to my left shoulder and walked in the direction that Harry had pointed.

I knocked softly on the door of 714. A young woman with large gray eyes with dark patches under them and medium brown hair that fell to her shoulders glanced over at me.

"Diane," I said, "I'm a—"

"You saved me. Us. You saved us."

I wasn't prepared for her to recognize me.

She held out her hand, reaching for mine. I crossed the room, grasped her hand, and sat in the chair next to the bed.

"Thank you," she whispered.

"You're welcome." I gave her hand a gentle squeeze and released myself from her grip. "I've come to save you again."

"What? Oh my God—"

"It's okay. Please, believe me, you're going to be safe. I just need you to be quiet and trust me. Okay?"

She nodded, her lips trembling and her eyes watering.

I reached into my pack, pulled out a Ruger SR9, checked that the ammunition magazine was full, and slung the pack's straps over my shoulders. "I'm not going to let anything happen to you."

She nodded again, biting her lip in anxiety.

I stepped behind her door with the pistol ready in my right hand. I was just barely tucked out of sight when a man entered the room.

Peering around the edge of the door I saw a guy built like the proverbial brick outhouse. Solid. Squat. Unpleasant. Buzzed, dark-brown hair. Squinty brown eyes. He was 4 inches shorter than I am, about five foot ten, with absolutely massive shoulders and his chest had the bulk of as a Panzer tank. His arms and legs were thicker than V2 rockets. His dark-gray suit was stretched tightly over his broad proportions.

"Hello," he said to Diane in a raspy tenor that was completely unsuited to his heavy frame.

Diane's eyes were wide with fear.

"I just wanted to see how you are doing," he said.

I stepped immediately behind him and shoved my pistol into the small of his back. "That's a 9mm Ruger." I jabbed a little harder to make sure he understood. "I want you to turn slowly and walk back into the hall."

Rolf turned, his hands at his sides, and walked slowly into the hallway. I was way too close to him. If you hold a gun on someone and actually make contact, you're too damn close. I was giving Rolf an opportunity to knock the gun away—all he had to do was spin around. His leading arm, let's say his left, would knock my gun hand to the side. His right would follow through with a punch to my jaw. Judging by the size of his prodigious paws, the punch would blast me into the afterlife. But given that I didn't want anyone in the hospital to know what was going on, which meant I had to stay close enough to him that our bodies hid the pistol from view.

"Take the stairs," I grunted into his ear.

He grunted assent and walked to a door with a small sign over it: Stairway. We stepped into the stairwell, the door closed behind us, and Rolf made his move. For a big guy he was quick, his left shoulder and arm spinning toward me like a drag racer bursting off the starting line.

But I had anticipated that he was going to make a

move. I took two steps back and yanked my gun up and out of his way as his arm brushed past my chest. He continued to spin until his face was opposite mine. Out of the corner of my eye, I saw his right fist coming at me.

I hit him in the middle of his forehead with the butt of the pistol. I hit him a hell of a lot harder than I normally would have butted someone, but this was no time for delicacy.

Stunned, he blinked. His fist slammed into my cheek, the blow sending me staggering back against the wall. My guess was that, due to the pistol butt to his head, his punch was only half-strength. I was struggling to focus but was grateful he'd only caught me at half-strength.

Before I could recover, he rushed at me, his body crushing me against the wall. He stretched his left hand up to grab the pistol from my right. I didn't let him get a grip on the gun, but that meant I only had one arm to protect my torso. And one arm was not enough: His right fist drove into my ribs like a piston, quick, short blows that made it impossible to breathe. Rolf was about to beat me to death.

I resorted to the masculine nuclear option: I kneed the Teutonic bastard in the balls. He bleated in his raspy tenor, stopped reaching for my gun with his left and halted the pounding of my body with his right. He stood hunched over in pain for a long second, trying to recover, and then I saw the fire reignite in his dull brown eyes. I was about to be on the receiving end of a violent encore. No thanks, I thought.

Rolf swung his right at my jaw. I ducked sideways, spun, and kicked, catching him on the right knee. It wasn't a great kick, but enough to stagger him. I pistol whipped him across the right side of his head. He dropped to his knees then toppled down the stairs. He kept bumping and thumping all the way down the flight, coming to a stop with a heavy thud on the landing below. He was on his belly, arms splayed wide, and he was bleeding from a cut on his forehead.

I took a few tentative steps down the stairs but halted as Rolf groaned. He slowly pulled his arms close to his sides, planted his hands on the landing, and with a groan pushed himself off the floor to a kneeling position. The left side of his face was covered in blood from the cut on his forehead, and he was groggily scanning the stairs, apparently trying to figure out what had happened. He reached for the railing, grasped it in his huge left paw, and agonizingly pulled himself to his feet. He continued to gaze this way and that until he spotted me.

Rolf stood up, his eyes focused on me. And once more, there was fire in those eyes. He flexed the fingers of both hands, grunted, and stepped to the bottom of the stairs, then began climbing toward me, grinning as he came toward me.

This guy was indestructible. Damn.

What I should have done was run. But I'm supposed to be a tough guy, and I was holding a gun after all.

I pointed the Ruger at him, "Stop right there."

He stopped. Grinned wider. "I don't think so," he rasped. And began climbing.

Like everyone who's been trained in close-quarters weapons use, I aimed at Rolf's center mass. None of this shoot him in the arm or leg baloney. The thing about Rolf was he presented so much larger a target than your run-of-the-mill bad guy. I adjusted my aim, going for his right shoulder, which seemed almost as big as a beer barrel. At this distance, I was highly confident I could hit him with a non-lethal shot.

But Rolf did not take me seriously and continued to climb the stairs. Well, he was warned, wasn't he? I shot him.

The bullet caught him exactly where I had aimed, spinning him around and sending him plunging down the stairs again to crash again on the landing.

He was lying face down, and a small pool of blood below his shoulder was spreading out on the landing. I took a few steps down and halted—

Rolf groaned and opened his eyes. Once again, he planted his hands, palms down, on the floor and pushed up. Between the forehead cut and his shoulder wound, he was a mess. A bloody mess. But he was still moving.

"Haven't you had enough?" I asked sharply, annoyed.

His response was a feral grin.

"What is it with you and Gerhard and all the damn

smiling?"

His mouth went wider. Placing his left hand on the railing, he pulled himself to his feet. He stood for a long moment—his glazed-over eyes indicating he was waiting for dizziness to pass. His eyes went tight and beady, once again locked on me. He took a step up the stairs, coming directly at me.

"Screw this," I said and kicked out hard with my left foot, which slammed into the wound in his right shoulder. He yelled in pain as he flopped backward, smashed his head against the far wall of the landing, and slumped to the floor.

Covering him with my pistol, I stood above him on the steps and waited, watching for movement. His massive chest was going up and down. He was breathing. Too bad. But lucky him. He was in a hospital.

I grabbed some plasticuffs from my back and bound his wrists behind him with two cuffs. I used his belt to bind his feet together. I undid his tie, not out of consideration for his comfort but because ties make handy dandy gags.

Once Rolf was trussed up, I spoke into the air, "Harry? Could I see you?"

Harry appeared.

"Could you arrange for Diane to be moved to another hospital. Immediately? Let her parents will know, but no one else, okay?"

"And you want it to be as if she was never here?"

"Perfect."

His eyes angled upward then at me. "It's already done."

"Wow. Thank you."

"What are you going to do with Rolf?" he asked.

"Is he going to die from the gunshot wound?"

"No."

"Would you mind whooshing him to Gerhard's place in Riverdale?"

"Don't you want the police to arrest him?"

"For what? Getting beat up and shot?"

"He was going to kill Diane."

"You know that, and I know that, but there's no evidence of his doing anything wrong."

Harry turned to Rolf's massive lump of a body. I watched as Rolf just . . . disappeared.

"That trick never gets old," I said. "And thank you for cleaning up the blood. The poor hospital staff would have wondered what patient had died in here."

"We couldn't have the staff worrying. Since I was removing Mr. Jäger, I thought: Why not clean up the blood, too?"

"You're so thoughtful."

He nodded.

"Diane recognized me."

"It was helpful for her to know you in that moment."

"It was nice . . ."

"I'm sure it was, but you know the conditions of your work for the Chairman."

"I do. I help people, and they forget me. I have to be selfless in my service to others. And I'm not trying to renegotiate that reality. But . . . it was nice."

"Yes, I can see that."

We stood for an awkward moment in the stairwell.

"Okay," I said for no other reason than to relieve my discomfort. "I suppose we should be going."

"Would you be interested in a visit with Detective Patrick Costello? I thought we might persuade him to testify against his corrupt fellow police officers at the 24th Precinct."

"When he talked to the other cops he sounded pretty determined not to 'rat out' anyone."

"Yes," Harry treated me to his Mona Lisa smile, "but he hasn't discussed it with me."

"Oh? You're confident in your ability to persuade this bad cop?"

"Yes. I'm capable of many things."

"You're always a surprise."

"After we talk to Costello, we can follow up with Naomi and Stewart and find out what they have discovered about Gerhard Fuchs."

"Sounds like an excellent doubleheader. I like that."

And whoosh . . .

7

Over the years, I've journeyed to a number of prisons. I can't speak for anyone else in law-enforcement, but I never became accustomed to the sound of a steel gate clanking shut behind me. The hair on the back of my neck literally prickled up. I could not begin to imagine the sense of despair that must overwhelm an inmate in such a place. But, every time I visited a jail or prison, it was on business, so every time I just kept my mind tightly locked on the business at hand. Which was my plan now that I was at the Benjamin Ward Central Visit Center on Riker's Island, about to see Detective Patrick Costello. The visitor center at Rikers had all the charm of overcooked Brussels sprouts. Without the weird green color.

To my complete surprise, Harry had volunteered to come with me to visit this dreadful place.

"Really?" I was stunned. "Why would you want to go to Rikers?"

"I didn't say I *wanted* to go. I suggested that I might be useful to you when you discuss the future with Detective Costello."

So, wearing navy-blue suits with white dress shirts and boring ties—doing our best impressions of criminal attorneys—we signed in and were led to an area that bore a striking resemblance to an extraordinarily depressing cafeteria. But no food. There were large spaces between the tables, which were bolted to the floors as were the benches at the tables. The walls were pale gray. Or maybe it was a very pale green. Or a very pale, very faded blue.

Harry and I chose a table to one side of the room, and a few minutes later Patrick Costello ambled in, dressed in gray coveralls with big white DOC letters on his back. He did his best to appear that he didn't have a care in the world. I found his performance unconvincing. Although maybe it was the swollen, blackened left eye that undercut his confident image.

Costello sat. Eyeballed Harry then turned to give me the once-over. After a moment, he said, "You. You put me here."

"Yup." I replied.

"Why the hell do you think I'd talk to you?"

"Well, I realize that we're interrupting your busy social schedule—"

"—Fuck you."

"I feel the same about you, but I'm actually here to help you out."

"Oh, yeah, and how are you going to do that?"

"Mr. Costello," Harry said, "within the next few days, all of Gerhard Fuchs's financial accounts, holdings, and transactions will be laid bare to the NYPD."

"Yeah, so?" Costello was a shade less belligerent with Harry. I had never seen Harry interact directly with a

117

bad guy before, and I was fascinated by his effect on this particular thug.

"Once the NYPD has this information, they will be able to tie you to Fuchs's prostitution house at 341 West 91st Street. They will also be able to tie any corrupt police officer in the 24th Precinct to Fuchs."

Costello shifted uneasily on his bench. "I don't know anyone named Gerhard Fuchs."

"Nice try," I said.

Harry continued, "You do, in fact, know who Mr. Fuchs is. Right now, before your former employer gets Fuchs's financial data, you can still strike a deal. You can give the police and the DA a great deal of information about the corrupt cops in your precinct. But after Fuchs's data is delivered, there will be no need for your information, and, therefore, no deal."

"You'll get bupkis," I said. "Bupkis is Yiddish, in case you don't know."

"I know Jewish slang. I'm not a neo-Nazi."

"You just take their money."

Costello glared at me. I glared back. He gave up and turned to Harry, "Like I said, I don't know Fuchs."

Harry nodded as if accepting that statement on its face. "Even if you don't know Fuchs, you are still going to jail for statutory rape. As a corrupt cop taking money from the prostitution house, you are criminally liable kidnapping and sex trafficking. And felony murder. In prison, you will be in the general population, where word will spread that you are a child molester. My understanding is that prison is an unfortunate place to be when you are a child molester."

"That's my understanding, too," I said helpfully. "Very unfortunate place. Not to mention you're an ex-cop. Prison can be downright horrible for ex-cops."

"You're full of it," Costello growled.

"Boy, you are one tough guy," I said with an insincere grin. "The boys in gen pop are going to love having you in attendance."

"You don't have the power to do what you say."

"Yes, we do," Harry said quietly. "Please believe me when I say that *every single thing* I've said to you will come true."

Costello turned from Harry to me then back to Harry. If I were Costello, and I thanked God that I was not, I would have believed Harry. He seemed divinely credible to me.

Apparently, he had persuaded Costello, too. "All right," the former detective said, "I'll cooperate."

"Contact your lawyer immediately," Harry responded. "Inform him that you are ready to make a deal. Move fast. You want to make the deal before the police get the financial data."

"I got it. I got it. I'll move fast."

We stood up to leave. "Nice seeing you again," I said.

Costello grimaced, flashed his middle finger, but

said nothing.

"I had no idea what a talented guy you are," I said to Harry once we were outside Rikers. "You sounded as if you've been negotiating with hardened criminals your entire life."

He arched an eyebrow.

"Would you mind using one of the abilities I am familiar with and whooshing us out of here?"

And . . . he did. To the hallway outside Naomi and Stewart's railroad flat. Naomi let us in and led us to Stewart.

"This guy Fuchs is like some kind of tropical skin disease," Naomi spoke as she walked. "Your skin's all messed up with a horrible rash, you're running a fever, and you're nauseous and diarrheic at the same time."

"But other than that . . ." I observed wryly.

"Other than that, he's worse than pond scum."

"Were you able to dig into his background while you hacked his laptop?"

"Of course we did. He's a rich white kid of German descent. His grandfather emigrated to this country in the 1920s with a pretty fat wallet. Daddy used the money to create a highly profitable real estate business."

"Gerhard made his first appearance in 1976 and when he was old enough, went to Groton and to Harvard," Stewart said, waving hello to us. "It must have been tough being a neo-Nazi at a place like Harvard."

"Maybe his stormtrooper alter ego hadn't fully

developed."

"No, he was a complete jerk already," Stewart was shaking his head. "The guy didn't belong to any clubs, didn't play on any teams. He took a lot of economics, history, and poly sci. And . . ."

"Wait for it," Naomi said, grinning broadly.

"He joined an off-campus group called 'Sons of Deutschland,'" Stewart finished his thought.

"I'm guessing they did a lot more than sing the Horst Wessel Song."

"No arrests for anything criminal, but they sold copies of *Mein Kampf* on street corners and held some demonstrations," Naomi added. "They were suspected of spray-painting swastikas on some Boston area synagogues and beating of some yeshiva students."

"Any witnesses to the beating? And how badly hurt were the students?"

"All the witnesses reported guys in masks. Luckily, none of the students got anything worse than a black eye or a broken nose. That's about all we know about his college days: He was a part of a group that was violently anti-Semitic."

Stewart chimed in earnestly, "But *now* we know what a despicable human being he is. And that he's kind of a genius when it comes to crime."

"What do you mean?"

"The guy's a wunderkind when it comes to financial sleight of hand. He's got a couple dozen corporations and offshore bank accounts. It's almost impossible to trace all of his money and properties."

"But you did?"

"Yeah, well, I said *almost impossible*," Stewart grinned in self-satisfaction. "Most people would have never discovered his crimes."

"Most people don't have help from Harry," Naomi pointed out.

Harry bowed slightly.

"Can you lay it out for me?" I asked.

"Sure," Stewart replied. "We hacked the laptop you brought us. It had all kinds of encrypted ledgers, and a ton of the entries were in a code, but . . ."

"We got him," Naomi said. "The house at 341 West 91st Street—Fuchs owns it. We had to slice our way through four different companies to discover his financial fingerprints, but we did it."

"Can you summarize everything in writing? Something I can give to the police along with the laptop? And maybe you could include instructions for how the police can get into the laptop?"

"I don't claim your expertise in law enforcement," Stewart said hesitantly, "but won't the police need a chain of evidence for the laptop?"

"Yes. But their chain will begin when an anonymous tip leads to their discovery of the laptop."

"Anonymous?"

"Completely and absolutely."

Naomi grinned and said, "There's more."

"Oh?"

"Yes," Stewart interjected. The two of them were like kids on Christmas morning—each one needing to show off the bright, shiny toys they'd just unwrapped. "You were right. Fuchs owns a drug lab. Processing and wholesale distribution of heroine laced with fentanyl."

"How did you figure that out from a bunch of numbers in his ledgers?"

"Fuchs, through about a half-dozen companies, owns a warehouse in Queens under the business name is König Raw Materials. The warehouse is pretty ratty, but it has almost immediate access to the Whitestone Expressway. Lots of chemicals being purchased, and some legitimate product being sold."

"Like what?"

"Raw building materials."

"Just what are raw building materials?"

"Concrete, caulk, sealants, epoxies, welded wire mesh, rebars, polystyrene insulation, waterproofing chemicals—" Stewart stopped when he saw the grin on my face. "You were going to see how long a list I could recite."

"Yes, I was. And I'm very impressed. You could have a career on late night TV as the announcer on low-budget commercials."

"Am I complimented or insulted?"

"Up to you."

Harry interrupted, "The important thing to comprehend about this business is that there is a great deal of cash coming in that doesn't seem to be connected to the raw-materials business."

"And . . .," Naomi said, beaming ear-to-ear, "thanks to Harry we were able to hack some local security cameras. Fuchs's warehouse seems to have a huge amount of traffic in and out at all hours. Not trucks, but sports cars and tricked-up SUVs."

"In other words," I said, "not the kind of transport one would use to pick up welded wire mesh and rebars."

Naomi acknowledged my statement by continuing to beam like a smart student being praised by the teacher.

Stewart interjected "Yeah, but there's something else going on, but we can't figure it out."

Naomi added, "Fuchs seems to be stockpiling cash. Why?"

"He's going to use it to fund his illegal activities," I replied.

"But what?" Naomi was frustrated by her inability to answer her own question. "He used the prostitution set-up to generate cash and to demean Jewish women. Most of the men who show up at his warehouse are people of color, so he's selling drugs to generate cash and while spreading addiction in communities of color. If his standard thing is to grab cash and hurt some group he hates, what is he going to do next?"

"As I mentioned to you earlier," Harry said to me,

"Fuchs has a team that robs banks."

"What?" Stewart was perplexed. "Why?"

"Yeah, why?" Naomi chimed in. "After all, banks are federally insured. How does robbing banks hurt any of the groups Fuchs hates?"

"For a long time, it was standard operating procedure for terrorist groups to fund themselves by robbing banks. Back in the 1970s, there was a German terrorist group called the Baader-Meinhof Gang, a very nasty bunch who pulled kidnappings and bank robberies, among other crimes. Besides, it's standard Nazi nonsense that Jews control financial institutions. In Fuchs's mind, robbing banks is another way to grab cash, literally, and hurt Jews."

"Isn't that a stretch?" Stewart asked.

"For a guy who kidnaps Jewish teenagers, enslaves them with drugs, and then prostitutes them? Really, what could you think of that would be a stretch for a character like that? Going back to Fuchs's ledgers, do you have any idea how much cash he's stockpiled?" I asked.

"About two million," Naomi said. "I'm not an expert at robbing banks, but two million seems like one hell of an expense fund to rob a bank."

"Maybe he's planning to rob more than one bank?" I wondered out loud.

Stewart added, "Maybe more than one at a time?"

"Oh God," I groaned. "I wish you hadn't said that."

"Why?"

"Because I think you're right."

Naomi asked, "Is that what you'd do?"

"You mean if I were a Nazi bastard planning to rob banks?"

She smiled and nodded.

"Yeah, that is what I would do."

"But that's going to make it really hard to stop him, isn't it? You'd need to know how many robberies, where and when."

"Yup. All the essential details."

I turned to Harry. "I don't suppose you can provide a lead."

"No."

"That's not very helpful." I didn't bother locking eyes with him—in my experience it was impossible to win a staring contest with Harry. Probably because he was an angel. "You know," I paused then continued, "if I were a master criminal, since after all I think I'm part of the master race, I wouldn't use two million dollars to rob a bank. I'd do something on a grand scale. Something horrific."

"Terrorism?" Stewart asked.

I nodded.

"Why terrorism?" Naomi asked.

"I think he's escalating. Using the Baader-Meinhof Gang as an example—they got more and more violent as the years passed. Not only kidnapping and bank robberies, but assassinations, bombings, even shoot outs with the police. Their violence peaked in the late '70s."

126

"I'm confused," Stewart said. "Is Fuchs somehow linked to them?"

"No, no, sorry, I didn't mean that. But I think he's probably operating on their pattern. He's already kidnapped girls and sold drugs. And as Harry just said, Fuchs is robbing banks. Seems logical for him to escalate to something even bigger. Much bigger."

"But why? He's already got money and hurting Jews."

"He wants to make a statement. Something huge that people will always remember."

"A terrorist strike," Naomi whispered.

I nodded and said to Harry. "Am I the victim of my own over-active imagination?"

"I wish you were."

No one said anything for a moment. A moment that seemed to last an hour.

Finally, I asked, "Anyone got an idea for next steps?"

Naomi replied, "We keep rolling up Fuchs's operations. Stewart and I will keep digging. You . . . you do what you do."

"Whack the Supreme Order like a piñata until the terrorist plan spills out."

Harry said, "I'm not certain that your piñata imagery is the best comparison to our situation."

"Did you know what I meant?"

"Yes—"

"Fine." I cut him off. I asked Naomi and Stewart, "Do you happen to know what the security is like at the warehouse in Queens? Guards? Cameras? Alarm systems?"

"No," Naomi said. "But we can find out."

Stewart added. "Call us later today."

"You guys are terrific."

"Yeah," Naomi agreed. "We are."

As soon as we stepped outside Naomi and Stewart's front door, Harry whooshed us to Buona Tazza. We were on the line waiting to place our order.

"Why didn't you ask me about security?" Harry wondered.

"You always tell me I get what I need from you. I'm pretty sure I don't need security info from you when I've got Naomi and Stewart to rely on."

"You're learning."

"You betcha. Speaking of need, why did you whoosh us here? Are you jonesing for cappuccino?"

Harry flashed me his Mona Lisa expression, but held it just long enough for me to be sure that he was, in fact, happy. "As we previously established, you've had a bad influence on me."

"How can introducing someone to the wonders of well-made cappuccino be exerting a bad influence?"

Once our drinks were ready, we retired to a table, barely large enough for our cups and the small plate of biscotti.

"Why don't you tell one of your contacts in the

NYPD about Fuchs's lab in Queens?" Harry asked.

"No evidence. No justification whatsoever for a search warrant. Just a lot of supposition by Naomi and Stewart. Now, I happen to think it was first-class supposition. But what I think won't be enough for the NYPD to get a warrant."

"What about the financial evidence that Naomi and Stewart are putting together?"

"That only shows the long, twisting trail that eventually leads to Fuchs as the owner of 341 West 91st Street."

"Won't the same trail indicate that Fuchs owns the drug lab?"

"Sure, but as Naomi and Stewart pointed out, there's no proof of criminal activity there."

"Does that mean you're going there to find something you can give the NYPD?"

"Yup." I paused to savor some of my cappuccino. Then chewed and swallowed a bite of almond biscotti. "I also need to get the laptop I took from Fuchs to the cops."

"I could get it to them. Anonymously."

"I know, but they have no reason to do anything with it."

"What about what you told Naomi and Stewart?"

"I didn't want them to worry about something they can't do anything about. But there's no chain of evidence for the laptop, which means no proof that it belongs to Fuchs."

"What if, after performing your usual destructive mayhem at the lab, you were to call 9-1-1?"

"All kinds of evidence, including the laptop, would be seized once the cops found the drugs and the lab paraphernalia. That might work."

We both mulled while we sipped more of our drinks.

"Do you think Naomi realizes that Stewart loves her?" Harry asked. "I ask because you know a lot more about human nature than I do."

"Since I am . . . human. And you're . . . not."

"Yes."

"Are you serious?"

"Yes. I watch over them as I watch over you. It seems to me that he loves her, but she cannot or will not see that."

"Unfortunately for Stewart, I think you're right. I'm guessing Stewart went to school with her older brother, he's known her for years and has had a huge crush on her for almost as long as he's known her. But she only thinks of him as her cute, Hobbitlike buddy and tech partner. Not the tiniest hint of romantic feelings for him."

"That is remarkably accurate. Although Stewart went to summer camp with her older brother, not school. How did you guess?"

"Hey, I'm a government-trained troubleshooter cum investigator."

"Do you think there's a chance they'll ever change

130

the nature of the relationship?"

"Probably not. Then again, the human heart is a complex and astounding thing. Maybe something will happen, and she'll see him in a whole new light."

"Do you think that's likely?"

"Likely? I don't know. I honestly don't. But, as Naomi is so fond of saying, 'when Harry is involved, anything is possible.'"

"The Chairman does not interfere with the exercise of free will. If he does not, I cannot."

"I would never suggest you *interfere*," I said with a wry grin. "But maybe you could *influence* . . ."

He closed his eyes and shook his head in disgust.

"Okay, sorry. Forget I said anything. Just remember: You brought up the subject of romance between them."

"As if you will let me forget."

We finished our biscotti and cappuccinos in silence. I left a heavy tip in the jar on the counter, and we strolled out of Buona Tazza.

"Are you planning to go to Fuchs's warehouse tonight?" Harry asked.

"I think it's best if I move as fast as possible. I need to get whatever evidence I can that will allow the NYPD to shut this Nazi clown down."

"Should I meet you?"

"Could you whoosh me to the lab at five minutes after midnight?"

"Yes. Are you going to Kim's for dinner?"

"Yes. Are you going to whoo—"

No, he was not. Harry disappeared as I was asking the question. I walked the few blocks from Buona Tazza to my apartment where I made myself a peanut butter and jelly sandwich on whole wheat bread, something I probably hadn't had in a year. It was quite the treat. Not quite as good as my once-a-year Coca Cola, which was so good it felt like a divine revelation, but the PBJ was very satisfying.

I spent the afternoon on the phone and e-mail with my current customers. All quiet on the client front. Just the way I liked it. They felt secure, and I received my monthly checks. So much safer than fighting with neo-Nazis. Steady paychecks and no midnight excursions, facing lethal dangers. I could get used to that life.

Harry would never interfere with the exercising of my free will to choose such a life, but he didn't have to. As much as I disliked getting shot, stabbed, and beaten up, I loved being of service to others. "Loved" was the wrong word—it was deeply satisfying to know I had helped people. People who had no one else who could help them.

I wrapped up my regular business around 3:00 P.M. and called the one and only Charlie Winfield, NYPD Detective First Grade, at the 6th Precinct.

"Hey, Charlie, I was hoping for a favor."

"After the tip you gave us on West 91st, sure. What's up?"

"I got a problem. The guy who owns 341 West 91st Street is a neo-Nazi. But it's going to take your tech experts and forensic accountants quite a while to connect the multiple shell companies to their owner."

"Yeah, got it. So, what's your problem?"

"I think this guy, Gerhard Fuchs—"

"—the neo-Nazi?"

"Yup. I think he's running a bunch of criminal enterprises. And . . . I think he's going to do something truly big and ugly. Along the lines of Baader-Meinhof. But I haven't a clue what or where or when."

"You're talking about an act of terrorism?"

"I think so."

"But no evidence?"

"Nothing."

"My old partner, Diego Quintana, is working NYPD's Counterterrorism Bureau. You should talk to him." Winfield gave me the contact info for Quintana. "Let me call him and set up a meet for you."

"How is he going to be able to help?"

"You never know. Maybe this guy Fuchs is already on Counterterrorism's radar. Regardless, once I tell Diego what a miracle worker you are, he'll listen to you, and then Fuchs will be on the radar."

"Sounds good. Thanks, Charlie."

"You're welcome. And, Jack?"

"Yeah?"

"Go get 'im."

"Will do."

* * *

About 20 minutes after my phone conversation with Winfield, he texted me and told me to call Quintana. I called, Quintana answered immediately, and we set up a meeting.

Excuse me, Mr. Tyrrell, have you thought through your Friday plans? Starting now and finishing at a Queens warehouse sometime after midnight? I examined my evening options and came up with the following agenda: prep for the excursion to Queens, go meet with Qunitana, have dinner and a visit with Kim, then off to warehouse. Very satisfactory. As long as I didn't get killed in Queens.

I showered, and dressed in my all black, cat-burglar outfit: turtleneck, cargo pants, and crepe-soled shoes. I threw on a black windbreaker over my black ensemble. There were black gloves and a balaclava in my backpack if I needed to disappear completely into the night. The pack also contained my usual assortment of goodies: two Ruger SR9s, extra ammunition magazines, eight grenades (four each of the smoke and flashbang varieties), and two-dozen plasticuffs. Yes, two-dozen. I always wanted enough party favors to go around.

"Harry?"

"Yes?" he said without my being aware of his entering my apartment.

134

"I'm going to meet an NYPD detective. Could I leave my pack here and—"?

"—I'll whoosh it along with you to the warehouse tonight?"

"Exactly."

"Of course." He disappeared as swiftly as he had appeared.

A few minutes after 5:00 P.M., I met Quintana at a coffee shop a few blocks from the Counterterrorism office at One Police Plaza. We shook hands, sat at the counter, and ordered coffee.

Detective First Grade Diego Quintana was about my height and lean, with neat brown hair and alert, dark-brown eyes. "Charlie tells me you are the real deal in every possible way. He also says you have amazing information and that I should listen to you."

"I guess he likes me."

"I've never heard him speak so positively about anyone."

I shrugged. Our coffee arrived. He added a packet of sugar to his. I drank mine black.

"Okay," Quintana said, "Charlie says you've got a real bad feeling about a neo-Nazi named Gerhard Fuchs."

"Real bad."

"But no evidence of any kind."

"Unfortunately, no."

"I ran a check on Fuchs after Charlie called. Nothing. He's got a clean sheet. Seems to be the owner of a couple of legit real-estate companies that he inherited from his father."

"Yup. That's exactly what I have."

"But you think he might be planning to attempt some kind of act of terrorism."

"I'm pretty damn sure, but all I have is this bad feeling in my gut. I don't have any idea of what, where or when."

"Charlie said to trust you, and that's good enough for me. I'll start digging into this guy. You do whatever it is that you do—Charlie tells me you produce amazing results—and I'll do what I can, and we'll let each other know as soon as either of us gets anything."

"Sounds like a plan. I appreciate your willingness to talk when I've got nothing but premonition to offer." I finished my coffee, stood up and extended my hand. "Thanks, Detective."

"Diego."

"Thanks, Diego."

My subway ride to Kim's neighborhood was swift and smooth. Her doorman looked me up and down when I entered. I guessed he didn't know what to make of my all-black ensemble. As I entered Kim's apartment, she cocked her head and squinted at my attire.

"Are we going out this evening?"

"I don't know about 'we,' but yes, *I* am going out."

"How worried should I be?"

Since I had no idea how many guards there would

be, or how many would be carrying big, honking assault rifles or submachine guns, I really couldn't give her an answer. On the other hand, I didn't think she wanted a dose of heavy reality, so I replied, "Not very."

"Really?"

"Really," I said in my most sincere, used-car salesman's voice.

"You ready for dinner?" she changed the subject because she knew I wasn't going to say anything reassuring.

"Yes, please."

I set the table as she whisked a salad to the table and served up plates with a half a roast chicken for each of us with new potatoes roasted in olive oil. Simple. Delicious.

"This looks great," I said. "Thank you."

"You're welcome."

We fell into desultory talk about her work and current clients and proceeded to a discussion of my work.

"Is tonight's excursion," she waved her knife at me, a gesture I understood to encompass my all-black garb, "for a client or is it the damn neo-Nazi thing?"

"The neo-Nazis. This guy, Gerhard Fuchs, makes infectious bacteria look like a higher form of life." My tone was hot and angry.

"Why are you so torqued up about him?"

"Because he is truly awful and despicable."

"You've dealt with some other people who met that

description. But I've never seen you this angry before."

"I'm passionate about my pro bono work."

Kim took a bite of salad. I could see that she was gathering resolve to bring up a tender topic. Stay calm, Tyrrell. Remember that Kim loves you and wants to help you.

"Come on, Jack, get real," she said. "You lost Laurie—someone incredibly important to you—just a month ago."

"Unfortunately, not the first time I lost someone."

"No, but this was a woman you couldn't save. And she was Jewish. And then you rescue a bunch of young Jewish women."

"And your point is?"

"This has got to bring up some issues for you."

"I've never been a guy who was issue-free. You know that."

"Now you're just being evasive."

"Hey, am I still grieving for Laurie? Yes, of course. Does that make me more dedicated to bringing down the bad guy? No. I'm always dedicated to bringing down the bad guy. Always."

"I'm worried about you. I don't want you to get hurt or worse because you're too angry to see what's coming."

"You don't have to worry. I'm a government-trained troubleshooter cum investigator. I can handle this."

She held up her left hand and wriggled her purple-yarn wrapped ring finger. "You'd better be careful, because

138

I intend to collect on this engagement ring."

"You will."

"Promise?"

"I promise."

*   *   *

Harry appeared in the living room at 11:30 P.M., a little while after Kim had gone to bed.

"Kim will be sorry she missed you," I said and glanced down the hall toward the bedroom. "Maybe she's not asleep yet."

"She is."

"Oh."

"I didn't want to increase her anxiety while we reviewed the security for the lab."

"That tough?"

"It's not easy."

He opened a large dark-brown leather briefcase and pulled out Fuchs's laptop, placing it on the dining room table.

"Naomi and Stewart copied all the data off the laptop so you can leave it at the lab. Once you manage to get the police to search the place, they'll find the laptop, and there will be no problems with the chain of custody."

"Assuming I find something tonight that will justify a search warrant."

"You will."

"I thought you were an angel, not a prophet."

He arched his left eyebrow in displeasure. "I cannot foretell events, as you well know. But, occasionally, I am given a general understanding of how things will turn out."

"Hmm. Once the police get their paws on the laptop will the cops be able to get into it?"

"Naomi and Stewart eliminated most, but not all, of the encryption. Stewart said that a kid in junior high could hack into the machine now."

I chuckled. "They seem to think of everything."

"Almost everything."

"Okay. Let's check out the layout and security of the warehouse."

Harry took a map and a diagram of a building from his briefcase and rolled them out on the table. "Fuchs's lab is inside a business called König Raw Materials." He pointed at the map, "It's this building on 123rd Street, a few hundred feet south of 31st Avenue in the College Point area. Mostly warehouses and wholesalers. Fuchs's building is only a few blocks away from the NYPD's Queens Tow Pound."

"Ballsy. And clever. Not that tow pounds have a ton of regular cops manning them."

"The front half of the building is a legitimate business, selling raw construction materials."

"And the back half?"

"It's the warehouse for the construction inventory.

The drug lab is in the basement. All of the lab's business goes through the back entrance."

"How secure is the building?"

"The front windows and doors are closed off with steel gates."

"So I'd need a bulldozer to get through them."

"Yes, that would do the job."

"What about the side walls?"

"No windows. No doors."

"And the rear of the building?"

"A loading dock—"

"With a steel gate?"

"Yes."

"I'm guessing the door used by the drug customer is steel-reinforced door with a peep hole. Probably two wide-angle cameras, monitored at all times from the inside. Impossible to sneak inside that way."

"Exactly. How did you know?"

"Don't sound so surprised. I do security consulting for a living."

"You assist illegal drug businesses with their security?"

"Touché. What about the roof?"

"Four steel ventilation caps."

"Any cameras up there?"

"None."

"Hmm." Fuchs's illicit business was going to be a tough nut to crack. "How many guards working tonight?"

"Eight. One stationed on the security-camera monitors. Two at the small back door for customers. One roaming the internal perimeter. The other four are sleeping downstairs. They take eight-hour shifts. A completely new set of four rotates in every 24 hours."

"When are the shifts?"

"8:00 in the morning to 4:00 in the afternoon. Then 4:00 to midnight and finally, midnight to 8:00."

"So we'll be getting there a few minutes after the midnight shift change."

"Is that a problem?"

"Well, they're probably extra fresh since they're just coming on duty. Then again, it might take them a few minutes to settle into their routines." I considered my options for entering the building then asked, "Would you be all right with whooshing me to the roof at 12:05?"

"Much as I disapprove of your expression 'whooshing,' yes, I'll transport you at 12:05."

"Thanks. What kinds of weapons are the guards carrying?"

"Each guard has a 9mm pistol and a Heckler & Koch submachine gun."

"Ugh. Any of these guys have special training? Ex-military or law enforcement?"

"A couple of former regular Army. No special unit veterans, no law-enforcement."

"What about alarms?"

"I am delighted to inform you that there is only an

142

internal alarm. If the guard watching the monitors or the guards at the back door are worried, they can summon the backup team in the bunk room downstairs. But you do not have to worry about alarms on any doors or windows. Mr. Fuchs seems to feel that steel barricades and human beings are enough."

"Does the drug lab operate 24/7? How many lab workers will be there in the middle of the night?"

Harry shook his head, "The lab runs from 9:00 in the morning till 9:00 at night."

"Why not 24/7? I can't believe Fuchs is trying to save on employment costs. He's probably paying people pennies."

"He is. But during the lab's hours of operation, he has extra guards in the lab supervising the workers to make sure they're not using or smuggling out his product. But he doesn't want to have extra guards 24 hours a day. Twelve hours is sufficient for the lab workers to produce the quantities of fentanyl-laced heroin that Fuchs sells at night."

I studied the map and the building diagram. "Are the four rooftop ventilation caps all in a single row or spread out in pairs?"

"Pairs. Two near the front, two at. The rear."

"Can you whoosh us directly in between the rear pair?"

"Certainly."

"Would you like to toss a grenade or two tonight?"

"What exactly did you have in mind?"

"You'll see."

8

At 12:05 A.M., Harry whooshed us to a spot on the roof of König Raw Materials, Fuchs's drug lab exactly in the middle of the two rear ventilation stacks. How did I know we were exactly in the middle? Because I was traveling with Harry, who did everything precisely.

We were very near the southern end of College Point. It was the kind of dull, slightly grimy neighborhood you would expect given that it was full of warehouses and parking lots. It was also, at that time of night, quiet. No automotive traffic. No pedestrians out strolling the less than scenic streets or watching planes land at LaGuardia Airport directly across Flushing Bay.

I turned my attention to my particular patch of the neighborhood and the 3-feet tall ventilation stacks, shaped like dull-gray, steel mushrooms. I tiptoed to the cap on my left, slowly and quietly shrugged off my backpack, and took out a small toolkit and flashlight.

"Would you mind holding the light?" I asked Harry, handing the flash to him, as I knelt by the cap.

He twisted the end to narrow the beam and tightly focus it on the stack. Less chance of someone detecting us thanks to a stray beam of light.

"Thank you," I said. "That's perfect." I leaned

toward the cap and used my fingertips to discover screw heads. The top of the ventilation stack, the round mushroom cap, was held in place by four Phillips-head screws. The base of the stack was attached to the roof by four bolts with heads the size of quarters.

Harry whispered, "You're too big to fit through the neck of these ventilators. You'll have to take off the entire unit."

"Thanks for that useful observation," I replied, also whispering. I took an adjustable wrench out of the tool kit, sized it to fit one of the bolt heads, and slowly began undoing the one closest to my feet. I had to turn the wrench slowly, and much as I wanted to grunt due to the bolt's tight fit, I couldn't. No noise, Tyrrell. None. Eventually, without any noise and not an undue amount of sweat I got the bolt out.

Ten minutes later, the other three bolts were out. I gently tilted the ventilation stack back and forth until it came loose without any noise. I lifted the unit up and put it down on the roof a few feet away.

I peered down into the hole left by the ventilation stack. Everything was black.

"What's at the bottom of this hole?" I asked. "Some kind of duct or grid?"

"There's a grid directly below us, about 18 inches lower than the roof. The air exhaust from the interior of the building. Through the grid and out through the cap."

"I don't want to shine a light down this hole—do I

need to unscrew the grid or cut a lock?"

"The grid is latched shut. No lock. You just drop and your weight will push the grid open."

"And bust my whatchamacallit when I hit the floor?"

"From here to the floor is less than 15 feet."

"Oh? Is that all? And where the hell will I be landing?"

"On the floor of a storage room with racks containing cement supplies."

"Why don't you go first? I'd be happy to follow your lead."

"You know that's not how it works."

"Really? Is this another leap of faith thing?"

He shrugged.

"You do remember that I need you to toss a couple of grenades, right?"

"Yes."

"You do know how to arm and toss a grenade, right?"

Harry's facial expression should have scorched the earth.

I acted unimpressed and handed him two grenades. "From the storage room, we'll go through the door into the warehouse," I pointed toward the rear of the building, "and head right and then left. You toss the flashbang and then the smoke grenades into the monitoring room. I'll keep moving and hit the guys at the back door with the same grenade combo. Got it?"

"Yes," Harry whispered with something highly acidic in his tone. He had the knack for displaying his displeasure with me through a fleeting expression or a single syllable.

"Okay, it's show time." I straddled the ventilator opening with my arms crossed over my chest, my hands in fists. If you're dropping 15 feet onto a hard surface, the ideal method is to bend your knees and roll as soon as you make impact. The rolling motion displaces some of the impact. Unfortunately, I was about to drop straight down into blackness so I'd have no warning when I was going to hit the ground.

I inhaled and exhaled very deeply. I whispered, "Please help me," closed my eyes, pulled my feet together, and dropped. My feet instantly smashed through the grid, popping it open with a dull thud. The millisecond I was clear of the grid, I bent my knees and tried to relax.

The impact was ugly. I thought my knees were going to come right up to my chin and knock my head clear off my neck. A jolting pain went through the soles of my feet to the top of my head. I rolled on impact and fetched up with my back against a wall or shelving unit.

The tiniest fraction of time later, Harry was next to me, shining the flashlight on me. "Are you all right?"

"Yeah, sure. Let's do it again." I slowly climbed to my feet. "Holy moly. Even my eyelashes hurt."

"Really?"

It was my turn to scorch the earth with a glance toward Harry. "Humor is wasted on you."

"What you call humor is definitely wasted on me. Are you ready?"

"Do I look ready?"

"You don't look any worse than you usually do at this stage of the proceedings."

"Oh, great." I walked to the warehouse door. It was not locked for which I was eternally grateful. I couldn't have picked a strawberry from its patch right then, never mind any kind of lock.

I pulled the door open. Soft light spilled into the hallway from the right. I took two grenades, one flashbang, one smoke, from my pack, pulled the pack back on, and stepped through the door.

"One last thing," I whispered. "Do all of these guards belong to *Oberste Ordnung*? No poor working Joes trying to make a living as security guards."

"Yes, they're all members of Fuchs's Supreme Order. Does that matter?"

"It'll make me less . . . reticent."

"Reticent about what?"

"Violence."

I tiptoed to the left along the hallway before Harry could respond. As I was about to turn right toward the monitoring room, a guard came around the corner toward me.

He was too surprised by my sudden appearance to

take action. I popped him with a quick jab, slid behind him, and applied a choke hold. It was the first time I'd ever tried that maneuver with a grenade in each hand, but it worked. After a few seconds he went limp, and I lowered him to the floor. I took his arms, Harry his feet, and we carried him back into the storeroom.

We laid him near one of the steel racks, and Harry shut the door.

"That was close," I whispered. I patted the guard down, removing his phone, a Heckler & Koch UMP submachine gun, as well as a Glock 17, and a stiletto. The guy had seen too many movies. What the hell was he going to do with a stiletto?

I shoved the knife in a pants pocket then plasticuffed his wrists behind his back, and cuffed his ankles, too. As was my usual method of operating, I pulled off his belt, and used that to secure his wrists to a storage rack. Then I tucked his weapons out of sight behind some sacks of cement.

"Feel better?" Harry asked.

"Yes, actually. Now I don't have to worry about the roving guard. One down. Seven to go. Let's hit it."

We exited the room and walked softly down the hall to the right. This time when I reached the corner, I made the left turn unimpeded. Ahead on the right was an open door. I peeked around the door frame and saw a guard at a desk watching a number of monitors displaying different areas of the warehouse/drug lab.

I held up ten fingers for Harry and mimed pulling the pin on the flashbang and tossing it, then did the same for the smoke grenade. He nodded.

I quickly tiptoed toward the back of the building, counting to ten in my head. I reached the small foyer at the rear entrance of the building. Two guards, dressed in long-sleeve, dark-gray shirts, sat on either side of a steel-reinforced door. In my mind: Nine. Ten. I yanked the ring on the flashbang and tossed it into the foyer.

At the same instant that my grenade made its loud, stunning bang, so did Harry's. My smoke grenade exploded about 2 seconds later. I stepped inside with a Ruger in my right hand.

I pistol-whipped the man on my right, backhanding him into the wall. He thudded against it then slid in a heap to the floor. The second guard made an effort to stop me, grabbing for the gun in its holster on his hip. I brought my pistol butt down on top of his skull and dropped him onto the floor.

Then I spun and ran back to the monitor room. The guard was coughing and groping his way toward the door, clearly unable to see or hear. I kicked him in the balls. He doubled over. I grabbed his shirt on the upper back, yanked him across the hall, and slammed him headfirst into the wall opposite. He also slid into a heap on the floor.

I rushed toward the rear foyer, stopping about 10 feet away from the door that led to the basement. I grabbed another smoke grenade from my pack, pulled the ring, and tossed it onto the floor directly in front of the door. The hall filled with smoke almost immediately. As the door swung open into the hall, I had my gun ready in my right hand and a flashbang in my left. I let three of the reserve guards step into the hallway before I threw the flashbang. The detonation felled all of them. I hustled the last few steps to the door and slammed it on the fourth guard as he tried to come through. The door bounced off of him and opened again, I grasped his shirt collar and tugged him into the hallway where he tripped over one of his fallen comrades and crashed to the floor.

My pistol butt served to pacify two of the guards, and I them of their submachine guns and Glocks and cuffed both their wrists and ankles. The other two guards were moaning but largely immobilized and didn't resist as I took their weapons. Maybe they couldn't resist. I have to admit, I didn't care what their health status was.

I hauled one of the two semi-conscious guards to his feet. "Okay, Sunshine, stand up. Who's the boss around here?"

"What?" I might as well have asked him to explain the theory of relativity. Those flashbangs really did a number on a person's cognitive abilities.

"Who's the boss? Who's the team leader of the guards here?"

He struggled to focus on my face.

"What's your name?" I asked.

It took him about 10 seconds to reply, "Otto."

"Otto. Listen to me, Otto. I know you're not feeling very well at the moment, but I need to know who's the chief guard?"

"The chief? Uh . . . I am. I'm the . . . senior man on the . . . guard team."

"Lucky me," I said. "I picked the man in charge right off the bat."

"Huh?"

"No worries, Otto." I whirled him around, cuffed him, and pushed him to the floor.

Harry was still standing outside the door of the security monitor room. "I thought I should wait for further instructions."

"Good thinking," I said. "Let's go downstairs."

The basement had a few long tables with drug-making paraphernalia. How did I know it was drug-making paraphernalia? Maybe I had seen too many TV shows and movies.

"Where should we leave Fuchs's laptop?" I asked.

Harry pointed, "I think the desk over there would be suitable."

"Yes, indeed."

Harry put the laptop in the center of the modern, stainless-steel desk. Very serious. It looked like a scientific instrument with its gleaming metal surfaces.

"Are we done?" he asked.

"Not quite. I need to ask Otto a few questions."

We climbed the stairs and discovered that Otto had

recovered to the point where he could answer simple questions.

"Who do you work for?" I asked.

"I'm not talking to you."

"I'm heartbroken." I circled him very slowly, maintaining eye contact the entire time. I allowed a grin to spread across my face, as if some devious yet satisfying thought had crossed my brain.

"What the hell do you want?" he grunted.

"Tell me who you work for."

"Get stuffed."

I leaned over him and tugged his shirt sleeve away from his wrist. There was a swastika tattooed to his forearm.

"You a fan of Adolf Hitler?"

"Yes."

"What about Gerhard Fuchs?"

"What about him?"

"He owns this place. And you work for him."

"So what?"

"Do you always work as a guard here, or do you do anything else?"

"Go fu—"

"Please don't tell me to do something anatomically impossible. It's unimaginative and a waste of time."

"Go to hell."

"After you."

He grinned.

I pulled the stiletto out of my pocket, pressed the release on the handle, and the blade flashed in the light of a single overhead bulb. "I never really appreciated how useful a blade like this might be. Have you ever considered its usefulness?"

He didn't answer.

"This thing is so sharp, it'll stab or slice through anything. Well, it won't go through steel, but then again, you're not made of steel, are you Otto?"

He said nothing. His eyes were locked on the blade as I nonchalantly waved it around as I spoke.

"I rarely indulge in torture. It's not productive. The poor victim will say anything to get it to stop. Since I already know a lot about your boss and his operations, telling me stories that you think I want to hear won't work. If you don't tell me the truth, I'll know."

I brought the stiletto to a fraction of an inch below his eye and laid the blade along his cheek. His eyes rolled down to look at the knife.

"What do you want?" his voice shook.

"Do you work for Gerhard Fuchs?"

"Yes."

"As a guard here?"

"Yes."

"Anything else?"

"Sometimes I'm on. . . ." his voice faded.

"Excuse me?"

"I can't tell you. He'll kill me."

This was the moment of truth for me. If I didn't make Otto more afraid of me than he was of Fuchs, he wouldn't tell me what I wanted to know. But I would have to do something I hated to do to make him talk.

"Sometimes you're what?" I asked.

He shook his head.

"Your mistake," I said.

I grabbed his wrist and sliced through the swastika tattoo. It wasn't a deep slice but enough for the wound to begin bleeding.

Otto began sobbing.

"The next one will be much worse," I whispered into his ear and laid the blade on his forearm, pressing down just hard enough that he could feel it.

He blurted, "I work on his bank robbery crews sometimes!"

"Did you say bank robbery?"

"Yes, yes—" he was sobbing hard now.

"When's the next robbery?"

"I don't know, I swear I don't, I swear. Please don't hurt me, I don't know—"

"What about Fuchs? Has he ever robbed a bank? In person, I mean."

"I don't know. I think so. I don't know. Really, please . . . I don't know."

"Okay, shut up."

Otto's sobbing faded. He jerked away from me in terror as I reached for his right arm with the stiletto.

156

"Hold still," I hissed. "I don't want to hurt you anymore."

He remained motionless, his face and body were drenched in sweat. Yikes, the poor guy needed a much more powerful deodorant. I sliced off his right sleeve and used it to gag him.

I staggered to a bathroom a few feet from where Otto lay bound and gagged, dropped to my knees and threw up into the toilet.

Harry followed me. "Are you all right?"

"Yeah, sure. I'm vomiting for recreational purposes."

"Is this an aftereffect of the torture?"

"What do you think?" I flushed the toilet, washed my hands at the sink, and flushed my mouth with cold water from the tap. There was a first-aid kit on the wall in the bathroom. I opened it, took out a few items, and walked back to the hall.

I gently dressed Otto's wound. "I'm sorry about this."

"Now are we done?" Harry asked.

"I hate to sound like a doubting Thomas regarding the quality of your work, but you'll make sure there's no video, DNA, or prints of mine, right?"

"Of course," Harry said impatiently.

"Hey, just being sure there are no loose ends." I pulled out my phone and dialed 9-1-1. As soon as the operator answered I began talking fast and breathlessly,

"There's been shooting and some explosions at König Raw Materials on 123rd, just south of 31st Avenue."

"Are you hurt?" the operator asked.

I disconnected and turned to Harry. "You may whoosh when ready, Gridley."

Harry frowned for the tiniest fraction of time possible, and then we were standing on West End Avenue in front of Kim's building.

"Sooooo . . ." I drawled. "Bank robbery."

"It would seem so."

"I don't suppose you could tell me when and where the Fuchs gang will strike next."

Harry glanced up and then back at me. "No."

"I wonder if Naomi and Stewart could find a pattern of deposits in Fuchs's financial accounts."

"That sounds promising."

"And while I'm at it, I'll ask them to research bank robberies in the last year or so. Especially violent robberies at local bank branches in neighborhoods with a lot of Jewish residents."

Harry nodded. "You're on the right track."

"Good. Thanks. Did you want to come up for a cappuccino or a glass of water?"

"No thanks." His Mona Lisa smile flitted across his face, then he disappeared from sight.

The doorman on the midnight shift greeted me with the weakest of waves. I knew how he felt. I was tired and achy. I could have given a more vigorous wave than he did, but that was about the limit of my physical abilities at the moment. In the elevator, I sagged against a wall and checked my phone for the time. It was almost 1:30 A.M. Holy moly, I thought. Harry and I had spent less than 90 minutes at König Raw Materials. Sure, the time had been packed with action and grenades and even a bit of torture—the thought of which sent a chill through me—but it hadn't even been 90 minutes. Not enough time to watch two entire episodes of *The Great British Bake Off*.

Once inside the apartment, I went to the second bathroom, the one off the hallway, and washed up, brushed my teeth, and gargled with some mouthwash. I knew it was probably in my head, but I felt compelled to gargle three times before the aftertaste of vomit was gone. I tiptoed into the bedroom and used all of my Green Beret training to slide into the bed with the softness of a leaf falling to the ground.

Kim rolled over. "Hey there," she whispered huskily.

"Hey there yourself."

"Are you all right?"

My aches and pains faded as she asked the question. "Yes, I'm fine."

"Rough night."

"In some ways."

"Did you accomplish what you set out to do?"

"Yes. Do you really want to talk about what I was doing in the middle of the night at a warehouse in

Queens?"

"No, I guess not. As long as you're all right and not too dissatisfied with your work this evening." She put her arm around my neck and pulled me close for a long kiss.

"Speaking of satisfaction . . . ," I said.

She grinned and kissed me again. Her hand left my neck and traveled down my chest, the tips of her fingers gently tracing a zigzag along my torso. By the time her hand reached my waist, I was . . . well, you get the idea.

We fell asleep, naked, in each other's arms.

*   *   *

NIGHT – GERHARD FUCHS'S HOME
PALISADE AVENUE, RIVERDALE

RAT FACE shifted uneasily from foot to foot. Greasy Hair's anxious gaze went back and forth from one Rottweiler to the other. Aschgrau's hard face and upright posture revealed no emotion.

"How the hell did . . . Wouk—or whatever the hell his name is—know about König Raw Materials?" Fuchs was very angry, but he wasn't wasting time with dramatic posturing. He didn't indulge in theatrical flourishes like hissing or shouting his words like his idol, Adolf Hitler. "There's no connection between 341 West 91st Street and König—or me, for that matter."

"Are you sure it was this man who calls himself Wouk?" asked Aschgrau.

160

Fuchs nodded, stood up from his desk, and walked to the bookcase. He stared at the books covering his safe. "The video cameras at König only showed a blurred image, but it was a tall man with obvious skills. It has to have been Wouk. But how did he manage to crack the encryption on my files? How do he figure out what was going on at König? He's just a talented piece of muscle with a pathetic sense of humor."

"So. . . ," ventured Aschgrau, "he must have a team with the necessary skills."

"Yes. An extraordinary team to hack my laptop. And to connect the dots between the raw materials business and the drug lab."

"Do you . . . do you want to postpone tomorrow?" she asked.

"No. Absolutely not. Even if the files have been hacked there's no direct evidence of the bank robberies."

Aschgrau nodded, accepting his direction. "In case Wouk somehow does figure out what we have planned and makes another appearance, what do you want our team do?"

Fuchs smiled. "Kill him."

"What about collateral damage? It's a public place, broad daylight . . ."

"Kill him."

9

"What are you up to on this rainy Saturday?" Kim asked as she placed a freshly made cappuccino in front of me.

"Harry and I need to talk with Naomi and Stewart."

"Your super hacker/forensic-accounting team?"

"That's them."

"You hoping for new information on your neo-Nazis?"

"More like we need to parse the financial info we have to see if there are patterns."

"Patterns that might lead you to criminal activities?"

"Exactly. You know, with a mind like yours, you could have a career with Tyrrell Security Consultants."

"You can't afford me."

"Well . . . maybe not with salary, but the fringe benefits are amazing."

"Don't flatter yourself."

"Ouch." I put my hand to my upper lip as if checking something. "Is my nose bleeding?"

"Not yet."

"Does that mean you're not done with me?"

"Maybe. Step away from the eggs," she said, elbowing me gently away from the stove. She took the spatula from me and stirred the scrambled eggs.

"I think I had the eggs under control."

"Please check the bacon."

I opened the microwave. The bacon slices were in between sheets of paper towel, and I could only see their ends, but they were dark brown and crispy, the way we both liked them. I grabbed the near corners of the paper towels and tugged them onto a plate, peeled back the top sheet of the paper towel and smiled. The bacon was dark and crispy throughout.

Kim used the spatula to shovel the scrambled eggs onto plates. I added the bacon, and the two of us sat down at the table with our hot breakfasts.

"The eggs are perfect," I said.

"That's why I took over. I didn't want you to overcook them."

"I wasn't going to over—" I stopped. What was the point, Tyrrell?

"So after giving Naomi and Stewart more instructions, what are you doing with your day?"

"Are you trying to insert a calendar item or two into my schedule?"

"Well . . ."

"Hey," I sighed, "I'd like to help out, but I'm going to be on a stakeout from about noon until I don't know when."

"A stakeout?"

"Yes, a place called *Gesellschaft der Deutschen.*

163

It's some kind of Nazi social club on East 85th Street near Second Avenue."

"There are still German businesses in Yorkville?"

"I guess so."

"Isn't it dangerous to hang out there?"

"I'm not hanging out there. I'm staking out the place. Taking pix of people coming and going. Trying to figure out what Fuchs is up to."

"What if Fuchs himself shows up? Would you go into the club then?"

"Why would I do that?"

"To provoke him."

"I'm not a high school kid trying to taunt the Nazi bully."

"You didn't answer me. Would you go into the club? Would you try to provoke him?"

"Why would I want to provoke him? What's the point of that?"

"To make him angry and force him into a mistake."

"Hmm. Now that you mention it, that might not be a bad plan."

"And totally in character. But please don't. Please."

"What can I do for you between now and stakeout time?"

"You're changing the subject."

"Do you want help or not?"

"We're hosting Thanksgiving on Thursday—"

"Wait! Thanksgiving is on Thursday? This

Thursday? Why didn't anyone warn me?"

"You're not as funny as you think you are."

I shrugged.

Kim shook her head and said, "I have to bake a few things. Could you pick up . . .?"

She listed a bunch of items she needed to bake cookies and brownies. I made her repeat them and noted them in my phone.

"Have you got them all?"

I read back the list.

"And you'll bring them here before you go on the stakeout?"

"Of course."

"Do you mind that we're hosting Thanksgiving?"

This was the fourth time she had brought up the subject of our hosting Thanksgiving. I smiled and pretended that she had never mentioned her concern before. "I'm fine with it. Really and truly. When it comes to your parents, I'm fully prepared to keep my mouth shut about the President-elect. It won't be easy, but I can do it. And, I've met your sister, and she's great. Your brother-in-law's not too bad. And their boys think I'm some kind of action figure."

"They're young and easily impressed."

"I love you, too," I said, grinning.

She responded with one of her dazzling smiles.

*   *   *

"You want us to check for violent bank robberies at local branches in Jewish neighborhoods and see if there's a correlation to cash influx into one or more of Fuchs's many accounts?" Stewart asked.

"Exactly," I replied.

"Could I ask why?"

"I'm trying to find a pattern between the types of bank that have been hit and the timing of the robberies."

"You hoping to intervene at the next robbery?" Naomi asked. "Give Fuchs and Company a bit of Tyrrell style?"

"I'm not sure 'Tyrrell style' is how I'd phrase it."

"Yes," Harry intervened, "'style' is not a word that is particularly appropriate for Jack."

"Thank you *very* much."

"I think it suits him," Naomi said. "Anyway, we'll see if we can't come up with what you want in a few hours."

"Yeah," Stewart muttered, "it's not like we had weekend plans."

"Sorry," I said. "If you want to wait until Monday that's okay. Lives might be hanging in the balance, but I wouldn't want to intrude on your weekend."

"Really? You're going with 'lives hanging in the balance?' Not too manipulative, Jack."

Naomi grinned, "I don't mind. I'll call when we have something."

"Thanks. By the way, do you happen to know if one of Fuchs's companies owns the building that houses the *Gesellschaft der Deutschen*?"

Stewart answered, "Yeah, one of his companies does. Do you need the name of the company?"

"No, as long as it—the company, I mean—belongs to our neo-Nazi person of interest."

"Yeah."

"Okay then," I said, looking at Harry. "I think we're done here." To Naomi and Stewart, I said, "Thanks again."

"Anytime," Naomi replied happily. At the same instant, Stewart groused, "Yeah, sure."

We walked out of their flat, and the second that the front door closed behind us, Harry whooshed us to a rental car office on the Upper East Side.

I had reserved a Buick Enclave (or "similar" in rental car lingo), an option-loaded mid-size SUV. It was bigger and more luxurious than what I probably needed, but since I was only renting it for a day, I decided to spring for the higher cost. You never knew how big a vehicle you might need on a stakeout. Ten minutes after walking into the rental office, I drove out in the Buick, my trusty angel sidekick in the front passenger seat, and my backpack full of the tools of violence on the back seat within easy reach.

It took all of 5 minutes to get from the car rental place to East 85th. We arrived at 1:00 P.M. and found an open parking space on the opposite side of the street about

50 feet from the front entrance of *Gesellschaft der Deutschen*. From this particular parking spot, I could see anyone who entered or exited the social club. This was a regular occurrence when I was with Harry—if I needed a parking spot to surveil someone, there always seemed to be an open space waiting for me.

The club was located on the ground floor of a brownstone, with a few short steps leading down from the sidewalk to the front entrance. The window blinds were down, making it impossible to see inside. I had a feeling the local zoning probably didn't allow for the club to operate in the small apartment building, but I was also pretty sure that the *gesellschaft* was so old it was probably grandfathered.

In addition to whooshing us to the rental car office, Harry had secured—in his role as my semi-divine concierge—lunch. Bottled water, roast beef on rye sandwiches, and chips. He'd also brought a digital camera with a long lens.

"You might want to take a few photos of possible bad guys," he said when he showed me the camera.

"Then have Naomi and Stewart run the pics through facial recognition?"

"Good thinking."

"You're only saying that because you thought of it first."

I ate my sandwich and chips and sipped water as we watched the comings and goings of the white men going in and out of the *gesellschaft* were white men. No one interesting appeared. No one wore a sign that declared him to be a bank-robber-to-be.

"Are they all good little neo-Nazis?" I asked.

"You mean the men entering and exiting the club?"

"Yes. Are they all neo-Nazis?"

"Yes."

"Probably all chowing doing on bratwurst and sauerkraut."

"Some of them."

"What's wrong with them?" I posed the question more out of frustration than an expectation that Harry would answer. "Why are they so hateful?"

"I know you aren't fond of my answering a question with a question—"

"Is anyone fond of that?"

"Probably not. But my answer is a question: Why do you think they are so full of hate?"

"My quickie psychological take is that they're all afraid. Driven by massive insecurity. They hate and then become enraged, and the rage empowers them."

"And they cease to be afraid."

"For a while. But rage as a solution to your fears is like booze—it's an extreme, short-term fix. As soon as the rage fades or the booze wears off, the fear comes back."

"You seem to have a good understanding of what is wrong with these men. Why did you really ask what is wrong with them?"

After a long moment, I asked, "Why does the Chairman allow them to become so broken and sick?"

"You're assuming He allows it."

"Doesn't the Chairman allow everything? Isn't He the ultimate? The Alpha and the Omega?"

"At the macro level you're referring to, yes, He allows everything. At the micro level, the personal level, He allows human beings to exercise free will. He honors their choices."

"Even the evil choices?"

"Even the evil choices."

"Why?"

"Humans wouldn't truly have free will if they could only make good choices."

I was quiet for a long while. It was hard to argue with free will. Damn.

A brand new, black Audi A8 sedan pulled to a stop in front of the *gesellschaft*. I had my camera focused and ready as Gerhard Fuchs and my old buddies Greasy Hair and Rat Face climbed out of the car and went down the steps to the front door. I got a couple of good shots of them before they went insider, and a couple of Rolf Jäger as he sat at the Audi's wheel and waited. Like Rolf, we waited.

After what seemed like an eternity of waiting but was probably only 5 minutes, Harry asked, "What are we waiting for?"

"I don't know. The likelihood of something happening is so small . . . well, it would take a miracle for something interesting to happen at exactly the moment we're sitting here waiting for it."

"You do remember that the Chairman is in the business of miracles?"

"I do remember that. I even believe it" I replied. "But a stakeout miracle? Really? You and I just happen to be sitting here when criminal action begins?"

"Would you rather consider it a coincidence?"

"As I've told you before, coincidence is just the Chairman's way of remaining anonymous. And, at the moment, nothing has happened so our entire conversation about miracles and coincidence is moot."

"Ye of little faith. And little patience."

"Yeah, right."

We lapsed into silence and stared at Rolf, who continued to sit and wait. After a few minutes, Rat Face came out of the *gesellschaft* carrying a brown paper bag. Rolf lowered his window, and Rat Face passed the bag through.

"Late lunch," I muttered. "Given Rolf's bulk, I would have figured him for a six-meals-a-day guy."

"Maybe this is his second lunch."

"Well said," I was grinning.

Rat Face went back inside the *gesellschaft*. Rolf dug into the bag and began eating. We waited and watched.

"That may have been the most exciting moment of the day," I said.

"Yes," Harry replied, not sounding convinced.

"Why do you hate them?"

"It's *always* okay to hate Nazis. Always."

"I think there's something more to your feelings."

"There are people in AA who say that alcoholism is a *disease of more*."

"Do you think that's true?" he asked.

"Well, it's definitely a disease of more for me."

"And that's why we're going after Gerhard."

"And his neo-Nazi polka kings."

"I thought the Nazis' favorite dance was the goose step not the polka."

I smiled but didn't respond to the comment.

After a long pause, Harry said, "Don't let the anger overwhelm you. Anger is corrosive; it will consume your entire life."

"Thanks," I replied, meaning it.

He nodded, and we went back to our waiting. But not for long. . . .

A weathered, dark-gray Chevy Express van with windows all around and passenger license plates pulled in behind Rolf in the Audi A8. At the same instant the van stopped, the front door to the *gesellschaft* opened. Fuchs, Greasy Hair, Rat Face, and four guys I hadn't seen before came out of the club and crossed the sidewalk to the vehicles. Greasy Hair climbed in next to Rolf while Rat Face held the rear door of the Audi open for Fuchs. As soon as Fuchs was inside, Rat Face scurried around the car and got in on the other side. The Audi pulled away, and the four other guys climbed into the Chevy van.

"I can't be this lucky," I muttered.

"Why not?"

"Stakeouts usually runs hours, days even. To catch them in the act after an hour or so . . . what luck."

"Luck?"

"Come on. Really? You expect me to call this a miracle?"

"No, I expect that you will call it whatever makes you comfortable."

This dialogue occurred while I pulled out of my parking spot and followed the van, which had caught the red light at Third Avenue. I stopped far enough away that we had a clear view of the license plate.

"Could you please take a picture of the license plate?" I asked Harry.

"No need."

"You have it memorized."

"Exactly."

"You sure you won't forget?"

Harry shot me a look that would have turned a lesser man into the glob of jelly at the center of a jelly donut. But I just ignored him.

The van turned right on Third Avenue and headed uptown. I followed keeping three cars between the van and us to avoid calling attention to our Buick SUV.

"Do you have any idea where he's going?" I asked.

"No, do you?"

173

"My guess would be to 96th Street, head east to the FDR, then head north."

"To Riverdale?" Harry asked.

"I kinda doubt that Gerhard would have his gang rob a bank in his own neighborhood."

"Where then? Why not go west on 96th Street and rob a bank on the Upper West Side."

"Maybe he will."

At 96th, the van turned east and got on the FDR, heading north, with us a discreet distance behind.

"You are right so far," Harry admitted. "Where do you think he's going?"

"My hunch is that he's heading to Scarsdale."

"Oh? Why?"

"It's relatively close and has a pretty significant Jewish population. And there are probably a few small banks."

"Why would Fuchs target small banks?"

"Fewer people in the bank at any one time. Easier to control the situation once the robbery begins."

"But wouldn't the getaway vehicle be more noticeable in a small town?"

"Yes." I pondered that challenge for a second. "If I were Gerhard, I'd have a car parked, ready and waiting, one town away. If I was robbing a bank in Scarsdale, I'd hop on the Bronx River Parkway, drive north or south to an exit at the next town, dump the van, and drive off in the backup vehicle. Or. . . ," I paused as I concentrated on my driving, keeping the Chevy van in sight. "I'd drive to the next town and split up. The money and two, maybe three, of the guys take the waiting car. The others walk to the train station and take Metro North back to the city. The police won't be hunting for two or three men in a car, and they *definitely* won't be hunting for bank robbers on the train."

"It does sound counter-intuitive."

"Which is the reason it will work."

"Only if they're not recognized."

"Ah, good point. They'll probably have disguises or masks of some kind. Maybe reversible jackets. Or a lightweight top that they can pull off and ditch."

"What about DNA on the masks or disguises? Unlike you, they don't have me to protect their identities."

"Assuming they've planned very carefully, they'll probably dump everything in a garbage bag, which they'll take back with the money. Burn it once they return to the *gesellschaft* or Fuchs's home in Riverdale."

The van was cruising in the right-hand lane of the FDR. I continued to keep at least three cars in between us.

"Aren't you afraid of losing them?" Harry asked.

"You would never let that happen, would you?"

"Your attitude is not reflective of a proper spiritual path."

"Oh well."

The van exited the FDR for the Willis Avenue Bridge, then the Bruckner Expressway, and finally headed north on the Bronx River Parkway. The Parkway paralleled the Bronx River—which, despite its name is a lowly little creek and definitely not a river. Our two-vehicle procession drove past the Bronx Zoo (no animals were visible from the parkway!) and the New York Botanical Garden, up into Westchester and eventually to Scarsdale where the van exited at Crane Road.

We exited by making a tight almost-U-turn onto a road called East Parkway. This was followed immediately by a very tight, hard left turn that put us onto Crane Road. Scarsdale dated back to America's colonial era, and the traffic patterns hadn't evolved much since the colonists first laid out the dirt roads. The van turned right onto Chase Road, and I was a hundred feet behind. We drove past Scarsdale's post office and a park opened on our left.

In front of us on the right was the Harwood Building, a towering, turreted Tudor-style edifice. Offices upstairs and stores on the ground level. I don't think I've ever seen a more impressive building in a suburban village. Opposite the Harwood Building was Boniface Circle, a tiny bit of green space with a series of plaques honoring the Scarsdale veterans who had died in World War I and II. For a small town, an awful lot of men had died in those wars.

The van cut left across the traffic lines—a common but frowned upon maneuver—and pulled into a parking space directly in front of the Schoonmaker National Bank. I drove past the van and found a parking space at one end of the Harwood Building, almost directly across the street from the bank. I turned off the engine and grabbed my pack from the back seat.

With one eye on the van, I dug out a Ruger SR9 pistol and three extra magazines. God, I prayed, please don't make me use these. Please? Too many innocent people strolling around. I slid the magazines into the left coat pocket of my Barbour jacket and the pistol into the right pocket. Underneath the jacket, I was dressed in my usual ready-for-action outfit of dark clothes and crepe-soled shoes.

As I climbed out of the SUV, four of the bank robbers stepped out of their van, all wearing hideous, over-the-head, latex clown masks. These were nightmare clowns like something out of a Stephen King novel. They were all carrying shotguns, held down at their sides.

"Holy shit," I muttered then shouted as I walked toward them, "Okay, you clowns, stop where you are and put your hands up."

The four horrific clowns all turned; their shotguns aimed directly at me.

I spoke to the sky, "A little help, please?"

10

The four gruesome clowns were pointing their shotguns at me as I stopped in the middle of the road. They held their weapons at the hip instead of taking careful aim with guns at their shoulders. That meant there was a microscopic chance they wouldn't hit me if they fired. On the other hand, their 12-gauge shotguns would be devastating at a range of 20 feet. Well, I was going to be in a world of hurt if any of them blazed away.

"Place your weapons on the ground and put your hands up," I said firmly. At least I hoped my voice sounded firm. "And tell the driver of the van to get out with his hands up."

"Who the fuck do you think you're talking to?" one of the clowns asked.

"A bunch of bank-robbing clowns. Don't make me tell you again. Weapons down, hands up, driver of the van out."

The clowns turned to one another as if conferring. A clown with a neon-green mohawk and a skull-like face jerked his thumb at me then pointed at one of the other clowns, "Take care of this guy." To the remaining two clowns, he said, "Come on, we have to get going."

Neon-green Mohawk twisted away from me, and

the other two followed him. The last clown, with lightning shaped scars running down both cheeks of his white mask, raised his shotgun. His finger tightened on the trigger. As he brought the shotgun up, I grabbed my pistol from my coat pocket and fired as soon as it was clear. Lightning Scars spun around and toppled to the ground, his shotgun going off as he fell. The blast from his weapon caught the rear right tire of a Mercedes sedan parked next to the van, and the tire exploded with a violent pop.

The three other clowns wheeled around, firing as they spun. Behind me, the huge plate glass windows of stores on the ground floor of the Harwood Building shattered and rained onto the sidewalk.

I dove to the ground in the middle of the street, desperately rolling out of the path of an oncoming Chevy Suburban. In a panic, the driver jerked to a stop, and I rolled to the passenger side of the vehicle, keeping its huge black bulk between me and the shooters. Buckshot peppered the other side of the SUV. Do something, Tyrrell, before the poor driver is killed.

I stood up, propped my elbows on the Suburban's hood, clutched my right wrist with my left hand, and fired. I swept from my right to left, catching the three clowns, one shot each, no pauses between shots.

All three went down. Keeping my pistol aimed at them, I walked around the SUV's hood, casting a glance through the windshield at the driver, who was the most frightened mother in history. At least in the history of

Scarsdale.

"Are you all right?" I asked loudly.

She nodded.

"Call 9-1-1."

Tires screeched and rubber burned. The robbers' van rocketed out of its parking space and crashed into the SUV, smashing it into me and sending me flying.

I bounced off the side of a parked car and fell face first onto the pavement. Giving myself a conservative estimate, I would have said that of the more than 200 bones in my body, about 180 of them were broken. Every single part of me hurt. If any one of the bank-robbing clowns were still vertical, he could easily have come over and shot me without a problem. Or the guy in the van could make a U-turn, and run me over, reverse, and run me over again, and then repeat the process. I was powerless to stop any of these potentially lethal exercises.

My right cheek was on the pavement, which meant that I couldn't see too much out of my right eye. But my left eye was still working just fine. Checking under the SUV, I saw the three clowns lying on the pavement. I also saw the van pull away from the SUV and drive off at high speed, retracing its journey along Chase Road.

Sirens wailed somewhere in the distance, but they were closing in rapidly by the sound of them. Several people crouched at my side.

"Don't move," a woman said, "help is on the way."

"I can hear that," I mumbled. My right cheek felt

180

as if it were pressed into the pavement, making speech difficult.

"Are you in pain?"

"Yup."

"Where?"

"Everywhere."

"Hang tight, the ambulance will be here in a minute. You'll be all right."

"I wouldn't bet on it."

She stifled a laugh.

The sirens stopped. The people around me backed away a few steps and two EMTs knelt down next to me. One of them flashed a light in my left eye then grabbed my wrist, feeling for a pulse.

He spoke into a radio microphone clipped high on his jacket, "Accident victim is conscious, pupils responsive, pulse elevated."

They placed me in a neck brace and lifted me onto a stretcher quickly and gently.

"Are you allergic to any medications?"

"No."

"Are you in pain?"

"All over."

"Can you squeeze my hand?"

I squeezed.

He grunted in surprise, "That's quite a grip."

As they lifted the stretcher into the ambulance, I passed out. Thank God.

*   *   *

AFTERNOON – GERHARD FUCHS'S HOME
PALISADE AVENUE, RIVERDALE

THE DRIVER OF THE VAN stood nervously in front of Gerhard Fuchs, who was glowering at him. Aschgrau stood to the side of the desk, watching the faces of both men. Her own face was devoid of any expression.

"I followed the plan," the drive whined.

"Oh?" Fuchs smiled. His voice smooth and reassuring, "In that case, where's the money?"

"We . . . we never got inside the bank. This guy shouted at the others as soon as they got out of the van."

"What did he shout?"

"I'm not sure. Something like stop and put your hands up, or maybe put your weapons down. I don't remember exactly."

"Are you sure it was only one man?" Aschgrau asked.

"Oh yeah, I'm sure. Big guy, six-two, maybe six-three. Athletic type. Moved like he had training."

"I gave orders that he was to be killed."

"Hey, we tried. Believe me, we tried. But this guy took out all of the other men. He shot each of them once."

"Only once?" Aschgrau asked.

"Yeah."

"Are they dead?"

182

"I don't know. But they were all down, no one was moving."

"How did you escape?"

"I slammed into a Suburban, which slammed the big guy. Threw him through the air. He banged off the side of a parked car and flopped onto the pavement."

"Was *he* dead?" Aschgrau inquired.

"I don't know. But he wasn't moving."

"After that, you drove to Hartsdale, abandoned the van, and drove here in the backup car that had been left there, correct?"

"Yeah. It's parked outside."

"Thank you," Fuchs said. He turned to Rolf Jäger, who was standing the door, listening. "Could you please pay him off and then deal with the car?"

"Of course," Jäger said.

The driver stood up and began walking toward the door. Jäger was a half-step behind him when his left arm snaked around the driver's neck. Jäger leaned back, pulling the driver off of his feet. There was gurgling noise as the driver tried to catch his breath, his hands uselessly pulling at Jäger's arms, frantically trying to break the choke hold. The driver's feet flailed about, slowed, finally stopped altogether, and dangled lifelessly.

Jäger lowered the dead man to the floor.

Fuchs said, "We need to find out if any of the others survived."

"I'll investigate that," Aschgrau said. "Mr. Jäger,

would you please take care of the body and then the car?"

Jäger looked at Fuchs who nodded his assent and asked, "Does the man who intervened at the bank sound like the man who stopped you at the hospital?"

"Yes."

"And probably the same man who confronted me here two nights ago. Apparently, he's quite capable. I want him killed."

"Yes."

"Be sure you do the next time you run into him."

*   *   *

I woke up in a hospital room. My immediate-last memory was of bouncing off of a parked vehicle and crashing face-first into the pavement. I was happily surprised to find out that I was not like the soldier in white, trapped in a full-body cast, in Joseph Heller's *Catch-22*. In fact, I didn't think there was a cast of any sort anywhere on my body. There was, however, an intravenous drip inserted into a vein on the back of my left hand. And some quiet monitors at the edge of my vision, no doubt recording my pulse and temperature. Harry was sitting in a chair near my bed.

"Am I dead?" I asked.

"What a drama queen," Kim said, stepping into my field of vision. She smiled and kissed me on the cheek. "No, you are not dead. I'm very happy to say you are alive." She kissed me again, this time very softly on the lips. "Not too bad all things considered. Why did you ask if you were dead?"

"Because Harry was the only one I saw. I thought he might be here to escort me to a face-to-face with the Chairman."

"How do you feel?" she asked. "Must be pretty bad if you thought you were dead."

"Actually, I don't feel much of anything, which is also why I thought I was dead. How bad am I?"

"Mr. Tyrrell," a slender, dark-haired woman in a white coat entered the room, walked to the bedside, and checked the monitors. She grabbed my chart from a pocket at the end of the bed and gave it a quick scan. "I'm Dr. Patel. And you are some kind of miracle."

"I am?"

"For starters, no broken bones. And . . . ," she paused for effect, "no torn ligaments or tendons, no lacerations requiring more than a Band-Aid."

"Wow."

"I'd like to keep you overnight for observation, but I don't think you have a concussion either."

"I really am a miracle."

"Don't get him started, doctor," Kim interjected.

"You've got a stunning collection of bruises," Dr. Patel said, grinning. "And if you're not feeling them now, you will."

"Should I ask why I'm not feeling them? Am I

about to become addicted to opioids?"

"No," she shook her head and pointed at Harry, "your friend was very persuasive. He said you'd be fine on prescription-strength ibuprofen. That's what I gave you."

"Thanks," I said to her, and Harry.

"You're welcome. I'm off shift in a couple of hours, but I'll see you one more time before I go."

"Thank you," I said as she left the room. "Harry, could you give me an update on the robbery? Besides me, who else was hurt?"

"Just you and the robbers. No innocent bystanders."

"What about the woman in the SUV? She got banged around a lot."

"Yes, she did. Scared out of her wits. And her car's totaled. But not a scratch on her."

I closed my eyes, too exhausted to keep them open, and smiled. "Too bad about her car, but that's what insurance is for."

"Yes, it is."

"What about the robbers? Please tell me I only wounded them."

"I'm sorry. Two of them are dead."

"What about the others? Do they know anything that leads back to Fuchs?"

"No."

"So the police won't be chasing Fuchs anytime soon."

"Unfortunately, that is correct. But your intervention at the bank probably saved a lot of lives."

I opened my eyes and looked at Harry then Kim.

"You did," she said softly.

"Thanks. What about the driver of the van?"

"He got away," Harry replied, "and reported back to Fuchs."

"And Fuchs had him killed."

"What makes you say that?" Harry asked.

"Fuchs doesn't leave loose ends, and the driver didn't bring any money back with him. No reason not to kill him. Right?"

"Yes, that's correct."

"These people are really ugly," Kim observed.

"Were you expecting tea and sympathy from neo-Nazis?"

"I just can't fathom how people like this think or behave."

"Be grateful that you don't." I closed my eyes again. It was amazing how hard it was to keep them open. "Not that it's all about me, but what about evidence of my being at the bank? And how am I registered here at the hospital?"

"They have your name. But no one witnessed your actions at the bank. As far as the police or media know you were an unfortunate bystander caught in the gunfire and street traffic. Your name has been withheld to protect your privacy. And there are no photos of you, no security video from the bank or any of the stores. Everything happened so fast that no one had time to take video on their phones."

"What? No one wanted a few shots of my bleeding body for their Facebook pages?"

"Oh, there are a lot of shots of you on Facebook," said Kim, taking my right hand in hers. "But all so far away I even had a hard time recognizing you."

I gave her hand a gentle squeeze, "Sorry to put you through all this."

"You were just doing your job. But don't make a habit of this."

"I'll try not to. I'm guessing Fuchs probably has a pretty good idea that it was me—well, he thinks it's the guy who visited him the other night at his lovely estate in Riverdale and stopped Jäger at the hospital."

"Yes, he does," Harry affirmed.

"Doesn't change anything, does it?"

"No."

"But Fuchs doesn't know your name, right?" Kim asked.

"No," Harry responded. "Fuchs does not know Jack's name. Or yours. The Chairman will keep you safe, Kim."

"What about this guy?" she casually waved her hand toward me. "The guy who got hit by a car."

"Wait a minute, I was hit by a Chevy Suburban—*not* a car," I corrected. "A really big SUV. Huge. *Ginormous*. Probably gets five miles to the gallon."

"And yet, you are here to tell the tale," Harry said.

"I suppose I have the Chairman to thank for my lack of serious injury."

"Do you believe you could have escaped that level of mayhem without some aid from on high?"

I gazed at the ceiling, imagined I was looking into the sky, and said "Thank you." To Harry, I said, "If I wake up tomorrow feeling miraculously better, does that mean there's more mayhem in store and the Chairman is making sure I'm fit to handle it?"

"That is a logical conclusion."

Kim said, "I don't like the sound of this. I really don't."

"It's going to be okay," I said. "Right, Harry?"

He said nothing.

Kim glared at him then faced me. "Oh, so that's the guarantee of your safety? The Silent Angel over there?"

"Not that I don't find all this stuff fascinating," I said, "but I've got to go back to sleep. Getting slammed by an SUV is exhausting."

Harry stood up. "I'll be here tomorrow when you're released." He whooshed away.

"What about you?" I asked Kim.

"I foolishly fell in love with you. Right this moment, I am acutely aware of how foolishly. But I do love you, so I'm here for the duration."

"You can't sleep in a chair."

"Watch   me,"   she   said   and   pointed   to   an

extraordinarily plush recliner on wheels. "The nurse wheeled that in a while ago. I'll probably sleep more soundly than you do."

She gave my hand another squeeze, stood up, leaned over me, and kissed me on the lips. A tantalizingly soft kiss that was better therapy than anything the medical professionals in the hospital could have offered.

"See you in the morning," I said. "I love you."

"I love you, too."

*   *   *

When it was time for me to be released, I made no protest about sitting in a wheelchair and being pushed out of the hospital. Given that I'm not exactly Tiny Tim, I thought the folks at the hospital should have assigned a large male nurse to my wheelchair. But, no, a tiny little Hispanic nurse was on duty. She smiled pleasantly, wheeled me around without any difficulty whatsoever, and deposited me at curbside outside the White Plains Hospital's main entrance.

"Take care, dearie," the nurse said to me and pointed to Kim, "and do what your wife tells you."

"Yes, ma'am," I replied.

Kim smiled, held up her left hand, and wiggled her ring finger with its purple-yarn engagement ring. "Do what I tell you."

"Yes, ma'am."

Harry thanked the nurse and informed her that we were all set. She nodded, smiled, and went inside.

"Did you just use the Jedi mind trick on her? Aren't they supposed to make sure I get into a car or ambulance or what—"

Harry whooshed us to Kim's in the middle of my run-on sentence.

"Want me to help you to the couch?" Kim asked.

"No thanks," I said, taking a tentative step toward the aforementioned furniture. It wasn't too painful. Kim hovered nearby in case I began to topple over. "I'm okay," I told her.

"Just making sure."

"Would you like a cappuccino?" Harry asked.

"Yes, please. A double."

"Coming up."

Kim sat next to me on the couch and took my right hand in both of hers. "How do you feel? Really."

"Surprisingly good. Really."

I could hear the expresso machine hissing loudly in the kitchen and smell the fresh-dripped beverage.

"Does the fact that you feel good mean you're headed into more trouble?"

"For sure," I replied. "I have to deal with your family at Thanksgiving in four days. Four days, right? It's Sunday morning, isn't it? Getting banged around by a truly enormous SUV is bad for one's sense of time."

"Ohhhhhh," she mock-groaned. "*Deal* with my

family? Remarks like that could mean you won't get any leftovers. No turkey and mashed potatoes the day after. No stuffing. Nothing."

"I'm not in my right mind. I must still be suffering from my injuries."

"When have you ever been in your 'right mind?'"

Fortunately for me, Harry appeared at that moment with a cappuccino. Perfect for what ailed me. I took a mouthful, savored the foamed milk and espresso flavor, and swallowed. "Thank you."

"You're welcome," he replied. "Will you be up for a visit to Naomi and Stewart tomorrow?"

"Have they got something on Fuchs's bank robberies?"

"They will by tomorrow morning."

"You've told me multiple times that you are not a prophet."

"Sometimes the Chairman gives me advance notice."

I nodded and drank more cappuccino. "Tomorrow then."

* * *

The next morning, Monday, Harry and I arrived at the railroad flat with hot beverages for everyone. Cappuccinos for Harry and me, a double espresso for Naomi, and a dirty chai for Stewart. Naomi and Stewart sat on swivel chairs, facing us, their backs to their large computer monitors. Harry stood, completely at ease.

I, on the other hand, could not find a good way to sit or stand. Naomi had offered me a chair, which I tried for a minute but had to stand up. I was as stiff as the Tin Man in *The Wizard of Oz*. I leaned against a door frame but shifted my position every few seconds.

"What's up, Jack?" Naomi asked. "You look bad."

"I got banged up in a car accident."

"Need anything? Aspirin? Tylenol? Weed?"

"That's very thoughtful of you, but no. I'm on enough ibuprofen to choke a hippopotamus."

"You should sit in a jacuzzi," she said with a sly smile. "Soak away your troubles."

"Yeah, if I sit there until I turned red like a steamed lobster I'd probably be pain free."

"Anyone mind if we talk about Fuchs's money?" Stewart asked. He was not a fan of Naomi's and my repartee. He was not a fan of *anything* between Naomi and me.

"Yes, let's talk money. What did you find out?"

"Okay, we had to do a lot of cross-checking and hacking to find out what you wanted to know."

"Thanks. I appreciate all the effort, I really do."

"Well, Harry helped a lot," Naomi said. "I'm not sure we could have pulled off some of the hacks that were necessary to get the information you wanted."

To Harry, I said, "Thank you."

"You're welcome."

"So, anyway," Stewart resumed, "we scoured through the files we had copied from Fuchs's laptop and discovered that your neo-Nazi buddy had sixty-three different bank accounts belonging to nine different phony companies."

"And Gerhard Fuchs is the president and CEO of each of the companies," I said.

"Yes."

"How do you know they're phonies?"

"Because none of these companies has any sort of regular revenues. They have no customers. They hire no outside vendors. The only thing they seem to have is whatever money is in those sixty-three bank accounts."

"Let me guess: the money tends to shift from one account to another."

"You got it."

"Lots of banking activity but nothing that actually produces income. That's pretty odd," I said.

"You're not kidding. Before you ask any questions, let's talk about what we found when we looked at robberies of small bank branches in neighborhoods with heavy Jewish populations." Stewart swiveled to the monitor behind him, reviewed something on it, and swiveled back to us. "There have been nine robberies over the last twenty months in the metro New York area that fit that description. One in New Jersey, a couple in Westchester County, all the others in New York City in different neighborhoods. They never hit the same neighborhood twice in a row. Never hit a branch of the same bank twice in a row."

"What's the M.O.?"

"Five men in rubber masks. Four go into the bank; one remains in the vehicle outside."

"Any violence?"

Naomi answered, shaking her head, "They shove people around and push them to the floor. They pistol-whipped the bank managers on two occasions. They did shoot a guard and a customer. Both survived. Usually they just shoot into the air. Never more than a couple of shots until an attempted robbery a few days ago in Scarsdale—" her eyes narrowed on my face. "Was that where you got hurt?"

"Yes."

"So you've seen them in action?"

"Yes. Operating just the way you described them."

"What do you need us for if you already stopped them?"

"I got lucky—it was a fluke that I spotted them on the way to the robbery. And I only stopped that particular robbery. Believe me, there will be more, and I still need your help."

Harry interjected, "Please, he really does need all the help he can get."

Ignoring Harry, I asked, "Is the interval between robberies the same?"

195

Stewart's face lit up. "Good question. Usually it's around two months. But there were two intervals of about three months."

"Why the variation?"

"Well, the first thing I have to say is that there's no absolute connection between Fuchs and the bank robberies you asked us to analyze. But there is a ton of coincidence."

"For my purposes," I said, "coincidence is just fine."

"Okay. Well, the intervals are the first coincidence we noticed. Every time there was a robbery, there were cash deposits to about half of the sixty-three accounts within two to three business days. All deposits for less than $10,000, which is the IRS reporting threshold. In another two or three business days, the banks that received the cash would transfer all of the money to other accounts. Finally, a week or so later, that second group of accounts would transfer all the cash to the accounts that seem to be the main operating accounts of the phony companies."

"And all of these deposits equaled the total amount stolen from the bank?"

"Pretty much," Stewart smiled. "Quite a coincidence, huh?"

"What happens when the cash finally gets to the phony companies' operating accounts?"

Naomi grinned, "Finding the answer to that took a lot of hacking by me, and a lot of analysis by Stewart. It seems that Fuchs is funding his neo-Nazi activities with money stolen from the banks and deposited to the phony companies' accounts. And, aside from that, as we told you before, he's also stockpiling money."

"A $2-million stockpile, as I remember. And the intervals between robberies is because . . .?"

"Because he runs out of operating cash," Stewart replied.

"Why not dip into his stockpile?"

"The stockpile is only used to buy trucks and gasoline, which are stored at Colgate Truck & Equipment Sales. Fuchs never dips into the cash to fund any of his other operations."

"Trucks and gas," I said. "A poor excuse for a lyric in a country western song."

Naomi smiled. Not much of a smile because it wasn't much of a joke. Stewart frowned because Naomi smiled.

"With a stockpile that large, I'm guessing Fuchs is cooking up something really huge and really ugly," I said.

"That's our guess. Stewart and I remembered what you said about the Baader-Meinhof Gang and their escalating violence," said Naomi. "A $2-million stockpile buys a whole lot of huge and ugly."

"Whatever Fuchs is up to, thanks for all your work. You guys are great."

"Thanks," Stewart said. He was pretty darn pleased with himself.

"But you've got a problem," Naomi said.

"Yeah, you do," Stewart added. "Since the last bank robbery was unsuccessful, Fuchs needs to replenish his cash. He's going to have to rob another bank really soon."

"What about the drug operation in Queens? And his prostitution business at 341 West 91st? Wouldn't they generate lots of cash?"

"Could you please refer to it as something other than a business?" Naomi asked.

"You're right, I'm sorry," I said. "I just don't know what else to call it."

"How 'bout sex slavery?"

"That works. Again, I'm sorry. I didn't mean to be insensitive."

"It's okay," she said, giving me a small smile. "You did bust up the 'business,'" she said, using air quotes around the word "business."

"What about the drugs and sex slavery?" I asked Stewart.

"They generate a lot of cash, but Fuchs has still depended on the bank robberies, on a semi-regular basis, to provide more. And feed his stockpile."

"What about his legitimate holdings? Didn't he inherit a healthy real estate business from his father?"

"He did. There are five real estate companies, and those bank accounts, eight in total, all seem to be on the up and up. No funny business. Gerhard Fuchs lives off his legitimate profits. He's got the huge home in Riverdale, plus a six-bedroom, four-bath home complete with an Olympic-sized pool and jacuzzi on the beach in a gated community in Florida. And a hunting lodge sitting on a couple hundred acres in Colorado."

"He lives very well for a criminal."

"Very well, and due to the real estate business, Fuchs appears to be a law-abiding citizen."

"What about the *Gesellschaft der Deutschen*, his Nazi-fan club?"

"One of his phony companies owns it."

"*Soooo* . . . not a legit operation."

"Well, assuming this guy is as rigidly disciplined as he seems to be," Stewart mused, "no, it's not legit. Fuchs keeps the legal and illegal parts of his life completely and absolutely separate. The *gesellschaft* is nowhere to be found in the legit books his real-estate companies keep. And I mean *nowhere*."

"But your immediate problem is the next robbery," Naomi reminded me. "I hacked into a couple of his accounts earlier today."

"You hacked into his bank accounts? You got through a couple of banks' computer security?"

"Harry was a huge help," she beamed at him. "But that's not the point, Jack. The point is that Fuchs's balance is hovering right around the level that usually triggers a robbery. Since the prostitution at West 91st has been stopped, and you foiled the last bank robbery, Fuchs has to have a cash infusion."

"You're sure?"

"Absolutely. This guy is so damn consistent, he's as regular as an atomic clock."

"I don't suppose you have any idea where and when he's going to strike next?"

"Well. . . ," Stewart hesitated, "it's just a theory."

"Let me have it."

"The guy is very careful about not generating a pattern," Naomi said. "But even so, we think he's unconsciously created a bit of one. Every time a bank is hit outside of Manhattan, the next target is on the Upper West Side. We think he'll hit on the Friday after Thanksgiving at a bank up there."

"Wow. Could you give me the bank branch while you're at it?"

She shook her head. Stewart interjected, "There are three banks that we think fit the usual target profile, but we have no way to figure out which one Fuchs will hit."

I turned from one to the other of them, absorbing what they'd just said. It was pretty damn good work.

"Why the Friday after Thanksgiving?"

"It fits his usual time pattern," Stewart said.

I said. "You guys are fantastic. Really. Fantastic."

They both grinned.

"Sorry we couldn't name the bank for you," Naomi said.

"No worries. Harry and I will figure something out. Could you just send me the info on the three banks?"

"Of course."

"Thank you very much for all of this. The CIA and the FBI couldn't have done better—and since I've worked with both of them, I speak from experience."

Naomi gave me a kiss on the cheek. She was quite petite and had to stretch to reach me. Stewart watched with a disapproving gaze but extended his hand and said, "You're welcome."

Naomi asked, "Do you want us to send the data from Fuchs's laptop to anyone? With our analysis, of course."

"Not just yet. After all, the NYPD seized the original laptop in the drug bust." I turned to Harry, "the police did get the laptop, didn't they?"

"Oh, yes. They did."

Naomi said, "But without Harry, it will take them a long time to figure out how to get into that machine and extract the data. Even with all the disabling of security that we did."

"It's fine if it takes them some time to get the data off that laptop. I still need to figure out a couple of things."

"Like what?"

"Like where is all this leading?"

"What's the huge, ugly thing?" Naomi asked.

"Exactly. He wants to kill a lot of people and make a huge, anti-Semitic splash. But I haven't a clue what the attack is going to be," I answered honestly.

Naomi spoke to Harry, "Maybe you could give us a

lead?"

"If you need it, I will give it," he responded quietly. "It's important that you work as fast as you can. As I told Jack, whatever Fuchs is up to is going to happen very soon."

Stewart, ever the accountant, asked, "Just how soon is '*very soon*?'"

"Days," Harry said.

"On that happy note," I said to Naomi and Stewart, "thank you for everything you've done, and have a Happy Thanksgiving!"

They wished us the same. Harry and I walked out to the hallway, and he whooshed us away.

11

"Is there a reason you whooshed us to Central Park?" I asked, as we walked north along the Mall, the bandshell on our right. The park was beautiful all year long, even when the trees were devoid of trees.

"I wanted to walk here. Does that meet with your approval?"

"Yes, definitely. I didn't know you needed my approval."

"To set the record straight: There is nothing I need from you."

"Ouch. Well, just to make you feel guilty for the gross insensitivity of that remark, on behalf of Kim and myself, I'd like to invite you to Thanksgiving dinner."

"Thank you. That's very nice."

"Was that a yes?"

"Yes."

"Kim will be thrilled."

"And you?"

I shrugged.

"What is your plan for dealing with the three different banks that Naomi and Stewart think could be robbed?" Harry asked.

"I was planning to ask you to ask the Chairman which one is going to be targeted."

Harry cast a quick glance to the sky then back at me. "No."

"But it is definitely one of the three?"

"Yes."

"I'm going to need surveillance of the banks. Maybe Naomi could check out the traffic cameras near the banks and/or hack into nearby security cameras?"

"If she can't?"

"I thought she could hack into anything with your help."

He ignored me, "You might want to consider setting up remote cameras focused on the front entrance of each bank."

"And, when the bad guys pull up in front of the lucky target, you whoosh me to the scene. Because you suggested it, you must realize that the cameras will only work if they can access WiFi and internet in the buildings they're set to watch."

"I do, in fact, realize that."

"Which means you'll help Naomi hack into the building networks, right?"

"If she needs my help. Will you spend all day Friday watching the feeds from the cameras?"

"All those video feeds on my laptop? I was hoping that Naomi and Stewart will watch the banks on those nice big monitors of theirs. And alert me as soon as the robbery begins."

Harry's Mona Lisa smile came and went. "When

should we plan on installing the cameras?"

"Tonight—actually the wee hours of tomorrow, Tuesday, morning. I can sleep late on Tuesday and still have almost two whole days to devote myself to helping Kim prepare for Thanksgiving. Obviously, I'll be too busy on Thanksgiving to set up surveillance cameras."

"Should I bring anything for dinner?"

I could feel my eyebrows climbing my forehead in surprise. "Are you offering to cook?"

"If Kim wants something cooked, yes. But I was guessing she might want me to bring something from a bakery. Or flowers. Or—"

"Maybe you should ask her."

"I will."

We crossed Terrace Drive and stood at the stone railing overlooking Bethesda Fountain and the Lake beyond.

"How will you find out what Fuchs has in mind for his big attack?"

"I'm not really sure," I said.

"Maybe a surreptitious return to the house in Riverdale? And/or a clandestine visit to the *Gesellschaft der Deutschen*?"

"Those are very good ideas."

"And dangerous, which, I suspect, is part of their appeal to you."

"Dangerous for me? Or the neo-Nazi bastards?"

"Whomever you prefer."

*   *   *

Naomi was excited about the surveillance was only too happy to assist me with whatever I needed. The first of the three banks was on the street level of the Ansonia Building on Broadway between West 73rd and 74th Streets. The Ansonia was built in the early 1900s in Beaux-Arts style and had been the home of the Sultan of Swat himself, Babe Ruth. Many years after the Babe had departed, the Ansonia housed the Continental Baths, which featured not-yet famous performers such as Bette Midler, Barry Manilow, and Peter Allen. The Baths were eventually replaced by Plato's Retreat, a sex club for "swingers." Unlike the Retreat, the modest little bank in the Ansonia had a neat, clean appearance. Given the Ansonia's proximity to the intersection of Broadway and West 74th Street, Naomi could easily watch its front door from traffic cams, which she could hack into without assistance from me.

The second bank was on the east side of Columbus Avenue just north of West 75th Street, and lucky for me, this one could also be watched through traffic cams.

The third bank was another story: It was located on the east side of Broadway, immediately south of West 85th Street. But there was construction underway, and scaffolding had been erected all along the front of the building. The nearest traffic cams only showed the scaffold, useless for our surveillance plan.

All of which explains why, at 2:00 A.M. on the rainy Tuesday before Thanksgiving, I approached the third bank. I was dressed in my usual cat-burglar ensemble: black cargo pants, black crepe-soled shoes, and a black turtleneck sweater under my navy-blue rain jacket. While navy blue didn't actually fit my cat-burglar uniform, I hadn't bothered to purchase a black rain jacket. I had two pairs of bullet cameras—why "bullet" for the camera name? They didn't have a bullet-like appearance. Must have sounded cool to someone in marketing—stuffed into my pants' cargo pockets and a role of duct tape jammed into one of the side pockets of the rain jacket. The other pocket had was a 12-inch, heavy-duty extension cord splitter. Over my right shoulder, I had draped a coiled, heavy-duty extension cord. I hadn't bothered with a gun. Who needed a gun when setting up surveillance?

I picked a spot about 10 feet uptown of the bank's entrance and clambered up the steel pipes of the scaffold. At that hour of the night, there was almost no traffic of the automotive or pedestrian kinds. Almost. But between the rain and the hour, I wasn't too worried about being observed.

The scaffold created a rough ceiling over the sidewalk. It didn't provide perfect rain-proof cover, but at least I wasn't soaking wet. Standing on a steel crossbeam on the curbside of the scaffolding, I could reach up to the ceiling, which was about 10 feet above the sidewalk. I used a liberal use of duct tape to hang the first pair of cameras next to each other, pointed in opposite directions, one focused along the uptown sidewalk, the other on the downtown sidewalk and the front entrance to the bank. I was able to nestle the black cameras close enough to the steel supports of the ceiling that most people wouldn't notice them. I twisted around, my feet still on the crossbeam, and taped the second two cameras at a 45-degree angle to each other, giving them a very wide view of Broadway.

A single string of light bulbs hung under the scaffold's ceiling, illuminating the sidewalk below. I found the nearest socket, unplugged the lights, swapped in my extension-cord splitter, and replugged the lights in the splitter. I strung the extension cord from one of the splitter sockets to the cameras and plugged them into the multiple sockets on the other end of the cord. I also turned on each camera's battery back-up power. Just in case. I climbed down off the scaffold, slipped my AirPods into my ears, pulled my phone out, and called Naomi.

"Jack?"

"Who else would it be at this hour? Thanks for being willing to take the call."

"For you, no problem."

I winced on behalf of poor Stewart. "I've opened the app you gave me, which is displaying the bank's network."

"Go ahead and press 'Connect.'" I could hear her

gently clicking a keyboard.

"It's asking for a password," I said.

"Right." There were a few more clicks, and then she said, "The password is Delta – Zero – Niner – Delta – Bravo – Zero."

"Okay," I said tapping in the appropriate letters and numbers. The WiFi icon on my phone displayed next to the phone service bars. "We're in."

"Connect the cameras to the WiFi using the app. Just like setting up lamps or appliances on a smart device in your home."

"The app is showing the cameras are connected."

"I can see the video feeds on my monitors. Nice work."

"All it took was lots of duct tape and your customized app. Thanks, Naomi."

"Duct tape? Really?"

"Hey, I didn't have to drill any holes or screw anything in."

"Go home. Get some sleep."

"Thanks. Good night." I disconnected and slipped my phone and AirPods into my pocket. I zipped up my rain jacket and took a single step uptown in the general direction of Kim's apartment.

Rolf Jäger stepped out of the front door of the lingerie store, the bank's immediate neighbor. The store windows were full of artsy photos of beautiful young women in bras and teddies. Rolf's massive, squat frame was a stark contrast to the nubile forms in the photos.

"*Guten morgen*, Rolf," I greeted him. "*Wie gehts*?"

Rolf, unimpressed by my Teutonic language skills, walked to within a few feet of me. Not quite within arms' reach. "Why are you pointing cameras at the bank?"

"Not that it's any of your business, but the bank is a client of my security firm. The executive in charge of the branch expressed some concern that the scaffolding was blocking the bank's own cameras."

"Do you always service your clients in the middle of the night?"

"That's the security business for you. When the client needs something, they *need* it. I'm sure you know exactly what I'm talking about, don't you? When Mr. Fuchs snaps his fingers, you jump. Right?"

His face was partially obscured by shadow, but I was pretty sure he was scowling at me. I was also pretty damn sure he was inching toward me. He was getting ready to make a move.

"Did Fuchs send you tonight?"

Jäger dove at me, head down, arms wide. I stepped to the side and chopped down at the back of his neck with my right hand, catching him at the base of his skull. I don't know about his neck, but my hand felt as if it was broken in multiple placcs. He staggered forward, his arms windmilling as he struggled to balance.

I planted my left foot and kicked up with my right, my foot slicing between his legs and mashing his gonads.

Rolf grunted explosively, his knees buckled, and he collapsed to the sidewalk.

Gee, that was a hell of a lot easier than I thought. I crouched next to him, grinning and rubbing my sore right hand with my left, and said, "I'll see you soon, Rolf. Give my regards to your boss."

Pride goeth before the fall, or in my case, arrogance went before Rolf slapped the crap out of me. As I finished urging him to give my regards to his boss, he raised himself on his left arm, twisted his torso, and uppercut me with his right. His fist was like a polo mallet. The punch straightened me up and sent me reeling. I crashed into one of the scaffold's support poles and flung my hand out to grab one of the cross braces. I held on like a nauseated drunk looking for a toilet.

I took a few deep breaths and blinked to clear my vision. Rolf was walking toward me. He grabbed me by my rain jacket, pulled me away from the scaffold, swung me around as if I were Ginger Rogers and he were Fred Astaire on steroids, and then released me. I reeled backward, banged off the scaffold again, and thudded to the sidewalk. Above me, a sexy angel of a woman wearing the merest wisp of a bra was giving me a come-hither smile. Get a grip, Tyrrell, or he'll kill you. Right here. Right now.

But I was too slow. Rolf clutched my arm, yanked me to my feet, and hit me again. I think he used his fist. And I think my face was his target. The only thing I was certain about was that I was lying on the sidewalk, my face pressed to the wet cement. I saw his feet coming toward me. If he decided to kick me, I'd be dead.

He didn't kick. He grasped my left arm and tugged me to my feet. Now or never, Tyrrell. Now. I felt a surge of adrenalin and stepped toward him, hitting him with a right jab that landed like Thor's hammer, Mjölnir. Caught him square on the huge slab of his jaw. His eyes rolled up in his head, and down he went. I wobbled out from under the scaffold and turned my face up into the rain. The water was a cool comfort. I could practically feel my facial swelling shrink. I probably stood that way for a minute. But eventually, all good things must come to an end. I had to make sure Rolf and I had concluded our affair for the evening.

Much to my dismay, we had not. Rolf was slowly getting to his feet. The damn guy was indestructible. He squinted this way and that, trying to find me. Once more unto the breach, Tyrrell. Once more. I rushed toward him. About 3 feet away, I jumped and grabbed a steel pole overhead, swung both feet, and kicked him in the chest.

He flew backward, smashing through one of the plate-glass windows of the lingerie store and flopping unconscious at the bottom of a poster-sized photo of a young black woman in a fetching teddy. An alarm bell started ringing. I clambered up into the window, put a finger to Rolf's neck, and found his pulse. Just to make sure he remained unconscious, I picked up his head in both hands and slammed it to the floor of the window display.

I thought about climbing down out of the window but gave up without attempting it. An arthritic old lady could have mugged me at that moment.

"Harry, please?" I panted. "Please?"

In the merest flick of time, I was sitting on the side of the tub in my bathroom, and Harry was handing me a couple of ibuprofen pills and a glass of water. As soon as I had swallowed the pills, he began ministering to me with the first-aid kit, cleaning my wounds.

My phone's electronic ringtone alerted me to an incoming call from Naomi.

"Jack, are you all right? Holy shit, Jack, what a fight. I saw the whole thing on the surveillance cameras. I wanted to call the cops, but I didn't want to make things awkward for you. You really messed up that guy!"

"You made the right choice as far as calling the cops. And you might have noticed that he just about killed me."

"Yeah, but he didn't."

"The alarm went off—did the cops come arrest him?"

"No. Right after you disappeared, a van pulled up, a couple of men got out, and they collected him. He's quite the load, isn't he?"

"You could say that. I cannot tell you how much I wish that guy had been arrested."

"But holy shit, Jack. You are the Man! You'll take him the next time, too."

"I'll rest much easier knowing you feel that way."

"Are you all right?"

"I'm fine, thanks. Harry's taking care of me."

"If Harry's taking care of you, you're going to be fine."

"You have an awful lot of faith in Harry."

"Yes, I do. You sleep tight tonight, okay?"

"Okay."

"Have a Happy Thanksgiving."

"Thanks, you, too."

We disconnected. I told Harry, "Naomi thinks you are the greatest thing since Spotify."

"I doubt she phrased it that way," he replied and gave the cut on my left cheek one final dab.

"Am I going to be healed by Thanksgiving? It's only two days away. I'm meeting some of Kim's family for the first time, and I'd rather not look like a refugee from *Fight Club*."

"You'll be fine."

"Meaning I'll be beautiful?"

"Only the Chairman could perform a miracle like that."

Harry continued his first-aid ministrations to my face, applying a topical antiseptic cream and, finally, for his pièce de résistance, a Band-Aid on my left cheek. He held onto my arm, led me to my couch, settled me onto it, and went into my kitchen. He was back in a flash (maybe he whooshed, I was too dazed to tell) with three ice packs.

One each for both sides of my face, and another for my right hand, which was propped up on top of a throw pillow.

"How do you feel?" Harry asked.

"Like a veal cutlet that's been pounded into scallopini with a meat mallet."

"And your hand?"

"Sore but not too bad. I'll be fine as long as I don't have to punch anyone with it in the next couple of weeks."

"You should probably assume that you will need to use your hand within that time frame."

"Does that mean I'm going to experience one of the Chairman's miracle cures?"

"If you need it. Do you want me to help you to bed?"

"No thanks. I'm just going to stay here for now."

"Are you sure?"

"I don't think I can handle the pain of moving from this couch."

Harry unfolded a wool, Black Watch tartan blanket and gently spread it over my legs and lower torso.

"Thanks," I said.

"Good night." He vanished.

I leaned back on the couch and shut my eyes. My last conscious thought was that the next time I ran into Rolf, I was going to shoot him immediately. Note to self: Until you've shot Rolf, don't leave home without a gun.

* * *

NIGHT – GERHARD FUCHS'S HOME
PALISADE AVENUE, RIVERDALE

ROLF JÄGER sat behind Fuchs's desk in the den. He checked his reflection in a vanity mirror sitting on the desk and cleaned the wounds inflicted in the fight at the bank.

Fuchs relaxed on the couch and petted one of his Rottweilers. "How does this man know what we're doing?"

Aschgrau, who was standing at attention in her usual posture, pointed out, "You said he took your laptop. Maybe he hacked it."

"I was speaking rhetorically, thinking out loud. That computer had world-class encryption. It would take a hacking genius to get in. And even if someone did hack his way in, he'd have to be an analytical wizard to figure out the bank accounts, review all bank robberies in the New York metro area, compare the robberies with our deposits, and conclude that we're robbing banks. Given Tyrrell's combat skills, it seems unlikely that he is also a super hacker and a wunderkind analyst."

"Do you think he's part of law enforcement?"

"He must be, but . . . ," Fuchs hesitated, puzzled. "If he were NYPD or FBI or DEA, a huge team of law enforcement would have already descended on us."

"So, he couldn't have figured out our operations by himself, and he hasn't arrested us, which means he's not the law."

216

"And as far as I know, someone is either law enforcement or not."

"Do you think," Aschgrau said, "that we should change things up?"

"Maybe wait a while before robbing the next bank?" Rolf asked.

"No, the operation for Friday is still a go. We'll just increase the team. Nine men, including the driver."

"Want me to supervise personally?"

"No," Fuchs smiled, "I have another job for you, Rolf. The men following Diane Eisenberg's father trailed him to another hospital and discovered that the girl has gone home. I want you to pay her a visit."

"To pay your respects? For the last time?"

"Precisely. Get some sleep, then go tonight."

*   *   *

When I woke up on Tuesday, it was almost noon. I opened my eyes as if the merest flutter of an eyelid might trigger a wave of pain. Nothing. I sat up on, and the now-warm ice packs that had been on my face dropped off onto the floor. The pack on my right hand followed suit. I didn't feel stiff and could clench and unclench my right hand without any painful tingling.

I got up from the couch where I'd spent the night and went to the bathroom where I peered in the mirror and surveyed the facial damage. There was a Band-Aid on my cheek and a small, scabbed-over cut on the left side of my forehead, just above my eyebrow. No black eyes, no broken nose. I checked my right hand—a couple of bruised knuckles.

"Not too bad," I said to myself. I tilted my head up and whispered, "Thank you."

I swallowed some more ibuprofen and took a shower in the hottest water I could handle. By the time I was toweling off, I felt close to 100 percent. Maybe the next time I saw Rolf, I wouldn't shoot him in the very first second.

Even though it was early afternoon by the time I finished dressing, I made breakfast. Scrambled eggs, well-done bacon, well-toasted English muffins, a small glass of OJ, and two cups of cappuccino.

While I was eating, I checked my phone for messages. There were several from Kim:

8:38 A.M.: Hope you had fun doing your surveillance. Since Harry didn't come wake me with bad news in the middle of the night, I'm assuming you're okay.

8:41 A.M.: Can you hit the grocery store and pick up some things for me? (A list of items followed.)

8:49 A.M.: Are you staying here tonight? That way we can watch the parade in the morning while we set up for dinner.

9:35 A.M.: Are you okay? Where are

you?

      10:01 A.M.: Should I be getting worried that I haven't heard from you?

      11:21 A.M.: Jack? This is getting scary.

      11:52 A.M.: ?????

I needed to work out a better system of letting Kim know I was okay after one of my little operations. I called her.

"Sorry, I was asleep until a little while ago."

"Oh. Are you okay?"

"Fine. A bit scuffed up. Nothing that will frighten anyone at the dinner table."

"I was really worried."

"I know. I'm sorry. I didn't want to wake you last night."

"Next time, wake me."

"Yes, ma'am."

Her tone was lighter when she said, "Will you stay here tonight?"

"Absolutely."

"Can you pick up that list of things I asked for?"

"Absolutely."

"Are you making fun of me?"

"Absolutely."

"You're not very bright when it comes to the right way of talking to your fiancée, are you?"

"Nope."

"You should get going to the store. I'll see you

soon."

"Okay. Hey—?"

"Yes?"

"Sorry I didn't wake you last night."

"Just don't do it again."

"I love you."

"I love you, too."

12

"Thanks for picking this stuff up," Kim said as I deposited the grocery bags on the kitchen counters.

"You're welcome." I kissed her on the cheek. "Do you want me to put the food away? You're not starting to cook till tomorrow, right?"

"Right. Everything can go in the fridge."

I carefully placed the food items in the refrigerator until every nook and cranny was filled.

"Can I count on you to do the mashed potatoes tomorrow?"

Please do not think that this request demonstrated any level of trust in my talents as a chef. Kim was requesting that I cook and mash the potatoes because it would save her time and required no skill whatsoever. "I will be delighted to help with the potatoes. And any other chores, culinary or otherwise, that you need done."

"Thank you." She kissed me.

There was a knock on the front door, but the doorman had not buzzed to announce a visitor.

"Please go let Harry in," Kim said.

"Yes, ma'am."

I answered the door. It was, in fact, Harry.

"You're early," I said.

"Unfortunately, I'm not."

"Bad news?"

"Yes. Diane Eisenberg is home from the hospital. Fuchs is sending Rolf Jäger to kill her."

"I hope there's an especially horrible corner of Hell reserved for guys who rape and kill women. And if there isn't, I'm sure I could come up with some ideas if the Chairman is interested."

"Maybe we'll discuss that some other time. You have a few hours to get ready."

"Where are we going?"

"The Eisenbergs live on Fenimore Road in Mamaroneck. Very near the Winged Foot Golf Club."

"Nice neighborhood," I said appreciatively. "Winged Foot has hosted the U.S. Open *and* the PGA."

"And that is significant for us because . . . ?"

"It's not. Just thought I'd mention it. Will you be providing transport?"

"Yes."

"Would you mind taking me to my apartment first?"

"Not at all."

"What time should I expect the whoosh from here to my place?"

"Mr. Jäger will arrive in Mamaroneck at about 9:30 this evening."

"Could you whoosh me at 9:00? That's plenty of time for me to grab some weapons and get up there and reconnoiter the place."

"I will see you at 9:00."

And then he was gone.

Kim chose that moment to walk out from the kitchen. "Where's Harry?"

"I don't know, actually. I guess that he had places to go, people to see."

"Do you have places to go and people to see?"

"I will. Later."

"You seem especially eager to get these people."

"I guess I am. And 'getting' these people is way too mild a term when you're talking about these neo-Nazi . . ."

"Bastards? Assholes?"

"Kim, please, watch your language."

"I didn't realize you were so sensitive."

"You, of all people, know I'm not so sensitive. No, my problem is there isn't a word vile enough or ugly enough to capture my anger *and* hatred toward these people. America went to war with the Nazis. How the hell do American neo-Nazis think they're patriots? It's impossible to be a Nazi and an American patriot. Impossible. Neo-Nazis are traitorous pissants."

"But that's not all, is it?" Her voice was quiet and sincere; she wasn't giving me a hard time.

"They're . . . *EVIL*. And I mean that with all the demonic and Satanic connotations of the word. They don't just hate Jews and people of color, they want to destroy them." I shook my head in frustration. "Hey, I'm not an idiot. I know that there's fear and prejudice, and the Nazis have more than their fair share of both, but . . . but these bastards kidnapped and prostituted young Jewish women. They enslaved them and forced them into a life of drugs and rape. Who the hell does that? What kind of monstrous shit does that?"

"Men like the ones you're going after."

"But why does this happen?"

"Do you mean why does the Chairman allow the existence of Nazis and Fuchs's Supreme Order?"

"Yes."

"Well . . . when I've asked you that kind of question in the past, you told me that—"

"—No, please, not free will."

"Yes," she said emphatically. "Free will."

"Are you telling me they choose to be evil?"

"They absolutely did. They know that America waged war against the Nazis and won. But they choose to ignore that inconvenient truth. They are aware that it is a crime to sell drugs, to kidnap and rape, but they choose to perpetrate those crimes. Choice is the definition of free will."

I mulled that over for a minute. "Well, I choose to exercise my free will by hating these evil men. By choosing to do everything I can to wipe them out."

"Kill them?"

"Probably."

"Don't you think they should go to prison?"

"I'm exercising my free will by choosing to ignore that possibility. They're evil. They *need* to be put down like rabid dogs. The difference being that dogs are blameless when they get rabies."

After a few minutes of uncomfortable silence, Kim reached out and took my hand. "I just want you to be careful. Well, as careful as you can be when you're out doing your government-trained troubleshooter thing. I do love you, you know."

"I love you, too."

"Are you going out soon?"

"Not until 9:00 tonight."

"Hmm." She grinned. "I know you slept late, but I was wondering if you would like to take a nap?"

"I'm not very sleepy."

"Who said anything about sleeping?" She took me by the hand and led me to the bedroom.

And we took a nap. Without sleeping a wink.

*   *   *

Harry appeared a few minutes before 9:00 P.M. "I just wanted to say hello to you." He said to Kim.

She gave him a quick peck on the cheek and said, "Hello to you, too. Are you going to keep my fiancé out of trouble tonight?"

"That is beyond my power."

"Wait—you're his guardian angel, and you can't

225

keep him safe?"

"He's an extraordinarily challenging assignment."

"Feel free," I interjected, "to talk about me as if I'm not here."

"Fine by me," Kim replied. To Harry, "I'm introducing him to my mother on Thanksgiving. I really need him to be presentable."

"He probably won't even guarantee that I'll still be alive by then," I pointed out.

Kim's eyebrows shot up her forehead, and she gave me a withering glance. She gave Harry much the same treatment. "Is he right? You can't even guarantee his safety?"

"You know that," Harry responded as soothingly as possible.

"I'm asking for a favor. I want Jack alive, ambulatory, and relatively unbruised for Thanksgiving. Please?"

"I will do everything in my power to deliver him to you in the condition you just described."

"Thank you," she said and gave him another peck on the cheek.

"Are you ready?" he said to me.

"What if I want a favor?"

"The answer is—

Whoosh—I was standing in my bedroom, next to the closet. Harry sat on my bed, finishing his sentence.

"—no."

"You're very pleased with yourself, aren't you?"

"If I was, I would be lacking in humility."

"Which would not be very angelic, huh?"

"Exactly."

I pulled the black backpack out of the space behind the false panel in the closet. The pack went onto the bed, followed by both Rugers—fitted with suppressors—twin shoulder holsters, four extra magazines, two smoke grenades, two flashbang grenades, and a blackjack as well as brass knuckles.

I changed into my all-black, cat-burglar outfit and slid into the holsters. Inserted the guns and shoved the magazines into mag carriers on the straps. The grenades, blackjack, and brass knuckles went into the pack.

"May I ask why you're taking weapons for close-quarters combat?"

"You mean the blackjack and brass knuckles? Have you seen Rolf Jäger?"

"You've managed to beat him twice without resorting to those kinds of . . . instruments."

"What's the problem with these . . . instruments? Other than the possibility I'll kill him with them."

"That is the problem. It indicates a level of savagery that I find disconcerting."

"Yeah, well, having Rolf crush my skull is disconcerting to me. I'm not going hand-to-hand with him again. I was very lucky to get off as lightly as I did."

Harry said nothing.

"Hey," I continued, "this has nothing to do with my faith in the Chairman. I realize He's the reason I survived the last two encounters with Rolf. I feel more comfortable if I have more options for dealing with Mr. Jäger. Besides, isn't it my responsibility to evaluate the situation and take the right tools for the job?"

"Yes, it is. But it seems to me that you wouldn't mind using one of those things on Rolf."

"That's not exactly right. I would *LOVE* to use one of those things on Rolf."

"Why?"

"I just had this conversation with Kim."

"You *just* had it?"

"Okay, we talked about it this afternoon."

"And . . . ?"

"To boil it all down for you: I loathe them because they did horrible things to a bunch of young Jewish women. And now it's time for them to face justice."

"And you are justice?"

"Well, it sounds pretentious of me to make that claim, but . . . hell yes, I'm justice. Tonight anyway."

"Are you planning on using the death penalty?"

"It's crossed my mind."

Harry asked, "How do you know that is what the Chairman wants?"

"I don't. I'm hoping for inspiration when the time comes."

Harry frowned and asked, "Are you ready to go?"

I grabbed my Barbour jacket from the closet, put it on, and slung the backpack over my shoulder. "Ready."

Within a microscopic fraction of time, I was facing the patio and the back door of a large white Colonial surrounded by large trees. A couple of lamps along the drive cast enough light for me to see over the side yard out to the front, where a Lexus sedan, an Acura SUV, and a Toyota Prius parked on the driveway.

"This must be the Eisenberg's house?" I whispered.

"Yes."

"Could you please point out north, south, east and west?"

Harry pointed at the house, "That is east of where we are standing." He gestured at the road that ran past the far side of the house. "That's Fenimore road, which runs east/west. More or less. The golf course—"

"Winged Foot?"

"Yes, Winged Foot, is a few hundred feet north of us."

"More or less?"

"Yes. May I ask this need for the compass points of this location?"

"I was trained by the U.S. Army. I like to know the north and south of my situation."

"Are all Green Berets as annoying as you?"

"No, not at all. I have a special talent for it." I treated Harry to a winning grin. Which was completely wasted on him. I continued, "I checked this neighborhood out on Google Maps. There's a short road called Dudley Lane that curves north of us here."

"Yes."

"If I were Rolf, and I thank God that I'm not, I would park there and walk through these trees. Assault the Eisenberg residence from the rear."

"Why not park at the end of the driveway? Just off the road?"

"What if the police happen to come by? What if Mr. Eisenberg is out with the dog—"

"How did you know the Eisenbergs have a dog? Two in fact."

"I didn't. Just seemed like the kind of neighborhood that's chock full of family dogs. I'm also going to guess that these are not big dogs, or I wouldn't be here to stop Rolf."

"How do you know Rolf isn't as skilled at handling dogs as you are?"

"Maybe he is. But I still think the Eisenbergs's are small. Aren't they?"

"Yes. Cocker spaniels."

"Anyway," I said, "if I were Rolf, I wouldn't park my vehicle at the target destination. Especially when I could park it in a less obvious location that is very close by."

"So you think Rolf will come creeping through the trees at the back of the house in the next 10 minutes."

"More or less," I replied. "Let's go."

I used all my government-instilled training to move

as silently as a ghost through the trees toward Dudley Lane. Harry traveled equally quietly, seemingly without effort. A streetlamp on Dudley Lane cast a faint glow, creating shadows under the trees in the Eisenbergs's backyard. I slipped behind a thick oak toward the left side of the yard, away from the direct route to the back door. Hopefully, Rolf would make a beeline for that door, focused intently on his mission, and give me an easy opportunity to spot him before he spotted me.

While we waited for Rolf to appear, I pulled off the pack, dug the brass knuckles out, and slipped them into my left jacket pocket. I tucked myself back into the straps of the pack. And waited. For about 30 seconds, when I heard the crisp crunching sound of a twig breaking.

"Our mystery guest has arrived," I whispered to Harry. I edged backward around the oak to keep it between me and Rolf.

He walked out from under the trees onto the back lawn. I pushed my left hand into the jacket pocket and inserted my fingers into the rings of the brass knuckles. I pulled out a Ruger with my right hand.

Rolf stopped, listened, and scanned the area around him. Deciding that everything was perfect for his assignment, he took two steps forward.

As he stepped toward the house, I stepped toward him. Instinct must have made him turn. He swept his arm up to parry my blow, but he was way too slow. I hammered him on the jaw with the brass knuckles. His head twisted, his knees buckled, and he went down like the proverbial ton of bricks. I leaned over him and slammed him in the jaw again. Upon straightening up, I kicked him in the gut to make sure he was really and truly unconscious. In the interest of thoroughness, I kicked him again. He didn't move. He didn't grunt. He was out cold.

Nice work, Tyrrell. You stopped Jäger from killing Diane Eisenberg. Maybe her parents as well. But now you're stuck with his huge body.

Harry stood on the other side of Rolf's recumbent form. "What are you going to do now?"

"Could I just kill him? If I don't, he'll keep trying to kill Diane. She can tie Fuchs to prostitution because he repeatedly raped her. If nothing else pans out for us good guys, Diane can still send Fuchs to jail for a very long time."

"And your feeling is that Rolf will not stop until his boss is safe."

"Yes."

"Perhaps you should kill him."

"Are you giving me permission?"

"What do you think?"

I looked down at Rolf and back to Harry. "I think you're waiting for me to make my own decision."

"Exactly."

"I need some guidance."

Harry said nothing.

I cursed under my breath then turned my eyes up

into the night. "Please help me?"

The instant I had uttered my little prayer, the knowledge that I couldn't kill Rolf washed through me. I searched my vocabulary and found only one single word that was appropriate to this situation. I whispered—hissed actually—a B-17's payload of F-bombs.

"I don't suppose you would consider whooshing me and this gigantic tub of goo to his car?"

Harry shook his head. I dropped more F-bombs, grabbed Rolf by the wrists, and started dragging him off the lawn into the trees. Man, this guy was a load. I was only capable of dragging his bulk slowly, which kept the noise to a soft rustling of dead leaves.

Our little procession was about 50 feet away from the Eisenbergs's yard when I stopped to catch my breath. I dropped Rolf's wrists and scouted out the area. We were in a thick stand of trees at least a hundred feet away from the nearest house. Dudley Lane was probably another hundred feet. Once on Dudley, I was going to have to find Rolf's car, heave him inside without giving myself a hernia, and drive off. My breathing was almost normal. Stop procrastinating, Tyrrell. Time to move this load.

I leaned down to grab Rolf's wrists, and he threw a quick jab at my chin. He was punching upward, not an ideal way to hit someone, so it wasn't a knockout blow. But it was a hell of a shot for a guy who had come to in the last 30 seconds. I staggered back away from him, stopping when I crashed into a tree. I blinked to clear my vision and saw Rolf roll over, push up into a standing position, and charge me like a locomotive. His head was down, arms swinging, legs pumping.

I waited till he was almost on me and dodged to the side. He slammed into the tree, but his shoulder caught my lower chest and spun me around. He stumbled back, arms out wide, stunned. Then he focused, saw me, and lunged, clutching my jacket at the shoulders. I seized his arms, dropped down into a backward somersault, pulling him up and over me. I thrust up with my legs, catching him in the gut and catapulting him into the air. I heard him thump to the ground as I finished my somersault and came to my feet. I twisted around to face him and ready myself for his next attack.

It turned out that I had gotten very lucky. Rolf lay crumpled where he had fallen, his head at an unhealthy angle. I crouched next to him and laid a finger to his twisted neck. No pulse. Not that I had thought there would be one, but I understood that with Rolf, you couldn't take any chances.

I searched his pockets, and Harry walked up, gazing down at Rolf. "You got what you wanted."

"Not exactly. What I wanted was to shoot him. Nice and neat. No roughhousing. No bruises for me." I found Rolf's phone and his keys.

"But you did the right thing by not murdering him earlier."

"Not sure that would have been murder, but let's

not argue." I was about to begin dragging Rolf toward Dudley Lane again but had a thought and straightened up. "Wait, are you saying this was the Chairman's plan?"

"Do you mean the Chairman gave you a justified reason for killing Rolf?"

"Yeah, that's what I mean."

Harry shrugged.

I glanced to the sky, "Thank you." To Harry I said, "Could you please whoosh me and the corpse to his car?"

"Excuse me?"

"We can't leave him here. The Eisenbergs have been through enough. I don't want them to hear anything that hints that Fuchs is trying to kill Diane. Imagine how they'll feel if a dead man is found in the trees behind their house."

Harry nodded thoughtfully.

A tiny bit of a second later, I was behind the wheel of an Audi A8 sedan, Harry was next to me in the passenger seat.

I checked the back seat. Empty. "Did you whoosh Rolf straight into the trunk?"

"It seemed appropriate."

"Perfect. Thank you." Before pushing the starter button on the dash, I asked, "Could you make Fuchs forget the Eisenbergs's address? Make it impossible for him to find them?"

"Yes. Do you want him to forget about them completely?"

"No. I want him to remember there's a young woman out there who can put him in jail for a long time."

"Sadistic, but proportionate."

"I'm not sure you can be either sadistic or proportionate with neo-Nazis."

Harry's Mona Lisa smile came and went. "What are you planning to do with the late Mr. Jäger?"

"I haven't decided."

I held up the Rolf's phone, "Can you help me get into this thing?"

"His password is 3-4-5-6-7-8."

"Not very secure." I commented.

"Given Mr. Jäger's physical assets, do you think keeping his phone secure was a major concern of his?"

"That's a good point." I logged into the phone and checked the call log. Gerhard Fuchs's number was listed multiple times. I pressed the button.

He answered immediately, "Rolf? How did it go?"

"Well, Gerhard, you're not going to like how things played out," I replied.

"Who is this?"

"Sorry, how rude of me. This is Herman Wouk."

"Ah, Mr. Wouk. I hope your calling me on Rolf's phone doesn't mean you interfered with my plan for tonight."

"I'm afraid it does, Gerhard."

"What's your motivation?"

"Motivation? How about the satisfaction of

wrecking your prostitution scheme, messing up your drug factory in Queens, and breaking up your bank robbery in Scarsdale? I think it's as simple as this: You're the bad guy. I'm the good guy."

"Did you kill Rolf?"

"Yes."

"And you think that qualifies as good guy behavior?"

"Well, to be fair, it was self-defense."

"You seem very pleased with yourself. But you'll have a hard time establishing any connection between me and the crimes you just mentioned."

"First off, my team has already cracked the security on the laptop I took from your home in Riverdale. They've hacked all of your data and accounts and can connect you to everything. Secondly, the young woman you sent Rolf to kill is still alive. Still capable of testifying against you in court."

"You have a resourceful team," he sounded mildly impressed. "Who do you work for?"

"You wouldn't believe me if I told you."

"Well, this has been very unpleasant, but I have to go now."

"Answer a question first?"

After a pause, he said, "Yes?"

"Is this Audi A8 I'm sitting in your personal car? It's really nice."

"It's one of my cars."

"Oh, *one* of your cars. That's good. You won't miss it too much when I torch it."

"How adolescent of you."

"Hope your insurance is paid up. Now, go get your beauty sleep. And remember that I'm going to put you out of business once and for all."

"Hmm." It was a soft, self-satisfied grunt. "Good luck with that."

"I don't need luck."

"Oh? Really? Are you so extraordinary that you don't need luck?"

"I believe in something better than luck."

"I don't know what you mean. I don't care either."

"You will," I said, and disconnected.

13

"Were you serious about burning this car?" Harry asked.

"Yes?"

"Not here, I hope."

"No."

"Where?"

"I know a house in Riverdale with a long driveway that is perfect for some automotive arson."

"What's the point?"

"Just sending a message."

"Wouldn't a well-timed F-bomb do the trick?"

"No."

We drove in silence. We encountered very little traffic, arriving at the Fuchs house on Palisade Avenue about 20 minutes after departing the Eisenbergs's neighborhood.

I parked on the avenue and looked up at Fuchs's dark Tudor Revival house. Mina Aschgrau, Rat Face, Greasy Hair, and the Rottweilers all must have been nestled snugly in their beds. I pressed the gas pedal ever so gently, just enough to make the Audi creep forward, and turned slowly into the driveway. I braked to a very soft stop about halfway up the drive. We climbed out of the car. I put my elbows on the roof and studied at Fuchs's home.

"What's wrong?" Harry asked.

"We shut down Fuchs's house of prostitution. And his drug factory. And stopped his most recent bank robbery. But we still don't know what he's going to do with all the money he's been stockpiling. According to Stewart and Naomi, he's been buying trucks and gasoline. What the hell is he going to do when he goes really big and ugly?"

"I'm sorry. I don't know."

I shook my head, "I was just thinking out loud. I didn't expect you to tell me what's going to happen. But we've got to figure out what he's up to."

"How are you going to do that?"

"Well, I've already stolen what I could from here," I pointed at the house. "I think I may have to hunt for Fuchs's plan somewhere else."

"The *Gesellschaft der Deutschen*?"

I nodded, "Sounds like a plan. We'll enjoy Thanksgiving, break up the bank robbery on Friday, then sneak into the *gesellschaft*, and finally, see if we can find the plans for Fuchs's big ugly finale."

"You make it sound so easy."

"I'm sure there will be bumps and bruises along the way. You wouldn't let me get killed a few weeks before Christmas, would you?"

Harry stared at me in silence.

"Okay. No guarantees."

"I'm sorry, but no guarantees. You know that."

I took a deep breath, exhaled sharply, and smiled. "Would you be amenable to helping me get Rolf out of the trunk and over to that patch of lawn?" I pointed to an imaginary spot on the lawn about 30 feet from the car.

"Yes—" Rolf appeared on the lawn as Harry spoke "—that seems reasonable."

"Thanks. My recent scuffle with Rolf seems to have reactivated every bruise and sore spot in my entire body. The prospect of lifting him out of the trunk was daunting, to say the least."

"You're welcome. What other assistance are you seeking?"

"How do you know there's something else?"

Harry gave me a withering glare. If I wasn't used to that particular expression, I would have melted like a pat of butter on a hot skillet.

I gave him a large, "What, me worry?" grin in response. "I think you might actually like what I have in mind."

"What could possibly make you think that?"

"I have a suspicion that you would like to engage in a little mayhem from time to time. But, because you're an angel, you can't indulge in violence. You'd probably kill the poor mortal you got violent with. But I want to offer you the chance to cause some trouble but not harm a soul."

"You want me to set fire to the Audi."

"How the—never mind. Yes. I don't have anything incendiary with me, and I was hoping that you—"

241

Harry raised his hand and snapped his fingers. I couldn't be sure if he whooshed us away from the car first, or the Audi burst into flames first, or they happened simultaneously. But we were standing on the lawn next to Rolf, and the Audi's windows exploded from the heat.

"Was the finger snapping for my benefit?"

"A little bit of showmanship isn't a bad thing," he smiled broadly. Something I'd only seen him do when talking with Kim. "And thank you for giving me the opportunity to do that."

"You're welcome."

Lights went on in Fuchs's Tudor. I looked through the trees at the houses a couple of hundred feet away. Lights were going on in three of them.

"What message are you trying to send with this little display?" Harry asked

"I just want to make Fuchs uneasy." I gestured at Rolf's body. "And Gerhard will have a hard time explaining this away when the first responders arrive."

Emergency sirens wailed in the distance, along with the deep, booming of fire engine horns.

"Should we make an—"

We were standing in Kim's living room.

"—exit?" I asked.

"Good night, Jack."

"Good ni—" I stopped in mid-word as he disappeared.

I hung my jacket in the front closet, dropped the

242

pack on the floor, and went down the hall to Kim's guest bathroom. In addition to the usual pre-bedtime routine of washing my face and brushing my teeth, I swallowed some ibuprofen and made liberal use of a lidocaine roll-on to ease the pain of my bumps and bruises. If I were a spiritually enlightened human being, I probably would have grieved the loss of Rolf's life. But I wasn't enlightened. Instead I was pretty damn glad that I wasn't going to fight with him anymore. I tiptoed into Kim's bedroom, undressed, put on a clean T-shirt and underwear, and slid into bed next to her.

"Are you all right?" she whispered.

"Sorry I woke you."

"Did you get into another fight?"

"Just a short one."

"And you won, or you wouldn't be here."

"Yeah, I suppose so."

"That's my tough guy." She kissed me. "How banged up are you?"

"Not too bad."

"You sure?" she whispered in between more brief kisses.

"I'm feeling better every second."

"Is that all that you're feeling?"

"Now that you mention it. . . ."

* * *

Kim's side of the bed was empty when I woke up on Wednesday morning. I got up, used the bathroom, splashed water on my face to help me wake up, and followed my nose to the freshly brewed coffee.

Kim was chopping onions. I gave her a quick peck on the cheek and stepped to the coffee pot to get a cup.

"How are you feeling?" she asked.

"Very well, thank you."

"You're not going to have to work before Thanksgiving, are you?"

"Not till Friday."

"Care to help me?"

"Absolutely."

"Can you please handle the potatoes?"

"Of course."

There was a large bag of Idaho potatoes on one end of the counter. I gulped down some coffee, grabbed a five-gallon pot from a cabinet, filled it with water, and set it to boil on top of the stove. I peeled all the potatoes, cut them into uneven smaller pieces, five or six per potato, and when the water was bubbling and boiling, delicately dropped the potatoes into the pot. Make no mistake, I did not think that my ability to mash potatoes demonstrated any level of cooking talent. Kim assigned me the job because it saved her time and required no skill whatsoever.

We chatted as we continued our prep, making all the foods that are best made in advance and easily warmed immediately before serving on Thanksgiving itself.

Cooking a big meal in a New York City-apartment kitchen was as much of an organizational challenge as a culinary one. Kim was up to the task.

When the potatoes were cooked, I drained the water, added some milk, butter, and chopped onions, and then applied my energies to the potatoes with a masher. I scooped up a tablespoon full to test for quality. My Irish forebears would have been very pleased with these potatoes. I spooned them into a Tupperware container to await Thanksgiving.

Kim was still preparing the stuffing and vegetables, so I dusted and vacuumed the apartment. By the time I was ready to set the table, Kim was done and joined me. It occurred to me that I hadn't done anything this domestic with someone since the last Christmas I had spent with my wife, Maggie. For a moment, I felt a wave of warm nostalgia for those days, followed by a stark instant of regret over my corrupt behavior that had led to Maggie's death. And I was surprised that I felt a twinge of guilt that I had moved on—never forgetting Maggie, but finally happy in the chance to start a new life and traditions with Kim.

For crying out loud, Tyrrell. Can't you just set the damn table and not search your soul while you do it? You've done your penance, caught Maggie's killers, and been fantastically lucky to find Kim, who's foolish enough to want to share a life with you. Time to get some gratitude in your attitude and celebrate Thanksgiving.

*   *   *

AFTERNOON – GERHARD FUCHS'S HOME
PALISADE AVENUE, RIVERDALE

MINA ASCHGRAU'S gray eyes were without even the smallest amount of emotional spark. Her posture was so upright and firm, she looked as if her body could cut through concrete. Greasy Hair and Rat Face sat to each side of her in front of Fuchs's desk.

Aschgrau said, "I checked into the man calling himself Herman Wouk. The two of you worked with a sketch artist to produce a recognizable picture of Wouk. I ran the sketch through facial-recognition software and got a match: Jack Tyrrell. He has his own security consulting firm. The only thing I could discover about it was a phone number. I tried tracing the number back and found nothing. Absolutely nothing. I've never seen anything like it. Tyrrell's own security is impenetrable."

"That's not possible," Fuchs replied.

"I would have said the same thing before I checked into Mr. Tyrrell."

"All right, so you weren't able to find his company's phone number. Nothing else? Any personal information?"

Aschgrau shook her head. "I couldn't find any current contact information for him. He's a ghost."

"That ghost is trying to destroy me. Did you find any information on his?"

"He has quite a track record. He was a lieutenant in Special Forces, in combat in Afghanistan, twice decorated. After his discharge, he joined the U.S. Marshals Service. Commended twice. He and his wife were shot on the front stoop of their brownstone. He lived; she died. He took disability from the Marshals."

"And lived happily ever after?" Fuchs asked.

"Apparently. There's no record of him at all since he was shot."

"When did that happen?"

"About six years ago, in 2010."

"Six years and nothing. Until he shows up and closes down my prostitution house and my drug lab, then thwarts a bank robbery. Just to make sure I got the point, he left a dead man and a burning car on my front lawn."

Aschgrau smirked. "How did you manage to explain that to the police?"

"There's no connection between me and Rolf. He's an employee of one of the many companies that I control, but the NYPD would have to unravel a massive ball of string to discover that he worked for me. And they have no reason to do that. Same with the car, by the by. And the car was reported stolen."

"Leaving the police to assume it was a bit of lethal vandalism?"

"Yes."

"All right, thank you, Ms. Aschgrau."

She nodded and walked out.

Fuchs looked at the two men. "We have to assume that Tyrrell is going to be on the scene tomorrow."

"Rolf caught him hanging cameras at one bank, but we're not going to go there, are we?" Greasy Hair asked.

"No, but how the hell did Tyrrell know about our last attempt in Scarsdale?" It was a rhetorical question. "We have to assume he'll be there on Friday."

"What do you want us to do?"

"You two are going with a very large team. One driver, three men on the street and five in the bank. If Tyrrell shows up, be sure you kill him."

"Is Tyrrell the first priority?" Rat Face asked, "Or the money?"

"Tyrrell. I've had enough of him."

*   *   *

Thanksgiving morning, Kim and I were up early. We threw on sweatpants and T-shirts, drank coffee, preheated the oven, did final prep on the turkey, and slid the twenty-pound bird into the oven when it was ready. We grabbed some more coffee and watched the start of the Macy's Thanksgiving Day Parade.

During the next few hours, I periodically basted the turkey. We pulled the other foods from the fridge, ready to be warmed later. We took turns showering and getting dressed.

"Will your dad wear a jacket and tie?" I asked.

248

"No, probably a dress shirt and sweater. Nice slacks. Loafers."

That decided me: a burgundy-striped dress shirt over gray-flannel slacks. Kim wore a royal-blue silk blouse; the color was perfect with her red hair. Black slacks completed her outfit.

Our guests were scheduled to arrive at 1:00 P.M., but Kim warned me that her sister and parents were liable to show up at any time.

And they did. Mr. & Mrs. Gannon had allowed more than enough time to drive down from Westchester and arrived at 12:05 P.M. Introductions were made, and a hearty handshake was exchanged by her dad and me. Kim's father was a trim sixtysomething with a receding hairline and silver hair brushed back from his face. He was about 6-feet tall and had a very firm handshake. Mrs. Gannon was a slender redhead. Kim had previously informed me that her mother's color was natural, originally, but these days came out of a bottle. Mrs. Gannon had same dazzling smile and blue eyes as Kim. She gave me an awkward hug and said she was *soooo* happy to meet me.

"Kim tells me you were in Special Forces," her father said. "And then the Marshals Service."

"Yes, I was."

"That's very impressive."

"That's probably why she told you."

He chuckled uncertainly, not quite sure if he was

amused by or annoyed.

"Oh, Walt, please," his wife said. To me, "Don't worry about him. He never likes any of Kim's beaux at first, but he'll warm up to you."

I looked past her at Kim, arching my eyebrows and widening my eyes. Kim replied with her dazzling smile. I said, "Well, Mrs. Gannon, I'll do my best not to be intimidated."

"Please call me Beth. And you don't strike me as easy to intimidate."

"He's not," Kim tossed the phrase over her shoulder as she walked into the kitchen. We all followed, and I asked them if they wanted anything to drink. Beth said a glass of Pinot Grigio would be lovely, if we happened to have it.

"Of course," I said. "Kim told me that's your favorite. Walt, what can I get you? Maybe a Heineken?"

"That would be fine. Did Kim tell you that's my favorite?"

"Yes, I did," Kim said. "Jack, are you having Pellegrino?"

"Yes, please. Do you want one too? In a glass? With ice?"

"Ye, please."

I got everyone's drinks, including Kim's Pellegrino with ice and mine without. Walt surprised me by declining the offer of a glass and drank his beer from the bottle.

"You don't drink, Jack?" he asked.

I almost said, of course I drink. Water. Instead I responded, "Not lately. Trying to lose a little weight."

"Really?" Beth said, surprised. She looked me up and down. "You seem to be in terrific shape. Other than the fading bruises on your face."

"Does the other guy look worse?" Walt asked.

"The other guy always looks worse," Kim said and patted me on the arm. "Jack is *tough*."

"The other guy *always* looks worse?" Walt seemed skeptical.

"Kim exaggerates."

"Do you see a lot of action as a security consultant?" Walt asked.

"My fair share."

"What do you think of as your 'fair share?'"

I grinned, "Now and then, there's a bit of action. Not much really."

"Walt," his wife interjected with a mother's worried tone of voice, "you're not talking about a sport here. This is Jack's business."

"I think it's time to baste the turkey again," Kim said.

I winked at her and set to basting the turkey, which was browning nicely. As soon as I finished, Beth put her arm in mine and led me away from the stove.

"I want to hear about your family. Are any of them joining us for today?"

"My sister lives near Boston and is entertaining her

in-laws."

"Oh. Don't you have a brother?"

"Yes, in California. And his wife has a lot of family there, so they always stay put for this holiday."

"What about your parents? Aren't they local?"

"They're both gone now."

"Oh, I'm so sorry. Have they been gone for a while?"

Kim had turned from the counter where she was putting together a platter of assorted cheeses and crackers. She mouthed, "Sorry."

I shrugged, "About eleven years ago. Auto accident. Drunk driver was going the wrong way on a highway and hit them head-on. At least they were together."

"That must have been very hard."

"It was. But my late wife helped me through." What I could have added, but didn't, was that Maggie's help was diluted by the enormous quantities of booze I consumed at the time.

"Your . . . *late* wife?"

Kim's eyes went wide with apprehension. Her mouth gaped open, but nothing came out. I smiled as reassuringly as I could, which seemed to relax her parents. "Yes, my late wife. Maggie. She passed away in 2010."

Beth and Walt looked perplexed, and troubled. Tyrrell, this was why you didn't go into *any* detail about your life.

252

"It's okay," I said. "I've been very lucky. I met your daughter. Things are looking up." Geez Louise, Tyrrell. *"Things are looking up."* Could you be any more of a cliché?

Kim handed me the platter. "Out into the living room. No more talk about Jack's past. Shoo."

Walt said that Kim had told him I was a Yankee fan, which I admitted to, and we began a conversation about the Yankees' prospects for the future. Beth sat there quietly, as I imagined she had for many years. How the heck had Kim become such a spitfire with parents who seemed to have stepped out of a 1950s sitcom? Maybe that was an unfair reading of their characters. Maybe the pressure of meeting their daughter's fiancé was too much for them. Then again. . . .

We finished our assessment of the Yankees, agreeing that there was promise for the team's future. Did any sports fans ever come to any other conclusion about their teams in the off season? And to be honest, we didn't really finish our assessment, we could have gone on forever like most baseball fans. But Kim's mother had other ideas.

"Pardon me for dragging you away from baseball, but when are you going to get my daughter a real ring?" Beth asked, smiling widely and innocently, "Not that I don't admire the quality and color of your yarn. I like your style. But I'm old-fashioned and would love to see a real ring on her finger."

"Me, too," I agreed. "As soon as she wants, we'll

go to a jewelry store and she can pick one out."

"You're not going to surprise her with a ring?"

"I surprised her with a proposal in Paris. But Kim should choose her own engagement ring. After all, she's going to wear it the rest of her life."

"Oh, well, now that you've explained it," Beth grinned, "I have to say I *really* appreciate your style." I saw a flash of Kim's spirit and humor in her mother.

"Thanks," I said, smiling.

Kim came into the living room and plopped down in the armchair nearest the kitchen. "I might just stick with the yarn." She held up her left hand, turning it this way and that, showing off the purple yarn tied in a bow on her ring finger. "How many people do you see wearing yarn engagement rings?"

"Wow," I said, "you are a *cheap* date."

"Excuse me?"

"I meant you are an incredibly reasonable and insightful woman."

"That's more like it." Her eyes sparkled, and if I hadn't been in love with her already, I would have fallen for her all over again.

The doorman's intercom buzzed, and Kim hopped up and answered. The doorman announced her sister's family.

"Send them up, please."

I stood up and walked to the front door to greet them. Kim gave me a quick kiss on the lips then whispered,

"Sorry about my Mom giving you the third degree."

"Oh that was nothing. Wait till you meet *my* sister."

"Well," Kim said, "at least we know that my sister and her family love you."

"Her boys do, anyway." I grinned.

We stood in the open apartment door. The elevator doors parted, and two little boys exploded out, ran down the hall at us, screaming, "Jaaaaack!" and tackled my legs. I pretended to fall down, and they pounced on me. Henry, the eight-year old, clung to my legs. Sam, the six-year old, grabbed me around the neck. They both had lean, little boy frames and reddish-brown hair.

"Give up!" Henry shouted. Sam echoed, "Give up or else!"

"Or else!" I grunted. They were laughing and pummeling me and demanding my surrender.

I overheard Kim say, "Your grandsons seem to think that Jack is a life-sized action toy."

Beth replied, "Jack seems to think so, too."

"Okay," said another female voice. Kim's sister, Jennifer. She seemed to be speaking to us, the tangle of wrestling bodies on the floor, "let Jack get up. Come on."

They stopped and stood up. Henry pointed a finger at me and said, "We're not finished. We'll get you later."

"I'm counting on it," I replied with a squint and a gravelly growl. I stood up and kissed Jennifer's cheek and shook hands with the boys' father, Dave.

"You don't need to let them do that," he said.

"I probably enjoy it as much as they do."

"It looks like you do."

We walked into the living room, and I asked if I could get them something to drink. Jennifer, a slightly taller version of Kim but with reddish-blond hair. She asked for wine. Dave, who had a well-defined jaw and brown hair, asked for a beer.

The boys were settled in front of the TV at one end of the living room. I wasn't certain, but it looked like they were watching the movie *The Incredibles*. I wouldn't have minded joining them. Infinitely preferable to the next round of questions about Kim's and my plans, which I was sure were on Beth's and Jennifer's agenda.

Kim and I went to the kitchen to get the new round of drinks and to check on the turkey, which did not need basting. I poured the drinks while Kim put crudités and a small bowl of hummus on a larger platter. We went back to the living room with the food and beverages.

"How did you two meet again?" Beth asked.

Kim and I exchanged glances, and I held out my hand in a "you first" gesture.

"We frequented the same café, which meant that we kind of recognized each other, and one day I decided to ask—"

"—this tall, handsome stranger to join her at her table," I finished for her. "And since Kim is a stunning redhead, I happily agreed."

"*Happily*," Jennifer amplified teasingly.

"Yes, *happily*."

"So it's all my doing," Kim summed up.

"Have you set a date, yet?" Beth asked.

"Mom, now is not the time for playing Mother of the Bride."

"Why not?"

Kim looked at me, and I shrugged and said, "Why not?"

"You are no help at all," she replied and turned to her mother, "Probably in February."

"February! When in February? That's only eight to ten weeks away. What kind of plans have you made? Do you need my help?"

"Mom, I can manage. Small wedding at St. Ignatius on the Upper East Side. Jack's got an old friend who's a Jesuit priest who'll perform the ceremony."

"Small wedding? But St. Ignatius is huge. That's was Jacqueline Kennedy Onassis's parish."

Kim responded patiently, "As I said, Jack has a Jesuit friend there. We don't really care about Jackie O."

"What about a dress? And invitations?"

"Mom, I'm 38-years old and run my own business. I can handle these things all by myself."

"Yes, but . . ."

"I would love your help. I'm going to wear a dress, not a wedding gown. And we'll send out invitations in a couple of weeks. I'll e-mail you the guest list, and you can review it."

"Are you registered anywhere?"

"No. We don't want any gifts, although we'd appreciate it if people made charitable donations."

Beth looked perplexed.

Jennifer jumped in, "Will you be living here?"

"Yes."

"Please," I said, "don't ask my opinion."

"Don't worry," Kim treated me to her dazzling smile. "I won't."

Dave grinned at me. "Welcome to a family of strong-willed women."

He and I laughed. Walt clearly wasn't comfortable with the implication that he was controlled by a strong-willed woman. "I don't see anything wrong with letting Kim organize her wedding. She knows what she wants and runs her own marketing-and-communications business, which, among other things, produces events."

"Thank you, Dad." She said with exaggerated emphasis, "Darling, could you please go check the turkey."

"Yes, ma'am," I leapt to my feet and practically ran to the kitchen.

I pulled open the oven and tugged out the turkey far enough so I could baste it, and did. When I finished and had shoved the bird back inside and closed the oven door, I found Kim waiting for me.

"You don't mind all this wedding talk, do you?" she asked, putting her arms around my neck and kissing me before I could answer.

"No, it's kind of funny."

"Good," she kissed me again. "How's the turkey looking?"

"It's a dark golden brown. And it smells fantastic. I think it'll be done on schedule."

Harry arrived on the exact dot of 1:00 P.M. Kim kissed him on the cheek, put her arm through his, and introduced him to everyone. The boys gave him a wave and returned their attention to *The Incredibles*.

Walt asked, "You and Jack work together?"

"Yes, we do."

"How did you team up?"

"Jack's late wife introduced us."

I smiled to myself. What Harry wasn't saying was that Maggie had, in fact, been dead at the time of the introduction. It would have been more accurate to say her ghost had introduced us. Just like the ghost of Jacob Marley introduced Ebenezer Scrooge to the Three Spirits of Christmas. But saying that your dead wife introduced you to your business partner, who was your *actual* guardian angel, well, it was a surefire conversation stopper. I admired Harry's nimble sidestepping of the issue.

"Just how dangerous is this security business of yours?" Walt asked.

Harry gave him a reassuring smile. To be honest, I thought it was supposed to be reassuring, but Harry didn't quite manage it. He said, "Nothing that Jack and I can't handle."

"I don't want my daughter marrying a man who could get killed on the job."

"Dad!"

"I'm sorry," Walt said, "but I don't think it's unreasonable for me to be concerned."

Kim patted her father's arm, "I appreciate the old-fashioned father routine, but please . . . stop."

Beth chimed in, trying to help rein in her husband, "Walt? Are you behaving?"

"Of course he is," Kim said, smiling at her father.

"I give up," he said.

I got Harry a Pellegrino and checked the turkey. Again. Not because the turkey needed it. I needed the break. Just a minute to take a deep breath while pretending to look after our dinner.

The turkey finished cooking exactly when Kim had scheduled it. (I think the bird was afraid of disappointing her.) Carving, serving, and eating passed in a blur. Our plates were empty but for a few crumbs of stuffing. After hours of work preparing the meal, eating the meal took almost no time at all. The swift consuming of turkey and sides was a phenomenon I had observed at every Thanksgiving in my life. Fortunately, there was dessert. And coffee.

Kim's parents, as she had predicted, were out the door on their way home at 4:30 P.M. About an hour later, Jennifer gave me a kiss on the cheek, Dave shook my hand,

and the boys clung to my legs as they all said farewell.

We were left with dirty dishes, leftovers to pack up and put away, and Harry.

"You've worked way too hard today," I said to Kim. "Go sit on the couch and relax."

"I might just have to keep you."

"Does that mean I passed the parental inspection?"

"My keeping you has nothing to do with their feelings."

"Really?"

"*Really.*" She kissed me, poured herself another cup of coffee, and went out to the living room to plop down on the couch.

Harry and I tackled the dirty dishes. I washed the fine china and crystal by hand, and Harry dried. He looked out to the living room where Kim had fallen asleep.

"Are you ready for tomorrow?" he asked me.

"I guess so."

"You do know that Fuchs will send a larger team with heavier weapons, don't you?"

"The thought had occurred to me. It's what I'd do if I were a perverted, neo-Nazi prick."

"Hmm." He paused, then continued, "The Chairman wants me to let you know that Fuchs wants you dead even more than he wants the bank's money."

"How flattering. Does the Chairman plan to give me additional help?"

"He will give you what you need."

"Ah, yes. What I *need*."

"I suppose you will want to load weapons into your pack before we go to whichever bank they attempt to rob."

"It's probably a good idea, given that they want to kill me. And that I'm going to *need* to protect myself. Could you whoosh me to my place at about 9:00 tomorrow morning?"

"Yes."

We finished washing and drying in companionable silence.

"I hope you had a nice Thanksgiving," I said.

"I did. Please tell Kim how much I enjoyed being her guest."

"I will."

"In the morning then."

"Looking forward to it. Nothing like foiling a bank robbery on the day after Thanksgiving."

Harry gave me his barely perceptible Mona Lisa smile and disappeared.

14

Harry and I stared down at the assortment of weapons on my bed. Guns, grenades, plasticuffs, and a backpack. I wasn't bringing brass knuckles or a blackjack this time. If I had my way, there would be no hand-to-hand combat.

"You said more guys and more guns, right?" I asked.

"Yes."

I took a Kevlar vest out of the closet, slipped into it, and snugged the vest tight. Not too tight, I needed to be able to move. I was dressed in my usual action outfit: a black turtleneck and charcoal-gray cargo pants with black, crepe-soled shoes. The outfit was topped by a charcoal-gray windbreaker that concealed the vest and holsters. In spite of the fact that the robbery was happening in the daylight, I felt more comfortable in my dark, cat-burglar uniform.

I slid my trusty Rugers SR9s into the twin shoulder holsters and placed four extra magazines in the pouches on the holsters' straps. Into the pack went an Uzi with extra magazines, and six smoke grenades. I added two flashbangs to the pack's precious cargo. The weapons I had not chosen for this mission were returned to the secret storage place inside my closet.

"Now we wait," Harry said.

"Yup." The time was 9:36 A.M. "Both of the banks are open."

"Both? I thought we had three potential targets."

I shook my head, "I can't imagine that Fuchs would send the crew to the bank where Rolf and I had the fight."

"Maybe he would rob that one because you would think it is safe."

"That would be a good play. But my guess is that he's going to go big this time. He's sending a heavier crew, loaded for action. And I think this might be his last bank robbery before whatever truly huge and ugly thing he's planning."

"What evidence do you have that this is his last bank robbery?"

"None. Just a hunch. But the bigger crew and more weapons, makes me think this robbery is the build-up to his grand finale."

"You talk about him as if he were producing a theatrical extravaganza."

"Hey, think about his hero. Hitler loved the big, dramatic, theatrical set pieces. The giant swastika flags hanging on buildings, the vast parades and assemblies, the shouted, crazed speeches. Gerhard Fuchs is a piker compared to Hitler. He could do something horrifically awful and still fall short of his Nazi god."

I sat on the bed, grabbed the vest on each side, and

tried to shift it to a more comfortable position on my torso. I failed. Come on, Tyrrell, you want it to stop bullets *and* be comfortable? Don't you think you're asking for a bit too much?

"He's going after the bank at the Ansonia," I said.

"How do you know?"

"More public. Not quite two blocks from the intersection of Broadway and West 72nd. Very busy. Lot of people around to see his crew jump out of the vehicle, wave their guns, make a lot of noise, and steal a ton of cash."

Harry pursed his lips but said nothing.

My phone rang; it was Naomi.

"Jack, a black Ford Transit van just parked on Broadway in front of the Ansonia. It's the extended length van with extra capacity, probably can hold a dozen people at least."

"Thanks, Naomi."

"Jack!" she said quickly. "Be careful, there's seven, no, eight guys stepping out of the van. All in horror-movie clown masks."

"Thanks. I'll be careful. And please call 9-1-1. Tell them there's a robbery in progress."

I disconnected, pulled out the Rugers, and looked at Harry. "Time to whoosh to the Ansonia. Please."

He nodded and—

We were standing directly behind a Dodge Ram pickup truck with a hardtop shell over the cargo bed. The shell was nowhere near bulletproof, but it was definitely vision-proof. The truck was parked directly in front of the bank entrance, about 25 feet uptown of the Ford Transit. I stuck my head just far enough around the corner of the truck's cargo bed to see down the sidewalk.

The bank-robbing, ghoul-faced clowns had picked a good moment to disembark the Transit. Three of them, wearing long wigs in bright yellow, red, and orange, stood next to the van. Five clowns were crossing the sidewalk toward the bank. A tall man in a long silver wig was in the lead. The four others, wearing neon green, neon blue, neon purple, and neon pink, trailed Silver Clown. Every single one of them carried a Remington 870 pump-action shotgun with a six-round magazine. That was enough firepower to make me very queasy.

Silver Clown was about 3 feet from the bank's front door. It was now or never. Once inside the bank, they'd have hostages. And once the police arrived and surrounded the bank, God only knew how awful the situation would become. The clowns might want a fire fight like the Baader-Meinhof thugs did in the 1970s.

I looked up to the sky and whispered, "Another round of help, please," and stepped out from behind the truck onto the sidewalk, guns at the ready in each hand. "Stop where you are. Put your weapons down."

The clowns stopped and swiveled toward me, with their guns leveled at my midsection.

Very loudly and firmly, I repeated, "Put your

weapons down."

Yellow Clown, the one nearest to me at the front of the Ford Transit, shifted and began to bring his shotgun up. I fired the Ruger in my left hand, caught Yellow Clown in the shoulder and sent him spinning into the Transit. He bounced off and fell onto the curb. Behind him, I saw the Orange and Red Clowns alongside the van, also bringing up their guns. I fired multiple times without hesitation. There clearly was no point in repeating, my "put your weapons down" admonition. These guys weren't going to pay attention.

Orange Clown fell against the Transit and slid to the ground, leaving a large streak of blood down the side of the van. Red Clown toppled into the street just beyond the nose of the Transit.

There was a loud blast from my right, and I felt shotgun pellets plucking at my right arm and leg and thudding into my vest. It was like getting stung by a swarm of very large, very nasty bees.

I dove behind the Ram truck, as buckshot peppered the truck's cargo bed just above my head. Peering under the pickup's chassis, I saw the clowns disappearing through the bank entrance, leaving Neon Pink Clown on guard. I crawled down Broadway, on the traffic-lane side of the Ram, and, when I got to the hood, I stood up. Neon Pink Clown twisted around, bringing his gun up. I fired the Ruger in my right hand five times. The glass of the bank's revolving door shattered, and Neon Pink flopped down, his torso outside and his legs inside the revolving door.

Four down, four to go. You know, Tyrrell, you might just want to take care of the Transit's driver. I holstered the gun in my left hand and rushed forward to the driver's door. I grabbed the handle and tugged on it.

Locked. The driver, a demonic clown with a white wig, spun toward me. I ducked as he fired a pistol through the window at me. The window glass exploded outward, the bullet flew into the distance. Crouching out of his sightline, I pumped four bullets through the door. I waited a few seconds, stood up, and looked through the window. White Clown was dead. I reached through the window, turned off the van, and took the keys.

I looked across the hood of the Transit at the bank but saw nothing through the windows or the revolving door. I scurried downtown, past two parked cars, then looped back up the sidewalk toward the bank, staying below the level of the windows. Keeping close to the wall, I stopped just short of the revolving door and peered through it. Neon Pink Clown was still sprawled in the door. Through the revolving-door frame, I spotted Neon Green Clown who was standing guard immediately inside.

The other robbers were shouting at their hostages. I checked the time on my phone. I had first engaged these clowns 72 seconds ago. The police probably wouldn't arrive for another couple of minutes. A lot of hostages could get hurt or die in a couple of minutes. I couldn't wait.

I pulled four grenades out of my pack: three

smokers and one flashbang. I inserted fresh magazines for both Rugers, took a very deep breath, and forced myself to exhale slowly. I tossed the flashbang through the revolving door at the feet of Neon Green Clown. It made a very nasty sound and I was pretty sure I heard the thump of Neon Green's body hitting the floor. I took a step to the door, tossed the smoke grenades inside as quickly as possible, and lunged for cover. I heard smoke hissing from the grenades and people coughing.

"Someone talk me outta this," I muttered and jumped through the shattered revolving door. I dove through the smoke onto the marble floor, skidding across it until I fetched up against one of those tables people use to endorse checks and fill out deposit and withdrawal slips.

Neon Purple Clown was closest to me, and as he aimed at me, I fired four times. His body jolted side to side as he was hit. He dropped the shotgun and fell over one of the hostages who was prone on the floor. Neon Blue Clown was running toward me from deep within the smoky bank, firing his Remington. I took cover behind the table as his buckshot tore up the table. Miraculously, I wasn't hit. I rolled across the floor, firing with both hands as I went. I must have fired seven or eight times and missed with most of those shots, but I hit Neon Blue Clown at least twice, and he went down. Because I had been shooting up at him, the bullets that missed had hit the far wall.

Unless my count was off, and with all the excitement, I couldn't honestly say it wasn't, only Silver was left. And I could hear police sirens closing in. Thank God.

I looked around at the hostages. "Get up and run," I said. "Outside as fast as you can."

The only response was scared faces with wide eyes and slack, open mouths.

"Outside, now!" I stood up and moved toward the back, where I presumed the vault was. The hostages began moving toward the door. "Wait outside, the police are on their way."

"Really?" came a low growl from deep inside the bank. The tall Silver Clown walked out of the back of the bank. He fired his shotgun in the air and shouted, "Everyone down on the floor!"

He leveled the gun at me, but before he could say or do anything else, I shot him. Three bullets, center mass. He staggered and collapsed.

Hostages were running past me as I walked over to Silver Clown and yanked his mask off. I'd never seen him before. I tugged off the masks off the other clowns and didn't recognize a one. Where the hell had Fuchs gotten all these guys? Were they all members of *Oberste Ordnung*? Or just thugs out for a paycheck?

The police sirens were very loud, and tires screeched as the patrol cars screeched to a halt.

"Harry, would you mind?"

Nothing happened.

"That's not funny, Harry. It's time for me—

I was standing in the bathroom of my apartment. "—to go." I finished lamely.

Harry stood in the doorway. "Do you want me to clean you up? Remove the shotgun pellets?"

"Yes, please. Do I have any serious wounds I need to worry about?"

"Don't you think you'd be in much more pain if you had a serious wound?"

"My adrenalin is so high right now, I'm not sure I'd feel anything."

He grinned, a teeny-weeny grin that came and went in an instant. "No, nothing serious."

I slowly peeled off my Kevlar vest and gently kicked off my shoes and pulled down my pants. I looked down at my arm and thigh. From where I sat, it wasn't a pretty picture. Harry swabbed my arm and thigh with alcohol, which stung much worse than the shotgun pellets. I gasped.

Harry said. "And Kim thinks you're a tough guy."

"That's not fair."

He shrugged, poured alcohol over a pair of tweezers, and went to work pulling out shotgun pellets. Maybe I'm prejudiced, but he seemed to take a grim satisfaction from the pain he was causing.

As he plucked a pellet from my neck, he paused and looked closely at the wound. "You were very lucky with this. An inch over and it would have cut into your carotid. You'd be dead."

"Someone was watching over me."

"Yes, He was."

Harry finished up, and in no time, he was swabbing the small holes with antiseptic cream.

"Take some ibuprofen, and you should be all set."

"Thanks, Doc," I replied. "Should I call you in the morning?" I grabbed the ibuprofen from the medicine chest and swallowed more than the recommended amount with gulps of water straight from the tap. I grabbed a small box of Band-Aids from the medicine chest.

"What's your next step?" Harry asked.

I began applying Band-Aids to the pellet holes in my skin. "Are you asking me how I'm going to figure out what Fuchs is up to for his big, ugly finale?"

"Exactly."

"Like I told you, I'm going to break into the *gesellschaft.*"

"When will you be doing that?"

"Soon. Depends on how I feel in an hour or so, when the pain of being gunned down on Broadway really hits me."

"You are so dramatic."

"I also think I need to talk with Naomi and Stewart."

"Would you like to go now?"

"Soon. I need to put on some clothes that have no bullet holes—"

"*Pellet* holes. They hardly qualify as bullets."

"Regardless, clothes with no *projectile* holes. And no bloodstains. And, we should get Naomi and Stewart some caffeine first."

"Them or you?"

"Can't it be both?"

Harry sat on my bed while I changed into clothes with no holes and no stains. Not surprisingly, the new clothes looked a lot like the old ones. I had multiple sets of my cat-burglar outfit.

"How do you feel?" Harry asked.

"Surprisingly well. Is that the Chairman's doing?"

Harry shrugged, "He doesn't keep me informed of every little thing He does."

"How about the bank robbers? How many dead?"

"None."

"What? That's amazing. Will they all be enjoying the hospitality of NYPD?"

"Six of them are in the hospital, handcuffed to their beds, guarded by New York's Finest. The other three are being treated and will be released into police custody."

"Taken to the 20th Precinct for printing and processing and then to Central Booking at 100 Centre Street. Right?"

"Exactly."

"And none of the robbers will be able to lead the police back to Fuchs?"

"No, they won't."

"Does Gerhard know what happened?"

Harry glanced up as if consulting the heavens and back to me. "Not yet. He had a man watching from across the street. That man is reporting to Fuchs at the *gesellschaft* in a few minutes."

"Speaking of watching—"

"Any and all video cameras in the area will only show you as an unidentifiable blur."

"Maybe that should be my nom de guerre: Unidentifiable Blur."

"At a moment like this, I think Kim would say you are an idiot."

"Hey, I'm a wounded man. Made delirious from an ibuprofen overdose."

Harry closed his eyes in frustration and slowly shook his head. "Are you ready to go see Naomi and Stewart?"

"Give me a second, please." I stowed my backpack in the special compartment in my closet and pulled out my Walther CCP, along with a couple of extra ammunition magazines. The CCP was smaller than my Rugers but fit more easily into my pants' cargo pockets. The Walther went into the right pocket, the mags into the left.

"Whenever you're ready," I said.

And we were standing outside Buona Tazza in the Village. We got our usual order and the usual for Naomi and Stewart—double espresso and a dirty chai tea—and then Harry whooshed us directly outside the front door of their lair.

"Why not inside?" I asked.

"Sometimes it's better if we knock and are invited inside."

"Oh? Are we interrupting something?"

"Get your mind out of the gutter."

"It's not in the gutter. I just know that Stewart has a thing for Naomi, and it would be great if she returned the sentiment. I was hoping that we didn't whoosh inside because . . . I don't know . . . maybe they were . . ."

"They are deep in conversation. Dealing with Fuchs, actually. I wanted to let them finish their thoughts."

"Oh."

"We can go in now." He knocked on the door, and Naomi opened it. As usual, she beamed at the sight of me. I hated to think that I was an obstacle for Stewart, but what could I do about it? I handed her the drinks.

"Good to see you guys," she said. "Thanks for the caffeine." She led the way through the railroad flat to Stewart. "We've been thinking about the plans Fuchs might be funding with his money stockpile."

"Hey, guys," Stewart said.

"Have you got any solid ideas about out what Fuchs is going to do?" I asked.

"Not exactly."

"I don't mean to push, but does 'not exactly' mean you've got a rough idea, or does it mean 'not a clue?'"

"Not a clue. Sorry."

"We need to go deeper. Think big. Remember, this

guy is a neo-Nazi terrorist. We've got to try to find connections between the trucks and gasoline and some of Fuchs's other businesses."

"And remember that the clock is ticking." Naomi said. "You've stopped Fuchs's cash flow. Harry told us that his big move is going to happen within days." She pursed her lips as she scanned through some files on a computer. "Fuchs just took another truck delivery right before Thanksgiving. It looks like it was an expedited order."

"Maybe . . . ," Stewart mused, "maybe an expedited order of gasoline just before Thanksgiving is all about the Christmas season? Fuchs wanted the gas on hand to do whatever the hell he's going to do."

"There are an awful lot of tourists in New York right now," Naomi said. "That could make for a very big finish."

"Shit."

"We'll get to work and call you as soon as we've got something," Stewart said.

"Thanks."

"What's your next move, Jack?" Naomi asked.

"Nothing much. Just a little breaking and entering."

"Anything we'd be interested in?"

"Actually, I'm going to visit a social club that Fuchs owns.

15

Harry and I exited the building normally, walking down four flights of stairs. I realized it was the first time I had ever been outside Naomi and Stewart's place, which was in Chelsea, on 17th Street just west of Eighth Avenue.

"My sister had a place on this block right after college," I said. "In fact, it might have been this very building. She was going through her bohemian phase."

"I imagine the rent was very reasonable."

"It was. Not anymore. Can't imagine how Naomi and Stewart afford such a place."

"Stewart's grandmother left the apartment to him. As you've noticed, he doesn't have much of an eye for decorating."

"That's putting it mildly. How did he and Naomi meet?"

"They both studied math at NYU. After graduation, they went different ways, Stewart into forensic accounting and Naomi into computer sciences. They helped each other out on a couple of freelance jobs, realized they were a great team, and set up a little business of their own. They make a lot of money."

"Not from me."

"No. They, like you, work for the Chairman, helping others."

"How did that happen?"

Harry ignored my question. "What next?"

I reciprocated by ignoring his question. "Does Naomi know that Stewart is interested in her?"

"Interested?"

"Don't play dumb. It doesn't suit you. Interested. Romantically."

"Ah . . . I don't know."

After a moment, I said, "I don't have to worry about Naomi's feelings for me, do I? It's just a crush, right?"

He shrugged. "I can't tell you. Sorry. Human emotions don't always make sense to me."

"They don't make sense to us humans, either." I looked up at the face of the building. "I'm pretty damn sure this is where my sister lived."

"How is that fact of any use to us in this moment?"

"It's not. It's just . . . it just seems like a cosmic coincidence."

"Whatever that means."

I began walking toward Eighth Avenue. Harry followed.

"Do you happen to know when the *gesellschaft* closes tonight?"

"Midnight."

"And when does the hired help clear out?"

"Usually about an hour after closing. Depends on how much cleanup they have to do."

"Would you mind picking me up at Kim's around 12:30 and whooshing me to the *gesellschaft*?"

"Not at all."

"Thanks, see you—"

He was gone. No fade away. No slowly dissolving out of sight. Just . . . gone. Neat trick. I walked downtown to my apartment. Once there, I put together my action pack for the evening's festivities at Fuchs's social club. Rugers with suppressors and extra magazines. Four each of smoke and flashbang grenades. Plasticuffs. Brass knuckles. Blackjack. A climbing harness, some carabiners, and a coil of ultra-thin, ultra-strong climbing rope. I also included a leather kit that was filled with what I thought of as my anti-security tools: locks picks, wire cutter and needle-nose pliers with insulated handles, and a pair of screwdrivers, one flat-head and one Phillips-head. I also added a number of cables with different jacks and alligator clips in case I needed to plug into whatever digital alarm system Fuchs had. Naomi could guide me through disarming the system.

I decided it would be very healthy for me to go to an AA meeting, so I used the handy-dandy meeting finder app on my phone to lookup the Friday, 12:15 PM meeting at the Perry Street Workshop. The meeting space had been a store once upon a time, a long rectangular space with its narrow, windowed end looking out on the sidewalk. The meeting space could generously be described as dismal, but it was only a four-block walk from my apartment, and there were a lot of meetings there from morning to night.

Some familiar faces were outside smoking cigarettes (one of the more unappetizing features of AA meetings—sometimes you had to go through a gauntlet of smokers to get to the meeting itself). I said hello and went inside to find a seat. The meeting got underway and everyone seemed to be talking about acceptance. About how you need to accept that some things won't ever change. Accept that you're not in control. Accept that you will have to live with some people and some situations just the way they are.

Accept.

Throughout the meeting, I kept thinking one thing: If I have to accept Fuchs, well . . . that just was not going to happen. I couldn't do it.

At the end of the meeting we prayed:

"God grant me the serenity to accept the things I cannot change, courage to change the things I can, and wisdom to know the difference."

I have to admit as I spoke all the words, the phrase that resonated for me was: "courage to *change* the things I can." I had some very severe changes in mind with regard to Fuchs's neo-Nazi Merry Men. Very. Severe.

After the meeting, I went home, made a cappuccino, and played *The Rites of Spring* by Igor Stravinsky. I sat in an upholstered armchair and wondered what the hell was Fuchs up to as Stravinsky's dark, striking music stimulated thoughts of violent deeds.

A neo-Nazi had a bunch of trucks. And gallons and

gallons of gasoline. Was he going to blow something up? But gasoline wasn't explosive. It was flammable as hell, almost literally, but not actually explosive. Fuchs would need true explosives to start a huge conflagration—he would know that, so he must have them. What was he going to target? Unfortunately, New York did not lack for targets that would appeal to terrorists. Maybe I should just go up to Riverdale and shoot the bastard. Stop the terror at its source. But . . . was that really what the Chairman would want me to do? If I knew an evil thing was going to happen, wasn't I supposed to do whatever I could to stop it and protect others? Including killing Fuchs in cold blood? Maybe just call Diego Quintana and let NYPD's Counterterrorism Bureau handle the problem? But what *was* the problem? What exactly would I be warning Quintana about?

Twenty minutes later, *The Rites of Spring* ended. I had finished my cappuccino, and still had *not* figured out a damn thing.

I was struck by the impulse to make another cappuccino and listen to more Stravinsky. Additional caffeine and *The Firebird* might help me discern Fuchs's big, ugly move. But . . . probably not. The real challenge in figuring out Fuchs's terrorist strike was that my thinking was clouded over by my hate. He despised people like Laurie Mandelbaum just because . . . wait a minute, I thought, Kim was right. I hated it when that happened. But she had pointed out that this mission was being driven by

281

my feelings for Laurie. That I could make things right for my dead first love by stopping a neo-Nazi. I wondered if it was spiritually healthy behavior to admit that to Kim. Maybe I'd admit it, maybe I wouldn't. In my experience, admitting to your fiancée that she was correct about your motivation —that you were out to stop a neo-Nazi terrorist because your first love was Jewish—well, maybe some things were better left unsaid. Aren't you being a wuss, Tyrrell? You're a government-trained private detective cum troubleshooter, and Kim is constantly declaring you to be a tough guy. Never mind all that, at the age of forty-four, you're supposed to be an adult. But you're too big a wuss to admit she was right?

I sighed, got into some fresh clothes (yes, another set of dark clothes that were part of my Cat Burglar Collection), slung my backpack over my left shoulder, and headed out. Since Harry was not around to provide me transport to Kim's, I did what millions of New Yorkers do every day, I took the subway.

Kim greeted me with a big smile and a quick kiss on the lips. She looked me up and down. "Are you going out later?"

"Unfortunately, yes. But not till after midnight, so we have a full evening of fun and frolicking."

"Frolicking? Don't get your hopes up," she said impishly.

"I'm always *hopeful* when I'm with you."

"Not sure if that's sweet or sexually obsessed."

282

"It's sweet, of course. Maybe a little obsessed."

"Can you be a *little* obsessed?" she asked. "Never mind, come into the kitchen."

I hung my coat in the front closet, left my pack on the closet floor, and followed her to the kitchen.

"Are you good with Thanksgiving leftovers for dinner?" she asked.

"Was Thanksgiving yesterday? I've lost all sense of time."

"Yes, it was yesterday. Did you get banged on the head this morning?"

"Nope. And, yes, I am very good with leftovers."

Kim was about to open the refrigerator when she paused, turned to me, and checked out my clothing. "And, you're going out later?"

"Yup. After midnight."

She arched her eyebrows. "Maybe we should take a nap."

"I thought I wasn't supposed to get too hopeful about frolicking."

"Do you want to take a nap or not?"

"A nap would be very nice."

Kim took my hand and led me to her bedroom. We tumbled onto the bed, and there was a lot of kissing and caressing, gentle laughter, undressing, and the bliss of sliding under fresh sheets with someone you love. Someone who happened to be naked.

"I'm sorry to interrupt our nap," Kim said, putting

283

her fingertip on one of my many Band-Aids, "but what are all of these?"

"Band-Aids. *Very small* Band-Aids."

"I can see that. Why are you covered in them?"

"Well, I was uncomfortably close to the discharge of a shotgun."

"What?" She pushed up onto an elbow.

"Well, to be precise, you could say I was shot by a shotgun. These Band-Aids are covering the pellet holes. Very minor, very shallow, all cleaned up. No worries."

"You were hit with buckshot? When did—" she stopped and thought for a second. "At the bank robbery?"

"Yup."

"The news said there were nine robbers."

"Yes, there were nine of them."

"Oh my God, you're lucky to be alive."

"It wasn't luck. When you said, 'Oh my God' I think you were right on target."

"The Chairman kept you safe?"

"That's what I believe. People as close to 12-gauge shotguns as I was don't usually get off this easy."

"I don't know whether to be frightened or reassured."

"Reassured. The Chairman's taken care of me so far."

"What if, someday, he doesn't?"

I smiled my most winning smile and said, "St. Ignatius of Loyola supposedly said, 'Act as if everything depended on you; trust as if everything depended on God.' And that's my plan for the future."

"That's not really an answer to my question."

"I don't have an answer."

Kim put her arms around my neck, pulled me close, and kissed me.

We kissed for a moment or two—who keeps track of time in the midst of intimacy—when Kim stopped and said, "I want to talk with you about something serious—"

"Am I in trouble?"

"Always. No, I want . . . oh, this is hard right after what we were just talking about." Kim took a deep breath and said, "What do you think about having children?"

"What a segue, from shotgun pellets to babies."

"Stop joking around. You know I worry about you. But that doesn't mean I don't want to have a future with you full of all the things any two people in love might want."

"Holy moly."

"What does 'holy moly' mean?"

"It means I'm . . . surprised and don't really know what to say."

"Okay, now that you've had—" she mimicked looking at a watch on her wrist, "thirty seconds to contemplate it, what do you think?"

"Uh . . . talking about having kids is not effective foreplay."

She smiled, "Since we're about to do the deed, I thought this might be a good time to discuss doing the deed

285

for something more than sexual pleasure."

"I really don't know what to say."

"You at a loss for words. Hmm. Never thought I'd see the day."

"While I attempt to compose my thoughts, may I ask what you think about having kids?"

"We should."

"Just like that?"

"Yes. I love you, we're getting married, and I want to have children with you."

"Don't you think we should be married first?"

"That's kind of 20th century, don't you think? We're not getting any younger. I'm thirty-eight. You haven't seen the sunny side of forty for years—"

"—Hey!"

"What are we waiting for?"

"Well, we're going to get married in February, maybe wait until the honeymoon?"

"Even if I got pregnant right now, I'd only be about ten weeks along by our wedding. I'd barely be showing anything. And who cares if I am pregnant then? Does anyone really worry about that anymore?"

"At a guess, I think your parents might look askance at such a situation."

"What are you afraid of?"

I opened my mouth, and nothing came out. Yeah, Tyrrell, what are you afraid of? "I'm not afraid of anything in particular. I'm *just* afraid."

She smiled at my honesty and stroked my cheek. "Come on, what could be better than a government-trained troubleshooter troubleshooting *his own* kids?"

We kissed for a moment. One of those long, slow, wet kisses that songs—or movie dialogue—are written about.

"So, ten weeks. Sounds like you've been giving this some serious thought," I said.

"I might have done the math once or twice."

"Or ten or twenty times?"

"Maybe. So . . . what's it to be?"

"Yes."

"Yes?"

"Yes. Absolutely. I love you, and I want to have kids with you."

Kim hugged me tightly and gave me another long, slow, wet kiss. A transcendent kiss. When we came up for air, she whispered, "Wanna get started?"

"Absolutely."

And so we did.

I had never made love to a woman without protection. But this time, attempting to create new life . . . was joyous in ways that I had never experienced.

After we both climaxed, Kim sighed theatrically and said, "Wow."

I agreed, "Wow."

We both laughed, but when I turned to kiss her, I saw that her eyes were watery.

"I love you," she whispered.

"I love you, too."

We lay on our backs, our arms touching, and stared at the ceiling. It was about 5:30 P.M., so it was pretty dark outside. A soft glow permeated through the windows from lights in other buildings and the streetlights.

"Why do you think the Chairman sends me after people like Fuchs?"

"Isn't this the kind of thing you talk to Harry about?"

"He'll go all Socratic on me, and I hate that. He knows all the answers, but he wants me to find them."

"Is that so bad?"

"No, but right now, I'd rather talk to you. We're both trudging along the road of happy destiny, trying to figure out our relationships with God. I'd much rather hear what you have to say."

"Okay, but . . . trudging the road of happy destiny? Where'd that come from?"

"It's a paraphrase from the Big Book, you know, *Alcoholics Anonymous*."

"Hmm. I like it."

"Me, too. Anyway, why do you think the Chairman sends me after people like Fuchs?"

"Didn't this case start with you trying to help someone else?"

"Yes. This little old lady, actually, she wasn't all that old. Anyway, Mrs. Schörner wanted me to find and help her nephew, a guy named Willi Axmann."

"And you found him, helped him, and that led to Fuchs?"

"Not quite. I found Willi at Fuchs's house of prostitution. The only thing I helped him with was an introduction to the NYPD."

"What did you tell his aunt?"

"I reminded her that I had said I would do what I could for him, and the only thing I could do was turn him over for arrest."

"And after dealing with the prostitution ring, you went after Fuchs."

"Yes. But he wasn't part of my original mission. I was done once I found Willi."

"Do you think it's a coincidence that the Chairman sent you after Willi and that led you to Fuchs?"

"I think coincidence is—"

"—God's way of staying anonymous."

"Yup."

"So you've always thought that the Chairman wanted you to straighten out Fuchs."

"Yup. I mean . . . oh, I don't know what the hell I mean. He's a neo-Nazi. It's all right to want to get this ugly bunch of neo-Nazis, right?"

"I think so. But you don't want to let your emotions run so high that—"

"—it clouds my judgment."

"Yes."

"I keep telling myself that, but I'm not sure it does any good."

"Why do . . . you think you feel this way?"

I sat up and exhaled in resignation. "I hate to admit it, but you were right when you asked me about Laurie. She's not directly involved, obviously. She's dead. And she wasn't killed by a neo-Nazi. But . . . somehow . . ."

"She was Jewish, and this guy hates Jews. You're still trying to defend her."

"I guess so."

Kim put her arms around my shoulders and pulled herself tight to me. "I love that you want to make things right for her, but you know that you can't."

"I know."

After a long pause, she said, "But you're going after Fuchs."

"Yes, I am."

"Then go get him. But first, Thanksgiving leftovers!"

The leftovers were every bit as delicious as they had been on Thursday. After dinner, we skipped coffee and dessert and hopped back into bed. Trying to make a baby was incredible for our libidos. And for the lovemaking.

Afterward, I left Kim asleep. I got dressed, grabbed my pack, and went to the roof patio to wait for Harry's whooshing. It was cold and clear, and the nighttime vistas were spectacular. South past Manhattan's midtown to the far shore of the Hudson River and the new towers of the

Jersey City skyline. North to the George Washington Bridge. I had seen these views many times, but tonight everything seemed completely different. I was on the path to fatherhood. Or maybe I was just experiencing a new sort of afterglow. Considering the normal, confused state of my emotions, anything was possible.

*   *   *

Harry whooshed me on the dot of 12:30 A.M. to a roof. Just your basic townhouse roof. There was a small shack-like structure at one end. A couple of ventilation stacks. Cable TV wires snaking this way and that around the edges of the roof. The Upper East Side neighborhood consisted of a mix of four- and five-story townhouses and large apartment buildings. Fortunately, no one was watching out the windows that overlooked the roof.

"Where are we?"

"On the building next to the *gesellschaft*," Harry replied, pointing east. "Fuchs's club is that way. It's one story shorter than this building."

I walked to the edge of the roof townhouse, looked down, and grunted.

"What was that for?" Harry asked.

"What was what for?"

"You grunted. 'Humph.' Why?"

"I guess I expected a big swastika painted on the roof."

"Are you disappointed?"

"Maybe a little." I scanned the *gesellschaft* roof. "No guards or dogs. Anything that I need to know about? Infrared beams? Pressure sensitive plates on the roof?"

"No."

"Boy, they should have hired me to consult on their security." I stared through the dark at the shack on the *gesellschaft*'s roof and the door that led to its stairway. Pointing at it, I asked, "Standard lock on the door?"

"Yes."

"Alarm system touchpad inside the door?"

"Yes."

"Did you brief Naomi and Stewart on this place?"

"Of course. They are waiting for your call."

I climbed over the short wall at the roof's edge, hung the full length of my arms, and dropped. I rolled as I hit the roof, more to keep the noise to a minimum than to lessen the impact. It wasn't that far, maybe 6 feet from the bottom of my crepe soles to the roof.

I came out of the roll onto my feet very quietly. I slipped in AirPods and called my tech team.

"Hey, Jack." It was Naomi, who was on a speakerphone.

"Thanks for taking this call. I know it's late."

"Not by our standards," Stewart said.

"Great. I'm going to pick the lock on the door to the stairs, then I'll have about 30 seconds to deal with the alarm system."

"Harry told us it's a Steel Vise 3000," Stewart said.

Naomi added, "Before you pick the lock, I want you to run the app I gave you. Plug in the cable to your phone, the one with the tiny alligator clips. Take out the smallest, flat-headed screwdriver you have. Once you pick the lock, find the touchpad, slide the screwdriver head under the center bottom of the pad and gently lift, popping off the front panel."

"Then I use the alligator clips on the electrical leads coming off the alarm's processor chip, right?"

"Yes."

"Does it matter which clip goes on which lead?"

"No. Just clip fast. The app on your phone will recognize the alarm system so I can disarm it."

"Thank God you're on my side."

"Thank me when I've disarmed the system *and* the alarm hasn't gone off."

"Remember, Jack," Stewart added, "move smoothly and swiftly. Every second you use is a second less for Naomi."

"Got it." I booted up Naomi's special app, inserted the cable with the alligator clips into the phone, and laid it and the screwdriver immediately next to the door. I took a very deep breath, put a small flashlight in my mouth like a light-spouting cigar, aimed the light at the lock, and set to work. The lock was a brand that was reputed to be impossible to pick, and I hadn't tried to pick a lock in a very long time. After a few minutes, the flashlight in my mouth felt like it weighed ten pounds. My jaw was clenching from the effort to hold it. But I forced myself to proceed patiently and was rewarded with the sound of the lock's tumblers falling into place. I reached down for my phone and the screwdriver, placed my hand on the doorknob, twisted, pushed the door open, and stepped inside. The touchpad was to my right, blinking and softly beeping in its thirty-second countdown.

Still holding the flashlight in my mouth, I put the screwdriver under the pad's front panel and popped it off. The alligator clips went onto the two leads. A progress wheel began spinning on the phone's app.

"I'm in," Naomi whispered.

Why the hell was *she* whispering?

A box-shaped icon was blinking red on my phone. Below the icon, a digital clock was counting down the seconds . . . 13 . . . 12 . . . 11 . . . 10 . . . 9 . . . and then stopped, frozen on 9. The icon was now blinking green.

"Plenty of time." Stewart said in a voice slightly louder than a whisper.

"Quick hands, Jack," Naomi said. "You gave me a lot of time to work in."

"Relatively speaking. Is the alarm system for the entire place disabled?"

"Yeah. It's just you and the night watchman. Maybe the janitor."

"Very comforting. And very nice work by you. Thanks. I'm off to pillage and plunder."

I disconnected the call, tugged the cable out of the phone, shut down the app, and packed the cable, the lock picks, and the screwdriver back in the pack. I tugged on my shoulder holsters and slid the Rugers, with suppressors, into their snug pockets. I also put the blackjack into my right cargo pocket. If you get up close and personal, a blackjack is very effective and often quieter than a gun with a suppressor. Depends on how much of a *SMACK!* the thing made when it connected.

It occurred to me that I hadn't seen Harry since I had dropped off the neighboring building's roof. I poked my head out the door; no sign of him anywhere.

I crept down the stairs, moving with extreme caution. I didn't want to alert any security personnel by stepping on a creaking floorboard. The staircase descended to a hallway that ran along the left side of building. At the far end of the hall, another set of stairs went down to the third floor.

There were two doors along the hallway, both locked, but it was much easier to pick those locks than the rooftop lock had been. Each door opened to a small apartment: living room/dining room, kitchenette, bedroom, and bathroom. The décor looked like something out of the Great Depression: faded, floral-pattern wallpaper and wall-to-wall carpets in a dark tan. No one appeared to be living in either place. I suspected that Fuchs used the rooms to house some of his henchmen. Were the members of a neo-Nazi gang properly called "henchmen?" I wondered. Hmm.

The third floor was the same as the fourth. However, one of the two apartment doors was open, and music was playing inside. It took me a long moment to recognize the song: "This I Promise You" by NSYNC. Seemed like an awfully drippy tune for a neo-Nazi. Which didn't mean the guy wasn't dangerous.

I pulled out a Ruger with my right hand, stepped to the door frame, and leaned around the edge. Two men were quietly chatting. One sat on the bed, the other in an over-stuffed armchair. Their heads snapped in my direction. I stepped quickly into the room, pointing my pistol at the guy on the bed.

"Be quiet. Kneel on the floor with your hands above your heads."

They did what they were told. Both men were medium height and build. The music was coming from a smart speaker. Much as I wanted to turn it off, this didn't seem to be the time to fool around with whatever device of theirs was playing the music just so I wouldn't have to listen to NSYNC. The men noticed that I was looking at the smart speaker and threw a knowing glance at each other.

"Don't do anything stupid," I said. "I'm not distracted by the music."

I eased out of my backpack straps and felt in a pocket with my left hand for plasticuffs. Pointing my Ruger at Bed Guy, I said, "Turn around, and put your hands behind you." I handed the plasticuffs to the other guy. "Put these on your friend, here. And cinch them tight."

He did as instructed.

"Now turn around, hands behind your—"

Instead of turning all the way, he rolled at my legs. I couldn't bring my gun down fast enough to knock him out. He caught me at the knees, knocking me to the floor. He scrambled on top of me, stretching for my gun hand. I hit him with a left jab—a short yet vicious punch that popped him off of me.

We both staggered to our feet, and he came at me again. He *was* a speedy little bastard. He tackled me with his arms around my waist and slammed me back into the wall. I brought my knee up hard, catching his shoulder, and straightening him up. I pistol-whipped the guy, and he slumped to the floor.

Unfortunately, while we had been fighting, Bed Guy had managed to pull his cuffed wrists under his feet so that now his hands were in front of him. Still cuffed, but dangerous, especially since he was on his feet. And grabbing a gun from a dresser drawer.

Bed Guy wasn't quite as fast as the speedy little bastard, but he was quick. He got off an errant shot that went through the open door and into the hallway wall opposite.

I fired three times, all three to his upper chest. His corpse dropped on top of the little speedy bastard.

The noise from Bed Guy's shot had alerted someone else in the townhouse. Footsteps pounded up the stairs, rounded into the hallway, and stopped. I heard the action being worked on at least two weapons. I dove for the floor as a torrent of bullets tore through the old walls. It would be ironic if a pair of neo-Nazis were shooting at me with Israeli-made Uzis but, in fact, it sounded like they were using Heckler & Koch UMPs, solid German weapons. All I knew was that bullets tore through the hallway, chewing up the walls. Then the firing stopped. It must have been time for a magazine change.

I rolled into the doorway, spotted two shooters, and fired until one Ruger was empty. One shooter, a woman, crashed backward into the wall at the top of the stairs and then slid down to the floor. The other shooter, a man, flopped down the stairs out of sight.

I stood up, slipping a new magazine into my pistol. I double-checked the two guys on the floor of the bedroom. The man I put three shots into was dead, of course. The other was still unconscious. I hurried down the hall to the female shooter. I grabbed her gun, and yes, it was a Heckler & Koch UMP. I made sure it was empty and tossed it down the hall.

The male shooter was sprawled about halfway down the stairs. Given the two bullet holes in his torso, the extreme angle of his head, and his wide-open eyes, it was a safe bet that he wouldn't be bothering anyone ever again.

I knelt next to the woman and put my fingers on her neck. She had a pulse. She'd also been hit twice, once in the right shoulder and once just below her rib cage. Both bullets had gone clean-through her. I picked her up and carried her back to the bedroom, stepped over the unconscious victim, and placed her on the bed.

I grabbed towels from the bathroom and Bed Guy's belt, which I used to wrap the towel tightly around her rib wound. Maintaining pressure on her shoulder wounds, however, was tough.

"Harry?"

No sign of my heavenly partner.

"Harry? I *need* you. This woman *needs* you. Please?"

"Just what do you think I can do?" he said.

"Well, if you felt like curing these wounds in miraculous fashion, that would be good. If not, I need you to sit here and keep pressure on both sides of her shoulder."

He sat next to me on the bed, reached over, and slid his hands under mine, maintaining the pressure on her shoulder wounds. "What are you planning to do while I save this woman's life?"

"I'm going to call 9-1-1 and then find what we came for. Find it in a New York minute."

"Next floor. Office at the back of the building."

"Thanks," I said, dialed 9-1-1, and hurried downstairs.

"9-1-1. What is the nature of your emergency?"

It was tricky stepping over the man sprawled on the stairs and talking coherently into the phone at the same time. The man was a broken, bloody mess.

"Gunfire at *Gesellschaft der Deutschen* at 230 East

299

85th Street. All suspects subdued. Send an ambulance." I clicked off.

On the second floor, I headed to the rear of the building and found the office door. Locked. Since I didn't have time to pick any more locks, I got through this door the old-fashioned way: I kicked it in. Inside, the room looked as if it had been an apartment similar to those upstairs, but the walls had been opened up, creating one large office. There were three desks and a couple of couches. Sirens were screaming in the distance and getting louder every second.

A Dell XPS 15 laptop computer, like the one I'd taken from Fuchs's home in Riverdale, sat in the middle of one of the desks.

Since maintaining a low profile on my expedition to the *Gesellschaft der Deutschen* was now out of the question, I was going to steal the laptop. My original plan was to copy the hard drive so that maybe Fuchs wouldn't realize security had been compromised at the *gesellschaft*, but as I often reminded myself: men plan, God laughs. I unplugged the laptop, tucked it into my backpack, and ran upstairs.

By the time I reached the third floor, the sirens were accompanied by the screeching of brakes. The NYPD had arrived.

Harry was still applying pressure to the woman's shoulder wound. Her eyes were open. I crouched next to the bed and took one of her hands in mine.

"The police and an ambulance are on their way. You're going to be all right."

"Thank you," she croaked in a whisper. "Why?"

"Why are we helping you?"

She nodded. As much as a person lying on her back can nod.

"It's the right thing to do," I said.

A door crashed open below us. I heard shouts from the police and seconds later, feet came pounding up the stairs.

Harry said, "I want to wait till the last second to keep the wound closed for as long as possible."

"Sounds good."

The woman squeezed my hand.

SWAT officers were rushing up the stairs. Harry looked at me and winked. A second later—

16

We were standing outside Naomi and Stewart's building in Chelsea.

"You're not going to make me climb all those steps, are you?" I asked. "I'm tuckered out from this evening's exertions."

"No, you don't have to climb. But I wanted to give you a second to catch your breath before we met with Naomi and Stewart."

"That's very kind of you. One might say it's almost angelic."

"One might. You won't."

"Not me—"

Harry whooshed us to Naomi and Stewart's front door. He knocked, and Stewart's voice came from behind the door.

"Harry?"

"Yes."

Assorted door locks clicked and tumbled open. I counted four different locks.

"Did you add a lock?"

Stewart grinned.

"You take your security seriously," I said, stepping inside.

"Yeah, and the door's steel-plated. You'd need a

battering ram to get through it."

"I never seem to be able to get my hands on a good battering ram when I need one."

Stewart waved at us to follow him. Naomi was waiting at the computer-laden tables.

"Hey, Jack. Harry."

"Hello, Naomi."

"Have you brought us a gift?"

"Yes, another one of Fuchs's computers." I handed it over to Stewart, who plugged it in and powered it up.

"Same kind of laptop as the last one," he observed.

"Yup."

"Bet Fuchs uses the same security on this one."

"Which would make your life easier, wouldn't it?"

"Yeah." Stewart's fingers moved quickly over the keyboard and touchpad. "There we are," he said he completed the logon, and the laptop's normal screen appeared.

"Do you guys want to wait?" Naomi asked.

"Won't it take you a while . . . ?"

"No, shouldn't be too long. We've already developed a theory based on some assumptions that—we think—aren't too far-fetched," Naomi said.

"*Too* far-fetched when you consider that we're dealing with a neo-Nazi terrorist?" I asked.

"Yup," Stewart said.

"All we need to do is check this computer for any data that would support—or better yet, confirm—our theory. Since we know what we're looking for, it shouldn't take too long."

"Great. Should I make myself useful and go get us some caffeinated beverages?"

"That would be fantastic," Stewart said. "The usual for me."

"Me, too," Naomi added.

"Harry do you want anything? Or do you want to come with me?"

"I'll accompany you."

As soon as the front door closed behind us, Harry whooshed us to Buona Tazza, which, true to its roots as a place to hang out in Greenwich Village, stayed open till 2:00 A.M. We had 30 minutes to spare when we walked in. We ordered a double espresso for Naomi and a dirty chai tea for Stewart. Mine was a cappuccino with an extra-espresso shot. Harry passed. His loss.

"Would you mind indulging me in a bit of speculation?" I asked.

"Just ask your question."

"Maybe you'll answer, and maybe you won't."

Harry waited.

"Right. Does Fuchs know about the break-in at the *gesellschaft*?"

"That's not speculation. That's inquiry."

"Call it what you want. Does he know?"

Harry looked heavenward for inspiration and said, "He will find out in a few minutes."

"Is he going to move up his timetable for the big finale? And that question, by the way, calls for you to speculate."

"It's not speculation if I actually know the answer."

"Do you know the answer?"

"No. But it I was to make an informed guess—"

"Yes, please, guess!"

"Fuchs will move in less than 24 hours. I'll give you as much advance warning as possible."

"Will your warning be early enough?"

"It will be what you need."

"Oh, please, stop with the need stuff. I bet he's going this morning."

"It is this morning. Saturday morning."

"Thank you," I said without the tiniest trace of gratitude. "As soon as Fuchs knows the *gesellschaft* was broken into, which you said will be in a few minutes, he'll want to activate his plot. Gives us less time to stop him."

"What do you think his timing will be?"

"He'll go as soon as he can prepare his trucks as bombs." I pondered the challenges facing Fuchs. "Trucks are only allowed to use certain designated routes into Manhattan. Fuchs wants to hit his targets; he doesn't want any of his trucks stopped by the police because they're traveling on a non-designated route."

"So?" Harry, my non-driving partner asked.

"So, from here, the drivers will take the Bruckner Expressway down to the RFK Triborough Bridge, then take local roads to get to whatever the hell the targets are. Fuchs will want to give them plenty of time, even on a Saturday morning. If the drivers leave the Bronx at 8:30 or 9:00, even with a minimum of an hour driving time, his drivers could hit places Times Square by mid-morning when the tourists are just beginning to congregate. Maybe Battery Park where the ferry for the Statue of Liberty and Ellis Island dock." I paused, considered the ugly realities, and said, "If I were a crazed, neo-Nazi villain, I'd go after the big, Jewish-controlled media like *The New York Times*, which is right across the street from the Port Authority Bus Terminal. And NBC, which is at Rockefeller Center. And probably some of the big synagogues."

"Why those places?"

"Anti-Semitic and high-news value. Terrorists want to use the media to frighten people and get their own twisted message out. Kill as many people as you can, then issue some anti-Semitic screed."

I stared at the barista then out the large window of Buona Tazza, shifting my weight from one foot to the other. Easy does it, Tyrrell. Easy does it, or you're going to have to switch to decaf.

"You seem more anxious than usual," Harry observed.

"Oh come on, I defeat neo-Nazi terror attacks at least once a month. This is just the same old, same old."

Harry focused on me and slowly shook his head. "Are you worried about the manpower, or the different trucks with all of their explosives or—"

"The evil nature of *Oberste Ordnung*?"

"Or the immediate and awful consequences if you fail to stop these trucks?"

I didn't say anything.

"It's possible that thousands of people could be killed and hurt," Harry said.

"Thanks for your encouragement."

"I'm not the one you should turn to when you need . . . *reassurance*."

"If I pray for the Chairman's help, will everything work out?"

"You know that's not how it works."

"No guarantees, right?"

"That's correct."

"This is one of those times I have to have faith."

"Yes, it is."

"But I want certainty."

"Ah, certainty. I believe you can find it in the dictionary. Somewhere between 'catastrophe' and 'chaos.'"

I glared at Harry in response—a look I had perfected in the Marshals Service. A facial expression that would wither the most hardened criminal. A glare that would make brutal fugitives stop and reconsider the error of their ways. It bounced off of Harry like bullets off of Captain America's shield.

The barista place our order on the counter. I paid, and Harry scooped up the recycled cardboard tray.

"Are Naomi and Stewart going to figure this out?" I asked.

Harry walked toward the front door and said over his shoulder, "Let's go see."

We were on the sidewalk for an instant, and then—

Whoosh. We were standing outside Naomi and Stewart's front door.

"Can I ask you something entirely different?"

"Yes."

I jerked a thumb at the door, indicating the two people on the other side of it, "They know about the Chairman, right?"

"Yes, they are aware that we all work for the Chairman."

"Do they know that you're . . . you know, a semi-divine being? An angel?"

"They know that I'm not like other men they've met. I'm not sure how deep or well-thought out their faith is. Everyone comes to know the Chairman differently."

"Okay, time to deliver the beverages and check out their theory."

I knocked, and Stewart let us in. After we had distributed drinks, and I asked, "Any luck?"

"Plenty," Stewart replied. "We found some things on the new computer you brought us that support our theory."

"Which is?"

"Remember we told you that Fuchs only used his

stockpile of cash to buy trucks and gasoline?"

"Yes."

"Well, he bought eight, severe-duty Freightliner trucks with tanker trailers. Each tanker holds about 9,000 gallons."

"And he's filled all those tankers with gasoline?"

"Yes, he has."

"So, you think he's going to turn the trucks into giant Molotov cocktails? Cause frankly, that's what I think."

Naomi said, "Well, you did compare him with the Baader-Meinhof gang. And we agree with you. Fuchs is a terrorist, and we think he's going to burn something down. Or several somethings. He might do a truck per target, or two or three trucks per target."

"But most buildings are hardened against attack these days. They have barriers on the sidewalks to prevent anyone from doing what Timothy McVeigh did in Oklahoma City," I pointed out.

"That's true, but an exploding truck spraying burning gasoline all over the place could still make a hell of a lot of noise and kill a bunch of people," Stewart said.

"But gasoline doesn't explode, it burns. Fuchs will need explosives to ignite the gasoline. And detonators to set off the explosions that will start the fires and—" I searched for the right word, "*hurl* the burning gas all over the place. Where's he going to get explosives and detonators?"

Naomi said, "That's what we wondered, but then Stewart remembered that the front for the drug factory in Queens was König Raw Materials, which sells construction supplies. We checked and discovered that the store has the paperwork necessary to sell explosives *and* detonators for demolition."

I spoke quietly, "Holy moly. I think you've got it. Where are the trucks?"

"In the Bronx, at Colgate Trucks and Equipment. All in one place," Stewart responded. "And that's probably a lucky break. If you can stop them before they leave Colgate, you won't have to worry about identifying their final targets."

"That's good. Really good."

"But," Naomi said and let the word hang in the air like a speech balloon in a comic book, "you've got a problem."

"And that would be?"

"Fuchs hasn't ordered any more trucks or gasoline. It looks like he's ready to go. These trucks could be rolling any day now."

"My colleague here," I gestured toward Harry, "has informed me that the trucks will be on the move in a few hours."

"Will you be able to stop them?" Naomi asked.

"Got to."

Stewart shook his head, "Better you than me."

"You all have special skills," Harry pointed out.

"You and Naomi are the brains. Jack is more the brawn department."

"Thanks for that ringing endorsement," I said.

"I gotta go use the facilities," Stewart said, standing up from his computer and walking to the rear of the apartment where the bathroom was located.

"The chai tea goes right through him," Naomi grinned.

I spoke softly, "This may come as a surprise to you, but he really likes you."

"I like him, too," she responded a bit too quickly.

"You know what I mean."

"Why do you care?"

"My mission working for the Chairman is to help others. Right now, I'm just trying to help the two of you."

"He's not my idea of boyfriend material."

"You might be surprised if you gave him a chance."

"What makes you say that?"

"He's smart. He *likes* you. He *respects* you. How many guys like that do you think exist? If the two of you ever left this apartment, you could probably have a nice time."

"Maybe . . . ," she paused for a long moment. "Are you doing this as a favor to him?"

"I think I'm doing it as a favor to both of you."

"What's in it for you?"

"If you go out with him, I get a month of

milkshakes."

"Chocolate or vanilla?"

"Chocolate, of course."

"Really, a month of milkshakes?" she asked, laughing.

"I wish," I chuckled.

Stewart walked back into the room at that moment. "What's so funny?"

"Nothing," Naomi said, which made both of us laugh more.

Stewart twisted his head from Naomi to me and back to Naomi.

She reached out and stroked his arm, "Sorry, it would take too long to explain. Don't worry about it."

He glanced down at her hand and immediately jerked his eyes away.

"Hey," I said, and pulled out my phone, "I'm sending you the contact info for Diego Quintana, a detective with NYPD's Counterterrorism Bureau. Please send him all the data you have on Fuchs. And send it soon."

"With a roadmap that explains how they can connect the data dots to lead to Fuchs?" Naomi asked.

"Perfect," I replied.

"Should we tell him we're friends of yours?" Stewart inquired. "Does he know who you are?"

"Yes and yes."

"Okay if we use a phony e-mail account?"

"Sure. Knock yourself out. Disguise your identity. Bounce the e-mail off of multiple servers and IP's—"

"Easy there, Jack," Stewart put out his hand as if to restrain me, "don't hurt yourself trying to make it sound like you know what you're talking about."

"That hurts my feelings."

"I know how to hide my identity from the NYPD. Don't worry about it."

"You're the man, Stewart."

Naomi chuckled, and Stewart and I exchanged tart grins.

"Do you have to go to Fuchs's place on Colgate Avenue?" Naomi asked. "Can't we just warn," she checked the information I'd given them, "Detective Quintana?"

I shrugged, "We don't have any hard evidence of a crime, so I have to go."

"But . . . it'll be dangerous, won't it?"

"Maybe a little." I looked at Harry and said, "We should let these kids get their beauty sleep. If you wouldn't mind, I need to go back to my place and grab the tools I'm taking to the Bronx."

"That sounds like a good idea," he replied. Too Stewart and Naomi he said, "Thank you for all your help."

"You're welcome," Naomi said.

"Yeah, anytime," Stewart added.

I said. "You guys have helped save a lot of lives."

*   *   *

313

Once Harry had whooshed us to my apartment, I went the express route for unpacking: I unzipped every pocket in the backpack, overturned it, and dumped everything on my bed. All of the climbing equipment I had so carefully included for the adventure at the *gesellschaft* adventure—and not used—was pushed to one side. Great planning there, Tyrrell. I also shoved aside the blackjack and brass knuckles. They didn't seem like the kind of tools I'd use to stop huge trucks. I also put the empty ammo magazines on the desk in my office, so I'd remember to reload.

I reconsidered the coil of rope on the bed and decided to tuck it into the pack along with my guns, holsters, and fresh magazines. I swapped out the partially used mag in one of the Rugers and inserted a fully loaded magazine in its place. I added more grenades of both the flashbang and smoke variety, giving me a total of six each. I also took a half-dozen burner phones—my entire supply—and tucked them into the pack. My pack was getting heavy and lumpy.

Finally, I went to the secret storage in my closet and grabbed an Uzi and several extra ammo magazines. The magazines went into the overstuffed pack. The Uzi itself I slung over my right shoulder. The pack was now too heavy and bulged in all sorts of ungainly ways.

"I don't suppose you'd like to carry a nice, little gun or two. Maybe a bazooka?" I asked Harry.

"You don't have a bazooka."

"That's right, I don't. Could you get me one? Now?"

"No."

"Got it. Do you want a gun or two of your own?"

"You know that's not how I do things."

"Listen, I don't mean to complain, but I've got to stop eight drivers and who knows how many others from blowing up a bunch of places all over New York City. Do you think you could change how you do things? Just this once?"

Harry gave me a long, pained look that seemed to indicate that he did feel I was complaining. I might go so far as to say he thought I was whining. To which my response was: REALLY? Eight guys with exploding trucks and probably guns, maybe other guys with guns, and all of the guys with guns also had truly nasty dispositions, and hundreds, maybe thousands of lives were at stake. How could my words be construed as whining?

Much as I hated doing it, I got rid of the Uzi and its extra magazines. I tucked a couple of the mags for the Rugers into my pants pockets. The pack was almost useable. I pared down the grenades by two each of the flashbang and smoke varieties. Damn, it was hard leaving such destructive hardware behind.

I checked the time; it was 6:22 A.M. "Is the balloon about to go up?"

"Excuse me?"

"It's a phrase meaning an operation is being launched. Do I have some time before Fuchs sets things in motion?"

"I believe so. The Chairman has not indicated I should alert you yet."

"Would you mind whooshing me to Kim?"

"She's asleep."

"I know. But I'd like to see her and give her a kiss."

Harry seemed perplexed. "This isn't like you. What's wrong?"

"I . . . I don't know. Fuchs is so . . . evil. It gives me the heebie jeebies."

"*Heebie jeebies*? Do you mean you're suffering from a premonition of impending disaster?"

"Yeah, sure, I'm having a premonition."

"And this leads to your wanting to say a final farewell to Kim."

"Well, hopefully not for a *final* farewell. But yes, I want a chance to see her again and say goodbye. Even if she's asleep."

Harry nodded and a second later we were in Kim's living room. I placed my pack on the floor and said, "Thanks."

Harry disappeared without a word as I walked to Kim's bedroom. She stirred when the door clicked open.

"Hey," she said in a husky, half-asleep whisper.

"Hey yourself. Sorry I woke you."

"You coming to bed?"

316

"Just wanted to stop by and give you a kiss. I gotta be somewhere."

She glanced at the ancient clock-radio by her bed. "At this time of morning?"

"Yup."

"The bad guys have early hours, huh?"

"Yup." I leaned over and kissed her gently on the lips. "Go back to sleep."

"Come back to me."

"I will."

I tiptoed out of the room, collected my pack, and went to the patio on Kim's roof. Across the Hudson, the Palisades loomed dark above the river. A lone tugboat pushed a long, ugly barge upriver.

I turned my head up to the sky. Not that I thought the Chairman resided in some spiritual zone in the sky. But after a lifetime spent in Catholic schools and churches, I was used to looking up whenever I sought God. I was also used to bowing my head, but that seemed more apropos when I was feeling guilt. Or sadness. When asking for help, it seemed to me that I should seek it from above.

When I had been an undergrad at Fordham, I had taken a course called "Prayer and Warfare," which had focused on the many cultures that had prayed and offered sacrifice while asking for divine assistance in battle. It always struck me as ironic that people appealed to their various deities for aid in killing their fellow humans. As part of the course, we had studied a prayer that Fr. James

317

O'Neill had written for General George Patton on the eve of battle in December 1944. It seemed appropriate to my situation, given that both Patton and I were about to engage Nazis:

"Graciously hearken to us who call upon Thee that, armed with Thy power, we may advance from victory to victory, and crush the oppression and wickedness of our enemies and establish Thy justice. . ."

Crush the wickedness of our enemies. Amen to that.

* * *

PRE-DAWN – GERHARD FUCHS'S HOME
PALISADE AVENUE, RIVERDALE

KATERINA ASCHGRAU spoke without any emotion, "The *Gesellschaft der Deutschen* was broken into."

Fuchs groaned softly. "Let me guess: a tall man, took out all my guards, no clear images on the security cameras, and he stole my laptop."

"Yes."

"Tyrrell strikes again." Fuchs's tone was not an admiring one. "I wonder what I have to do to stop him?"

"I'm sorry, I don't have an answer to that."

Fuchs swiveled in his office chair and stared out the window into the night. "I don't think I can afford to wait anymore. Time to strike out at the Jewish establishment and hit them in a way no one will ever forget." After a moment, he swiveled back and said, "Give the order. Have the trucks prepared."

"When do you want them to go?"

"As soon as they're ready." He stood up. "Alert them that I'm headed there now. I'll do a final check and give the order myself." He left the room with a quick, precise step that was almost a march.

Aschgrau picked up the phone on his desk. "Start the preparations. Fuchs will be there in 15 minutes."

17

Harry and I stood on the sidewalk outside of Colgate Truck & Equipment Sales on Colgate Avenue, just south of the Bruckner Expressway and a bit east of the Bronx River. Across Colgate from us stood a row of bare trees, a parking lot, and an apartment building. There were a few lights on in some of the apartments but not many. Still way too early on a Saturday morning for most of the residents.

We were standing next to an 8-feet high wall made of corrugated metal panels, topped by multiple strands of razor wire. It wasn't a thing of beauty, but it was a simple and damn effective deterrent for someone with my stealthy inclinations.

"I don't suppose you'd consider whooshing me to the other side of this wall," I said.

"I'd consider it."

"Okay, after careful consideration, will you whoosh me inside?"

"No."

"You are a. . . ," I stopped short of expressing my full thought. I wasn't on the brink of a profanity, but there was no point in going negative. Assuming Harry had feelings, my being insulting wouldn't hurt them in the slightest. Besides, what was the point of my trying to hurt his feelings? Tyrrell, you can be such a child . . .

I walked to the south end of the wall and peered around the corner. "Does this wall go all the way around this place?" I asked Harry who had followed me.

"Yes," he replied.

"Ohhhhhhhkay," I sighed and headed back up Colgate Avenue, sizing up the trees that ran alongside the road. There was a large maple with several thick branches stretching out over the razor wire. The lowest branch looked like it could support my weight and was about 12 feet above the sidewalk. It also might as well have been on the far side of the moon as there were no hand- or footholds up to that branch.

I dug the rope out of my pack, ran one end through the trigger guard of a Ruger, double-checked that the safety was on—no point in shooting myself in a climbing accident—swung the rope like a lasso, and released it. The Ruger sailed over the branch with the rope trailing it like the tail of a kite. I caught the pistol, untied it, and holstered it.

Grabbing both strands of the rope and planting my feet against the trunk, I climbed up the tree, hand-over hand. I hauled myself up on the branch and steadied my back against the trunk. I pulled in the rope, coiling it as I did, and tied one end around the left strap of the pack. I looped the rest of the rope over a branch about 4 feet above the branch where I was standing.

I checked the sidewalk below. No sign of my

guardian angel. "Okay, you don't have to be Philippe Petit to handle this," I muttered. "Let's go."

I began walking gingerly along the branch. Every few feet, small branches growing out from the chest-high branch I was using as support forced me to un-loop and then re-loop my support rope. With each step, the branch under my feet creaked lower and lower, bringing me closer and closer to the razor wire. One quick slip, and I'd be in a world of hurt.

As soon as I was past the top of the wall, I swung down and stepped onto the roof of an old school bus that was painted in a weathered lime green. I pulled the rope down, tucked it back into my pack, slid down the windshield, over the hood, and jumped to the ground. I wasn't completely silent, but I was damn close. I carefully peeked over the hood of the bus and scanned the Colgate Truck & Equipment compound.

To my right, battered old SUVs and pickup trucks were parked along the Colgate Avenue wall. There was a gate cut into the wall at the northeast corner of the compound. "Gate" might have been a grand word for what was just a large section of the wall that had been mounted on dolly tracks and was opened and shut by pulleys. At the moment, the gate was closed. To my left, along the southern wall of the compound, stood more parked SUVs and trucks. I couldn't see the far wall because the entire center section of the compound was filled with the eight Freightliner trucks with 9,000-gallon fuel tanks trailing

322

behind them. They had been parked in a diagonal row with their cabs pointed at the gate.

The cabs seemed to come in white, dark-gray, and pale blue. All of the tanks were about 40-feet long cylinders, some silver, others white. All of them had small ladders on the back that went from the rear bumper to the top of the cylinder. At the top of the cylinders was what looked like walkways that the length of each cylinder. All of the tank trailers had the same tire configuration: a pair of double wheels up front where the trailer connected to the truck cab, and then six double pairs in the rear.

Four three-person teams were working on the four trucks nearest me. From what I could see, they were duct-taping explosive packets just ahead of the rear wheels on the right side of the cylinder, a bit more than halfway along its length. As I watched, the team closest to me finished up by attaching a cellphone to a cable coming out of the explosive, then duct-taping the phone into place. The team then screwed a metal flap to the frame to hide the explosive device from prying eyes. They moved forward the gate and stopped to work on the fourth truck in the row.

I waited for the next couple of teams to move forward, then scurried to the recently armed, last truck in the row. I whipped out my phone and photographed the truck and license plate. Because the trucks were parked on a diagonal, the tank screened me from view of anyone working on a truck closer to the gate. Crouching near the now-armed explosive, I sent up a silent prayer that everyone would continue concentrating on rigging his or her detonator explosives. What a good bunch of Hitler Youth, I thought.

Using a screwdriver from my pack, I removed the metal flap, shot a photo, and unplugged the cellphone/detonator. The phone? An iPhone. Gee, if they had just used the Galaxy Note 7, it might have exploded all on its own. I powered off the phone, tucked it into my pack, and replaced the metal flap.

I crawled forward to the next truck, and repeated the process: photos of the truck, license plate, and the explosives, which I disarmed by removing the phones. No one saw me, no alarms sounded, and the explosives were rendered safe.

The fifth and sixth trucks, (fifth and sixth farthest from the gate) were now unattended, so I crawled to them, did my photography bit, and dealt with their explosive packages. However, I added a new wrinkle. I replaced the bad guys' phones with the burners I had brought. Then I popped in my AirPods and called Naomi on my phone.

"Ready to activate?" she asked me without bothering with hello. She seemed excited at the prospect of blowing up some trucks.

"Ready," I whispered.

I watched the burner on the fifth truck as its screen changed to a solid blue color, and a large timer wheel spun on its face. Then a giant checkmark replaced it on the screen.

Naomi said, "Both phones are activated."

"Looks good from here."

I hid the burner by screwing its metal flap back in place. There were voices nearby. I guessed that at least some of the teams had finished, and they were congregating around the truck closest to the gate. I went around the rear end of the fifth truck and went to work on the fourth and third trucks from the gate. With Naomi's activating the phones on those trucks, we had successfully disarmed or taken control of the explosives on six trucks. But if even one truck got loose, it could wreak havoc. All or nothing at all, as Frank Sinatra once sang.

I crept to the truck second closest to the gate. I heard several people discussing the merits of different European soccer clubs. I knew absolutely nothing about soccer other than it is mostly played by kicking a round ball, and that it is the most popular sport on earth. Give me baseball any day. Fortunately, the discussion seemed to be completely engrossing the neo-Nazi explosives crew. No one was paying any attention whatsoever to the second truck. I did my thing, barely breathing the word "Go" to my tech wizard. Naomi did her thing, and one more truck came under our control.

The voices continued, apparently debating which club had the best striker. Whatever the hell that was. One man suggested that strikers were really just high-scoring forwards and that there was no need to designate a "striker." A woman explained that he didn't understand what the hell he was talking about. As long as they were standing and debating at the hood of the truck closest to the gate, I couldn't perform my takeover of the truck's explosive device. I didn't know how much time I had before the trucks started to roll, but a very loud countdown clock was ticking in my head. How dare these neo-Nazis waste my valuable de-sabotaging time?

I dropped to the ground, crawled under the truck, and peered around the tires under the front of the tank. I counted four pairs of legs near the front of the Freightliner closest to the gate. If the explosive package was mounted on the right side of this truck, there was no way I could get to it without being spotted by one of the soccer fans.

"Jack?" Naomi asked. "We ready to go on the last one."

I didn't respond; I was too close to the bad guys.

"Okay, you can't talk," she said. "I'll wait."

A motor whirred on one side of the compound, and the gate slowly began cranking open. A dark Audi sedan drove through, pulling past the nose of the first Freightliner and stopping directly in front of the truck I was hiding under. Out stepped Gerhard Fuchs and Mina Aschgrau. Seeing Fuchs made me extremely anxious. His appearance was too much like that of a commanding officer come to send his troops off on their mission. As Fuchs and Aschgrau walked toward the first truck, the men and women there turned toward them.

Now or never, Tyrrell. I slithered out of my hiding-

326

place, moving slowly as I crossed the open space between the parked tankers. Fuchs and his pack of fanatics were about 20 feet away from me; fortunately, all attention was on Fuchs, the perfect Nazi leader.

"You know why we're here," he began. "You know how important our mission is." He delivered his speech clearly and crisply, but without a wisp of inspiration. "Today, you are going to strike against the Jewish media, in the midst of the Jewish sabbath. You are going to stab the heart of Jewish Manhattan."

As he was speaking, I shot a quick photo of the last truck's license plate then wriggled under it. I sent texts with all the photos I had just taken to Diego Quintana along with the message:

> Fuchs has readied 8 trucks, each carrying approx 9000 gallons of gasoline and explosives. Giant Molotov cocktails. Targets unknown, probably media, NYTimes, NBC large synagogues. Current location: Colgate Trucks & Equipment on Colgate Avenue in the Bronx. Have disarmed 7 trucks. Hope to get last one before too late. Hurry.

As soon as I saw that all of my texts had been sent, I tucked my phone into my coat pocket, wriggled to the far side of the truck, and found the explosive package. I was reaching for it when I heard a harsh voice growl, "Freeze! Or you're a dead man."

Given that I was outnumbered and probably outgunned by a ridiculous margin, I did not freeze. I rolled away from the voice, going back under the truck. Gunfire and ricochet pings filled the compound. Nothing hit me, thank God, and the instant I was clear of the truck, I pushed up to my feet and pulled both Rugers from their holsters. During my under-the-truck roll, I heard Fuchs shouting at some of his thugs to circle the truck and trap me with a pincers movement. He shouted at others to get into the trucks. It looked like he was going to set his plan in motion, at least with some of the trucks.

"Naomi!"

"Yes?"

"Get ready to detonate."

"Are you clear?"

"Just detonate when I tell you to."

"But—"

"—Can't talk. Gotta shoot bad guys."

Footsteps came pounding around each end of the truck, trapping me.

I whipped my head right and left and back again. The split second I saw someone come around the front of the truck, I fired twice. The woman who was leading the charge from that direction crashed back against the Freightliner cab and dropped to the ground.

I twisted back and fired at the man coming around

328

the rear bumper. He went down after three shots. I ran for cover among the trucks and SUVs parked along the compound's western wall.

"Jack? Jack, are you all right?" Naomi almost shouted over the phone.

"A little busy now, Naomi."

Two more gunmen edged around from each end of the truck, moving very slowly, presenting only the tiniest of targets. They both paused as they scanned the pre-dawn darkness. Scanned for me.

Fuchs was still shouting, directing drivers to their trucks. I heard truck doors opening and thunking closed. Engines coughed to life. The engine in the Freightliner closest to the gate, the one with explosives I hadn't disarmed, roared to life.

"Oh, hell," I grunted and ran for the truck. I had one of my Rugers in each hand, arms spread wide, firing to my right and left at the bad guys. This was the kind of action that looked incredibly cool and deadly in the movies. In reality, it was a terrible way to shoot. Taking aim was impossible, unless, like a fish, you have eyes on both sides of your head. Like most humans, my eyes faced front, so running, firing, and hitting a target at my sides was a ridiculously difficult proposition. My only hope was that my shots would force the bad guys to take cover and hinder the effectiveness of their shooting.

It mostly worked.

As I neared the rear bumper of the first truck,

something tore at my right arm, knocked me off balance, and sent me sprawling to the pavement. My right triceps burned like hell, which probably indicated a sizable flesh wound. Not deep or serious, but it felt like someone had taken a blowtorch to my skin. I cursed because everyone knows that cursing has immense curative powers and rolled. I fired with my right hand at the guy who'd shot me. I ignored the ricochets from the other gunman, even though his shots were pinging off the pavement all around me. It only took four shots, but I got the guy who had shot me. I turned to look in the other direction.

The guy on my left had gotten frustrated and was walking toward me, shoving a fresh magazine into his pistol. He lowered his weapon at me from about 10 feet away. I emptied the Ruger in my left hand into the guy. I probably hit him center mass four or five times.

I saw the red glow of brake lights from the rear of the tanker. I heard the transmission being worked and the deep cough of the engine as the lowest gear engaged. The truck started to roll toward the open gate. Fuchs's lead truck, the one with an intact explosive package, was about to get away.

I stood up and tried to avoid thinking about how much my right arm hurt. At that moment, my sleeve was not soaked with blood, which probably meant I wasn't bleeding too much. Probably. Blood loss would exhaust me and, thereby, impede my ability to stop the truck. Not that I was confident I *could* stop the truck.

The driver shifted gears, and the truck picked up a tiny bit of speed. Its front end was passing through the gate as I ran toward the back. I almost reached the rear bumper and the ladder on the rear of the tank, when gunfire forced me to dive for the ground. Aschgrau was firing at me with a submachine gun. This time there were no parked vehicles anywhere near me—no place to hide.

I still had two or three shots left in the Ruger in my right hand. At least, I hoped I did. I pulled my right arm around in front of me and took careful aim while trying to ignore the bullets spewing from her weapon. I shot her three times; my pistol clicked empty on the fourth trigger-pull.

The truck had cleared the gate and swung left to the north, heading to Bruckner Boulevard. The second truck was rolling, right at me. I dove out of the way, somersaulting as I hit the ground and rolling up to my feet. The second truck was almost to the gate.

I ran for the Audi sedan and shouted into my phone, "Blow the trucks!" I yanked the back door open, plunged inside, and scrunched down on the floor.

"What?" Naomi sounded frantic. "Are you clear?"

"Blow the damn trucks!"

The second truck blew up in the middle of the gate. The Audi rocked, and the glare of the fireball rising from the blown tank lit the car's interior. In almost immediate sequence, the next four trucks blew: Boom! Boom! Boom! Boom!

The Audi's windows burst inward, showering the entire interior with little pebbles of safety glass. The explosion's debris pelted the side of the car and rained down on the roof, hood, and trunk. Towering flames turned the pre-dawn light into the equivalent of midday sunshine. And, of course, it was very hot.

I climbed out of the back seat, slid into the driver's seat, and found the key fob in the center console next to the gear shift. I started the car, shifted into drive, and rolled toward the gate. I had to scrape the side of the sedan along the gate's pole to get past the burning truck, but at this point in the proceedings, messing with the Audi's paint job seemed to be the least of my worries. I turned north and gunned the engine. From a mechanical standpoint, the Audi seemed to have survived intact.

Ahead of me, Fuchs's truck was passing under the Bruckner Expressway and continuing north. I followed, flooring the Audi, racing through intersections, desperate to catch up.

"Your genius for making a mess is unsurpassed," Harry said, who was now sitting comfortably in the passenger seat.

"Thank you."

"Does your arm hurt?"

"Does a penguin wear a tuxedo?"

"Well, actually—"

"—Shut up," I said, not really feeling up to our usual, sparkling repartee. "Could you patch me up? Just a

332

quick-and-dirty job to keep the blood loss to a minimum."

He tore open my sleeve and produced several white handkerchiefs, seemingly out of thin air. He wrapped them very firmly around my upper right arm and tied the ends together to keep it in place.

"How is that?" he asked.

"Not bad. Thanks."

"You're welcome."

"Is Fuchs driving that truck?"

"Yes, he is."

"I don't suppose you could disarm the explosive on that truck?"

"No," he replied then added, "What is your plan?"

"My plan is to get really close to the back bumper of that damn truck. Then you are going to switch seats with me—"

"—How do you suggest I do that?"

"If I were you, I'd use magic. But if you insist, we can try to slither over each other and the console while maintaining our high-speed pursuit of the bad guys' explosive-laden truck, and—"

"—I understand. Magic it will be. What next?"

"You drive. I climb out through the shattered windshield and jump from the hood of this car to the ladder on the back of that truck."

There was a very long silence. We had turned right on Morrison Avenue, heading south toward the Bruckner Expressway. I had closed the distance to within twenty

333

yards of the truck. I was going to have to enact my plan very soon. Very, very soon.

"I have to say," Harry finally commented, "that you are not mentally competent."

"Because of my plan?"

"Exactly."

"Fine. We can do it your way. What *is* your way?"

There was another long pause. We had halved the distance to the truck. Only about ten yards to go and closing. . . .

"Maybe you should magically disarm the explosives," I suggested. "Or magically whoosh the explosives away. Or whoosh me into the truck's cab, so I can hijack the truck from the bad guys."

More silence. We turned right again, entered the Expressway, headed toward Manhattan.

"Wait," I said with a huge, insincere grin on my face, "I don't *need* that kind of help. The Chairman is completely comfortable with my plan."

"I'm not certain that the word 'comfortable' means the same thing to the Chairman as it does to you."

"At any rate, in His estimation, I don't *need* help. Maybe that's because He's decided it's time for me to go. When I leap for the ladder, I'll miss, fall to the asphalt of the Bruckner Expressway, and you'll smush me with this car. You, my guardian angel, will be the agent of my death."

"I think it's time for us to switch places."

"So, wait a minute! You're not the least bit worried that you're about to kill me."

"I wouldn't say the 'least bit.'"

I stifled a curse and said, "Let's go." I had barely finished the words when I found myself sitting in the passenger seat.

Harry had pulled the nose of the Audi to within about 3 feet of the rear ladder.

"Oh, shit," I muttered, reached out, grabbed the wiper at its base, and pulled myself through the windshield. It's a hell of a lot easier to think this crap up than it is to do it, believe me. Getting through the windshield's gaping hole was tough enough, but once out on the hood, there was nothing to hang onto. No handholds. Just a smooth metal surface bouncing at forty to fifty miles an hour along a roadway in dire need of repaving. And then turning into a long curve as the boulevard turned southeast. The expressway was climbing to become an elevated highway directly above the boulevard. Harry was keeping the Audi tight behind the truck, but the slope of the climbing entrance ramp made me slide back toward the windshield.

Come on, Tyrrell, the valiant taste of death but once.

I don't know how valiant it was, but I was able to slither forward on my belly to the front of the car. I stretched out my hand toward the ladder—just beyond my reach. I waved Harry forward. He accelerated a tiny bit more, closed the gap by about 6 inches, and the fingers of my right hand curled and locked around the ladder, followed a second later by my left.

I hauled myself up, swung my left leg over the gap between the tank and the car, and planted my foot on the bottom rung of the ladder. Harry stepped on the brakes, the Audi dropped away, and my right foot followed my left to a safe place at the bottom of the ladder.

The truck finished its climb to the elevated expressway. I carefully climbed the ladder, rung by rung. A couple of cars passed us, and I saw wide eyes and hands pointed in my direction. The Saturday dawn traffic was light, and we would reach the RFK Triborough bridge in a few minutes. I really needed to hustle. And do . . . what? I didn't have a clue, I answered myself honestly.

I reached the top of the tank and the gridded walkway down the center. I dug my fingers into the grid and hauled myself up. Was it my imagination, or was my right arm screaming in protest? I could hear the raw voice of a 12-year-old male inside me shouting, "Ow, owww, OWWWW!"

Oh, shut up, I thought. I crawled forward on the grid until I was—by my guesstimate—over the spot where the other explosives had been attached to the other tanks. Okay, Tyrrell, what's next? Keep crawling forward, launch a surprise attack on the truck's cab, and hope you can overpower the two armed men in it? Or tie one end of your handy-dandy rope to the grid, slide down the side of the tank, and disarm the explosives while dangling above the road as it hurtles below you at fifty miles an hour. And, pray that the truck driver doesn't see you in his right sideview mirror. . . .

I dropped my head until it was resting on the metal grid. Mr. Chairman, just what is it you expect me to do? A little divine guidance would be extremely helpful at this point in time. My arm hurt like crazy. I was exhausted. And afraid. And freezing. Riding around at highway speeds in cars without windshields or on the top of a tanker in late November was chilling. I sent my prayer to heaven, wherever that happened to be and waited. Immediately ahead of us was a steel trestle and a digital sign announcing the bridge coming up. Miles away, the towers of Manhattan gleamed in the early morning sun. No time for sightseeing, Tyrrell.

There was also no answer to my prayer. The clouds in the sky did not part and a booming voice did not give me direction. The Freightliner hit a big pothole, and the entire vehicle vibrated. The truck passed under the steel trestle and a sign pointed us to the Manhattan-bound Triborough Bridge about a quarter-mile ahead. Time was running out. I just could not face the prospect of getting to the cab and taking on Fuchs. And probably a Nazi henchman, too. If I took the rope-over-the-side route, I'd get a gravity assist. My fervent hope was that gravity wouldn't assist me straight under the tanker's wheels and directly to my grave. But it seemed the path of least resistance.

Keeping a firm grip on the grid with my left hand, I

wriggled out of the pack's right shoulder strap, dug inside the pack with my cold-numbed right hand, found the rope, and pulled it out. I decided—gambled might have been a more accurate term—that 15 feet of rope was all I needed. Getting a knife out of the pack and cutting off what I guessed to be the correct length of rope and returning the remaining rope and the knife into the pack was tricky. Threading the rope through the grid and tying if securely was quite the challenge with frozen, fumbling fingers. I only made it work by clamping the end of the rope in my teeth and pulling the knot closed. About now, I was having second thoughts about trusting my life to a rope given the givens of this situation. Hell, I was having third and fourth thoughts about it. Enough procrastinating, Tyrrell.

I looped the rope around my waist, secured it to my belt, slowly swung my legs down, and lowered myself hand-over-hand down the side of the tank.

"Lord, if you could keep the driver from looking in his sideview mirror, I'd really appreciate it."

All I needed was a few seconds to get below his line of sight. I was almost at the bottom of the tank. Don't look down, Tyrrell. Don't look down. I looked down. The pavement below whizzed by in a dark-gray blur. A tsunami of anxiety washed over me. Hold on tight. Don't look down. For God's sake, hold on tight. I focused on keeping a firm grip on the rope and felt with my toes for the frame that cradled the giant tank.

My right foot touched a narrow flat surface. I

looked down. I was standing on the edge of the tank's frame. The truck hit another pothole, and my body swung free of the tank's side, my fists clamping tighter than ever around the rope. I swung back in and bumped against the tank. I again found the top edge of the frame and lowered myself a little farther. I was able to slide one of my legs through the frame and sit awkwardly. I was still clutching the rope, but most of my weight now rested on the back of my right thigh. I eased off my grip on the rope and felt the muscles of my shoulders and upper arms burning with the effort I'd been expending to hold on. I looked forward, trying to use the sideview mirror to see inside the truck cab. Nothing. Okay, Tyrrell, get to work. No dawdling. Disarm the bomb on the side of the speeding truck.

*   *   *

DAWN – FREIGHTLINER CAB

FUCHS checked his right sideview mirror and said, "Well, well, well, I believe that bastard Tyrrell is hanging off the side of the tanker."

The Nazi thug compressed his lips and responded, "What's he doing?"

"Hard to say. He's climbing down the side of the tanker. Toward the explosives." Fuchs slowly shook his head, staring out through the windshield at the towers of Manhattan a couple of miles to the south. "You need to get out there."

"What?"

"Get out there. Stop him."

"Why don't we just pull over? Then we get out and shoot him."

"We can't stop if we're going to hit our target."

"Maybe we should abort the mission."

"No," Fuchs pointed a gun at his underling. "We're going through with it. Those explosions back at Colgate probably mean that we're the only truck with a chance of striking the Jews. If you don't get out there, I'll shoot you where you sit and dump your body on the highway."

The underling thought it over, realized he had no choice, released his seatbelt, opened the door and stepped out. He clung to a steel handle at the rear of the Freightliner's cab then climbed down to the trailer hitch, the platform extending over the truck's rear four wheels, where the tanker was connected. Fuchs leaned over the passenger seat and slammed the door shut. He placed his pistol on the passenger seat, dug his phone out of his coat pocket, and placed it next to gun.

Fuchs checked the rear and sideview mirrors and saw his henchman kneeling down as close to the tank as he could get. He was steadying himself with his left hand, a pistol in his right. He extended his arm, taking aim.

*　*　*

I had my legs scissor-locked around part of the

metal frame about a foot from the iPhone detonator. My left hand steadied me against the tank. I reached for the phone with my right hand. The truck bounced and both my hands flew backward, my back arched out from the tank's side, my legs squeezed incredibly tight, and the rope around my waist snapped taut. It hurt like hell.

But I was still riding the truck, still had a chance to disarm this one last explosive. I put my left hand back into position as a brace to stabilize me. My right hand wrapped around the iPhone. I wanted to pull the slender cord connecting it to the explosive package but didn't think I could manage it. Instead, I shoved my index finger into the gap between the phone and the duct tape securing it in place and tugged. And tugged some more. I worked the phone almost an inch away from the side of the tank, shoved a couple of fingers in between the phone and the tank, and—

A bullet pinged and banged through the framework. I had no idea where it went, but it missed me. Another clanked much nearer then ricocheted off of the road. One of the rear tires immediately behind me burst, sending chunks of tire flying everywhere.

The truck zagged close to the right-side guard rail of the RFK Bridge, but Fuchs was able to haul it under control and straighten it in its lane.

Never mind the gunman, Tyrrell, get the damn phone. I tugged it out of its duct-tape cocoon, yanking it straight out until the detonator cable yanked free and dangled uselessly from the explosive. I tossed the phone onto the highway and saw it shatter on the road. Another bullet whined past.

Still maintaining a scissor lock on the frame, I grabbed the frame at a point closer to the front of the tank, pulled a Ruger out of a holster with my right, took a very deep breath—don't look down—and swung so I was suspended under the tanker low over the road.

I ignored the tires spinning so fast I couldn't see the tread, ignored the cold wind in my face, ignored the infinitesimal distance between me and the expressway surface. I focused on the guy who was clinging to the rear end of the cab's trailer hitch. His eyes were wide with fear and his knuckles were white with tension as he gripped the hitch. He was aiming a 9mm pistol in my direction. Well, approximately in my direction. Clinging for life to a speeding tanker truck was far from an ideal shooting solution. Believe me, I knew exactly what challenges he was facing.

He fired again. I saw the spark of contact as the bullet ricocheted off the expressway, heading into the unknown.

"God, help me," I gasped, as I took as careful aim as the circumstances allowed, and fired.

The bullet caught him in the neck. He jerked backward about a foot, let go of the hitch, flopped onto the expressway, and was smashed under the massive wheels on the left side of the tank. The truck continued to roar forward, and I was grateful I couldn't really see what was left of him.

18

I tucked my Ruger into its holster and gripped the rope to haul myself back up to my awkward seat on the frame. It took every bit of strength I had. Panting, I clung to the side of the truck for a minute or so. We were on the Manhattan bound leg of the bridge, curving to the right, headed toward the drawbridge section of the RFK which spanned the Harlem River.

What now, Tyrrell? You can't exactly get off of this speeding vehicle unless it stops. And if it stops, maybe Fuchs will get out and rearm the damn explosives by using his own phone. Or maybe he's got a special, gold-plated, swastika-stamped backup phone for just this purpose. The bad news, I thought to myself, is you're not done, yet. I have to get to the cab. Have to stop Fuchs. Once and for all. And, I didn't have a hell of a lot of time to do it.

My eyes followed the rope up the side of the tank and out of sight to the top. It was only about 10 feet. My shoulders still burned from the exertion of ducking down under the truck and shooting Fuchs's gunman. I honestly wasn't sure I could make it.

"I'll pull you up," shouted a voice.

I looked up but didn't see anyone. "Harry?"

"Who else?"

Talk about *deus ex machina*. Although, to be

precise, this was *angelicus ex machina*. "You're going to haul me up?"

"Come on, Jack. Time for a leap of faith."

"This is more of a hauled-like-a-sack-of-dirty-laundry kind of faith."

"Do you really want to have this discussion now?"

I took a deep breath, gripped the rope with both hands, and shouted, "Ready!"

Harry was strong, I had to give him that. He pulled me up swiftly and easily. He was not breathing particularly hard when I reached the top and grabbed the grid.

"Thank you," I gasped, still panting from earlier efforts. "I think you just saved my life."

"Maybe for the moment." *And* . . . he was gone.

"Now? Really?" I wondered. "Couldn't you just stop the truck?"

There was no answer, of course. I took some more deep breaths, gave myself a two-second pep talk: "You go! Tyrrell!" and began crawling forward. The truck was approaching the eastern tower of the Harlem River drawbridge. There were signs on the tower; the left-hand sign for the FDR Drive down Manhattan's east side. The right sign directing people toward Second Avenue and 125th Street. The truck engine growled deeply as the driver downshifted and the truck slowed. We were descending off the bridge to the streets of Manhattan. I had reached the front end of the tank, just above the Freightliner's trailer hitch.

I swung my legs down the front end of the tank, retaining my grip on the grid, extended my arms as far as they'd go, and dropped down to the hitch. The instant I landed, the truck bounced again. I lurched sideways and was a second away from toppling off the truck when I was able to grasp one of the electrical cables connecting the cab to the tank trailer. Probably supplied power to the trailer's signal lights. Or the brakes. Or the heated swimming pool. I didn't care. What mattered was that it was strong enough to allow me to pull myself back to safety.

Still holding the electrical cable, I stepped to the back of the cab and glanced through the rear windshield. Fuchs's concentration on driving the huge rig was more tightly focused than that of a politician who was about to count his first bribe. I thought about shooting through the windshield, but there was a good chance that even at this short distance, the safety glass would deflect my shot wide. Or, the shot might kill him, and the truck would careen out of control, killing God knew how many people in the ensuing crash.

Stopping the Freightliner posed a potentially lethal conundrum: It was close to a certainty that I would have to use violence to wrest control of the truck from Fuchs. But that would almost certainly cause a crash. We were coming off the bridge onto East 125th Street or Dr. Martin Luther King Jr. Boulevard. Even though 125th Street is a major traffic artery, the early morning hour on a Saturday meant there was very little auto or pedestrian traffic. But if the truck slammed into the front of a building, a couple of dozen people could die before they knew what hit them.

On the other hand, if I didn't gain control over the truck, Fuchs would try to blow it up somewhere with even more people.

The conundrum was solved by the most mundane thing in New York City: a traffic light. A red light at Second Avenue. Fuchs—ever the law-abiding Teuton—stopped. I wasted no time on shock and surprise. My Ruger was in my left hand as my right grabbed the door handle on the cab's passenger side. I swung through onto the passenger seat, knocking a pistol and phone to the floor as I sat. My Ruger went into Fuchs's ribs.

"*Guten morgen, mein herr*," I said. "Pull over and turn off the engine."

He smiled and said, "I don't think so." He shifted into gear and stepped on the gas, driving through the red light.

"You are a hard man to kill," he said. "Which isn't going to help you now."

"If you don't stop this truck right now, I'm going to shoot you."

We were barreling west, crossing Third Avenue.

"You're bluffing" Fuchs said. He was as confident as a poker player with four aces. "You won't shoot me. You're afraid of crashing and what the results could be."

"I'm more afraid of what you're planning to do with this truck. Stop now."

His grinned wickedly, and he signaled a turn downtown on Lexington Avenue. "Please feel free, shoot whenever—"

I lowered my Ruger and shot him in the right thigh. He screamed, and his right leg spasmed, pressing the accelerator to the floor. He tugged the steering wheel hard to the left. I don't think he knew what he was doing he was hurting so badly. The truck didn't care whether he knew or didn't. As the angle between the cab and the tank became too acute, the truck jackknifed and skidded. There was a tearing of metal as the tank banged down on its side and then rolled onto its top, still skidding, its tires now up in the air like a dog's legs when lying on its back.

When I had first scrambled into the cab, I hadn't put my seatbelt on. Boy, was that a poor decision. I had banged off the door and thumped hard onto the roof of the cab, where I now lay crumpled like a discarded rag doll. I felt as if every single bone I possessed had been hit with a hammer. Every last one of them. I looked up and saw Fuchs hanging upside down in his seat, held in place by his seatbelt. Blood was dripping slowly from his thigh.

Fuchs opened his eyes and scanned his surroundings. His eyes lit up on something next to me. I twisted and saw his pistol and phone lying about a foot from my right shoulder. He stretched out his arm, toward his gun, but I swiped it away from his reach.

Something hard was pressing into the small of my back. I reached around and found my gun. His was a good

348

pistol, a Glock 17, but I preferred my Ruger SR9. I wondered if he liked the Glock because it was from Austria just like his dear *Fuhrer*.

I pointed my Ruger at Fuchs. "Go ahead, unbuckle your seat belt."

He did, and though he tried to avoid it, he slammed down onto the ceiling of the upside-down cab. He groaned.

"I'm getting out now," I said. "You're welcome to climb out, too, and please feel free to make a run for it."

"With a hole in my leg?"

"You can give it the old *guter soldat* try." I gently pulled myself through the broken window of the passenger door and stood up once I was out on the pavement. I was pleased that despite my diagnosis of a minute ago, every bone in my body was not broken.

I walked around the truck, checking it. Gasoline was leaking all over Lexington Avenue. But since I had disarmed the detonator, no spark had been struck, and it was just a giant, smelly, fuel leak. There were no casualties except for Gerhard and me. No crushed bodies or cars.

"Thank you," I said with a skyward glance.

I walked back around to the cab to find Fuchs crawling out of the driver's window, grunting as he moved. As soon as he was clear of the cab and on the sidewalk, he pressed his left hand on top of the thigh wound, the right hand under the thigh.

"Are you going to let me bleed to death?"

"I wish. But the police will get here too soon."

The air was full of sirens, coming east along Dr. Martin Luther King Jr. Boulevard. Ah the irony. Here, Fuchs, a neo-Nazi hatemonger, had crashed and metaphorically burned just a stone's throw away from a road named after one of America's great civil rights leaders.

"If you want to join us, I'll make it worth your while," Fuchs said, his voice rough with pain.

"Not a freakin' chance."

"You're a white Christian of European background. You'd fit in, even if you're not Aryan. And the money will be very, very good."

"I'm a veteran of the same Army that beat the shit out of Adolf Hitler. The only thing you and I have in common is that we're both filled with hate."

"Well, that's something to build on."

"Not really. You and yours are the people I hate."

"That's too bad," he said, forcing a grin. He swung his right hand swung up, and he aimed a small automatic pistol at me. I was shocked by how fast he moved.

We fired simultaneously.

A bullet slammed into my left shoulder, sending me staggering backward. I lost my footing and fell to the street. My left shoulder burned with the telltale pain of a flesh wound. I started to curse but realized I'd better deal with Fuchs. I rolled over so I could see him, aiming my Ruger at his torso.

I struggled to my feet and walked over to him. A Glock 42 was lying on the pavement just out of his reach.

Not that he was going to be reaching for his gun any time soon; my bullet had gone through his left eye.

"I told you it wasn't easy killing a man." I leaned over him and shot him twice in the chest. "Hope you won't think I overdid it, but I don't want you to be late for your reservation in Hell. Maybe when you get there, you'll be lucky enough to sit right next to Adolf."

The police sirens were awfully loud. I dropped to my knees, very close to passing out.

"Harry?"

"It's okay, Jack. I'm here."

"Well, if it's okay. . . ."

*   *   *

The rich yet biting aroma of espresso woke me. Kim was sitting by my side with a cup of cappuccino.

"I promise, it's perfect," she said as she extended the cup to me.

I held my hand up in a stop-right-there gesture. "Hold it, let me sit up." I propped myself up against the pillows and took the cup from her. She leaned in and kissed me. "Do all of your invalids get a kiss and a freshly made cappuccino?"

"All of the current invalids do." I raised the cup to my lips and took a long sip. It was perfect.

"Just how much of an invalid am I?"

"How do you feel?"

"Not too bad, all things (or in this case, wounds) considered. Hell, I wasn't even sure I was going to wake up. When you get shot and collapse next to a tank leaking 9,000 gallons of gasoline, things could go sideways in a hurry."

"But that's all it was: a big leak. Blocked traffic for hours. Great news footage from helicopters of the clean-up effort on Lexington Avenue."

"It's satisfying to think I provided such a terrific spectacle for the people out in Television Land."

"Television Land? What are you, from the 50s?"

"My Dad used to say that. He was using it ironically."

"Of course he was."

"Not to change the subject—"

"—But could we return to the topic of you?" she grinned.

"Yes," I admitted. "What's my health update?"

"Harry said you have a lot of bumps and bruises. You needed some stitches in your right triceps and your left shoulder, which he took care of. No broken bones, no torn ligaments or tendons, no hemorrhaging. And . . . I say this with love, but your face is a mess."

"Is the wedding off?"

"It will be if you make more jokes like that. Anyway, it sounds like you got off light for a guy fighting Nazis on a truck loaded with explosives."

"They were only *neo*-Nazis, not actual Nazis—"

352

"—Oh, that makes it so much safer—"

"—and the truck was full of gasoline, not explosives. Gasoline does not, contrary to what you see in the movies, blow up. It does, however, burn like crazy."

"Burns like crazy. That's so much better than exploding."

"You are so frustrating sometimes."

"Fine, no more cappuccino for you."

"Wait, I'm sorry. I almost got blown up. I'm halfway to Crazy Town. Please, may I have another cappuccino?"

I gulped down the last of it and handed her the mug. She left the room shaking her hear but chuckling. When she returned, she was accompanied by Harry.

Kim handed me the cup and said, "I have informed Harry that I am seriously displeased by his returning you to me in this condition, and that he should do whatever he has to do to prevent it happening in the future."

"Did he give you a satisfactory response?"

"He did not."

"Did he utter words to the effect that the Chairman would decide what I needed in the future."

"He did. I hate to sound like you, but I said that I wasn't sure the Chairman and I define the word 'need' the same way."

"Good to know you're in my corner." To Harry I said, "Thanks for stitching me up. And for pulling me away from the accident."

353

"You're welcome. I noticed that Fuchs had four bullets in him. Leg, head, two in the chest."

Kim looked surprised. And unhappy.

I spoke quickly to block her reaction, "Wow. Really? Four? I don't even remember in all the confusion of the crash."

"It was kill or be killed," Harry said.

"Yeah, that sounds right."

Kim asked, "You didn't murder him, did you? It was self-defense, wasn't it?"

"It was self-defense. Not to mention justice." I said calmly. Turning to Harry, I asked, "What about all his men? And the corrupt cops at the 24th Precinct? Did Naomi and Stewart send off all the financials to Diego Quintana?"

Harry ticked the items off using his right index finger to fold the fingers on his left hand. It was a highly theatrical gesture by his standards. "All of Fuchs's men are in jail, the hospital, or dead. The corrupt cops are all in jail. Costello, the detective you encountered at 341 West 91st Street, is cooperating fully with Internal Affairs in the hope of avoiding jail."

"I hope he doesn't succeed."

"He will be a sick, old man by the time he leaves prison."

"You told me you're not a prophet."

"I pass along whatever the Chairman tells me to pass along. If that's prophetic, so be it."

354

"I'm too weak to engage in a theological debate."

"All evidence to the contrary."

"What about Naomi and Stewart?"

"They sent a very full package of information to Detective Quintana. The NYPD will spend a large amount of time and energy analyzing it all, but in the end, all of Fuchs's operations and bank accounts will be seized."

"Will the victims receive compensation? Not that anything can compensate the women he abused, but some money is better than no money."

"Yes, there will be compensation."

"Then the *Oberste Ordnung* is *kaput*."

"Yes," Harry said.

"No way for some other Hitler Youth type to come along and resurrect it?"

"No."

"So everything is wrapped up?" Kim asked sounding hopeful.

"Not quite," I said slowly, eyes fixed on Harry. "Will she remember me?"

"For a little while longer."

"Thanks." To Kim, I said, "You up for a road trip?"

"When?"

"As soon as my face doesn't look like a Halloween fright mask."

*   *   *

355

A week later, with my face looking almost normal—or as Kim described it, "Quasimodo-lite"—Kim and I drove out of Manhattan in a rented Hyundai sedan. It was a cold, crisp December day. The leaves were long gone from the trees, but the drive through the parkways of lower Westchester was still very pretty. Forty minutes later, we reached Fenimore Road in Mamaroneck, and I pulled into the driveway of Diane Eisenberg's home.

"Are you sure you don't want me to wait in the car?" Kim asked.

"No. You heard all about the horrors of my mission with regard to Gerhard Fuchs and the Supreme Order. Now I'd like you to see the other side."

We climbed out of the car. I was dressed in khaki slacks, blue oxford button-down, and a rust-brown tweed jacket. I had left the tools of my trade, guns and grenades, at home. Kim wore dark-blue slacks, with a cream smocked blouse, topped off with a heavy, long, charcoal cardigan. Neither of us had bothered with a coat, although we both wore gloves.

As we walked up the driveway, the front door opened, and Diane and her parents stepped outside to greet us. Diane threw her arms around me and buried her head against my chest, pulling me tight. Kim and the Eisenbergs had tears in their eyes. After a minute or so, Diane loosened her grip on me. Her father shook my hand, introductions were made, and we were invited inside.

Mrs. Eisenberg offered coffee, tea, and cookies. We both accepted coffee. Kim declined the cookies, but I gladly accepted. I needed the calories; after all, I was still recovering from my injuries. Diane's parents went into the kitchen, leaving Kim, Diane, and me in the living room. Diane sat with me on the large couch, holding my hand.

"He saved me," Diane told Kim.

"Well, I happened to be in the right place at the right time."

"Don't do that. Don't minimize what you did. You *saved* me."

"You're worth saving. Listen, I can't begin to imagine what you've been through. But I do know what it's like to go through a traumatic experience, and I know how hard it is to return to so-called 'normal life.' I was in combat in Afghanistan, and I came back suffering from PTSD."

"Did you . . . get help?"

"No, and that was a mistake. Not getting any help just made it harder. So please, be sure you talk to someone. Ask your parents to set you up with a psychiatrist or psychologist. Don't try to muddle your way through this on your own."

"I won't."

"Promise?"

"Yes, I promise." She smiled, "Besides, my parents already scheduled me for an appointment with a shrink."

"Good. Very good."

Diane focused on Kim, "You're lucky to be

engaged to him."

"I think so."

Diane's parents returned with coffee and butter cookies. As everyone nibbled and sipped, Diane asked Kim about how we'd met and how we got engaged. I only half-listened, mostly watching Diane. There was color in her cheeks. She'd put on a little weight, just enough to eliminate the gaunt, drawn appearance she'd had in the hospital. It was incredibly satisfying to see her with so much happy energy. I didn't assume that she was all better. She never would be *all* better in the sense that she could return to the life she had before Fuchs. But I hoped she had started her long journey back to health and happiness in the life she did have.

Kim and I stayed for an hour. Then we drove into Mamaroneck village, got miraculously lucky, and found parking on Mamaroneck Avenue not too far from Sal's Pizza. To say Sal's had no frills didn't capture its ambiance. It was one of the ultimate old-school pizzerias, the kind that you found in certain neighborhoods in the Bronx. To be in Sal's was to know you were at the real deal.

We sat at one of the tiny tables and ordered a pizza with pepperoni and mushroom. When the pie came, we savored the first few hot, fresh bites in silence—except for the appreciative moans.

When each of us was about halfway through our first slice, Kim said, "Do you feel . . . better about Laurie?"

"Now that I eliminated the neo-Nazi bad guy?"

"Well, yes. I don't mean that this was all about her. It was about Diane and the other girls. And all the people Fuchs was selling drugs to. All the people at NBC and the *Times* who were targets of his bombing. But Laurie was a large part of what was driving you." She paused to sip some Coca Cola. "So, do you feel better?"

"Yes, I do. It doesn't make sense, but I feel like I did something for Laurie."

"You *did* do something. Something in *memory* of her."

I smiled, "Thank you."

"You're welcome." After consuming more bites of pizza, Kim asked, "From now on, Diane won't remember you?"

"If this mission works like the others, she and her parents have already forgotten me. And you, for that matter."

"Why does the Chairman make them forget?"

"These missions aren't about me. They're about the people I help. The missions are completely other-directed. Completely selfless. No rewards, no honors."

"But what will the Eisenbergs think? What replaces the memory of your saving her?"

"Diane will have some vague memory of a brave, handsome man beating the bad guys and rescuing her."

"Vague but brave and handsome."

"Of course."

"Where did this vague savior come from? How did

he get there?"

"I'm guessing they think he was one of two or three undercover cops who burst into the place and rescued all the girls."

"Two or three cops?"

"Three."

"Three cops?"

"Yeah, three. It had to be three guys. Maybe even more. You don't think anyone would believe that one, lone, brave and handsome man could defeat all those neo-Nazis and save all those girls, do you?"

She grinned broadly. "Actually, I do believe it."

ABOUT THE AUTHOR

Geoff Loftus is the author of the thrillers *Murderous Spirit*, *Dark Mirage*, *The Last Thing*, *Dangerous Purpose*, and *No Traveler Returns* (all Jack Tyrrell novels), as well as the thrillers *Double Blind, Engaged to Kill*, and *The Dark Saint*.

Loftus also wrote *Lead Like Ike: Ten Business Strategies from the CEO of D-Day* and was the 2010 Keynote Speaker at the Eisenhower Legacy Dinner at the Eisenhower Presidential Museum and Library. In addition, he blogged for FORBES.com on leadership for about ten years.

Like many authors, he once dreamed of writing the great American novel but instead tried to write the great American screenplay. The closest he came to that lofty achievement was writing *Hero in the Family* with John Drimmer for *The Wonderful World of Disney*. He has been a member of the Writers Guild of America, East for more than thirty years.

Acknowledgments

As with all the Tyrrell novels, I have to thank the three men who inspired me to write these thrillers: Charles Dickens who wrote my favorite book, *A Christmas Carol*; Philip K. Dick who wrote the short story *Adjustment Team*; and George Nolfi, the writer-director of the movie based on Dick's story: *The Adjustment Bureau*.

Many thanks to my editorial team: Alice Siempelkamp and Ted Berk. They have done their best to shape and sharpen this novel and clean up my many mistakes. Despite their Herculean efforts, there are some remaining errors in this book, and those errors are solely my fault.

My friend, mentor, and editor, Tom Seligson, has continued to support my work, and I'm very grateful to him.

Thank you to the many friends who have helped me through the Tyrrell novels and all of the rest of my life: Tom and Judy Galligan, Ted Canellas and Bob Roth, Erica Fross, Katie Ryan, Jill Quist, Marcia Menter, Sal Vitale, Ted West, Steve Pitts, and Lindy Sittenfeld.

My feelings for my wife, Margy, and son, Greg, have always been beyond my ability to express. I'll just quote Charles Dickens to them: "you have been the last dream of my soul."

Made in the USA
Las Vegas, NV
22 March 2022